PUFFIN CLASSICS

JOURNEY to the
CENTRE of the EARTH

'Oh, no!' I cried, leaping to my feet. 'My uncle mustn't know about this! It would be the last straw if he got to hear of a journey of this sort. He would want to follow suit, and nothing would stop him, he is such a fanatical geologist. He would set off in spite of everything, and he would take me with him, and we should never come back. Never! Never!'

JULES VERNE

JOURNEY to the CENTRE of the EARTH

Translated by Robert Baldick

INTRODUCED BY
DIANA WYNNE JONES

PUFFIN

PUFFIN BOOKS

Published by the Penguin Group
Penguin Books Ltd, 80 Strand, London WC2R ORL, England
Penguin Group (USA) Inc., 375 Hudson Street, New York, New York 10014, USA
Penguin Group (Canada), 90 Eglinton Avenue East, Suite 700, Toronto, Ontario, Canada M4P 2Y3
(a division of Pearson Penguin Canada Inc.)
Penguin Ireland, 25 St Stephen's Green, Dublin 2, Ireland (a division of Penguin Books Ltd)
Penguin Group (Australia), 250 Camberwell Road, Camberwell, Victoria 3124, Australia
(a division of Pearson Australia Group Pty Ltd)
Penguin Books India Pvt Ltd, 11 Community Centre, Panchsheel Park, New Delhi – 110 017, India
Penguin Group (NZ), 67 Apollo Drive, Rosedale, North Shore 0632, New Zealand
(a division of Pearson New Zealand Ltd)
Penguin Books (South Africa) (Pty) Ltd, 24 Sturdee Avenue, Rosebank, Johannesburg 2196, South Africa

Penguin Books Ltd, Registered Offices: 80 Strand, London WC2R ORL, England

puffinbooks.com

Voyage au Centre de la Terre first published in Paris 1864
This translation first published in Penguin Books 1965
Published in Puffin Books 1985
Reissued in this edition 2008

11

Set in Minion by Palimpsest Book Production Limited, Grangemouth, Stirlingshire
Printed in Great Britain by Clays Ltd, St Ives plc

British Library Cataloguing in Publication Data
A CIP catalogue record for this book is available from the British Library

ISBN: 978-0-141-32104-2

www.greenpenguin.co.uk

INTRODUCTION BY
DIANA WYNNE JONES

Journey to the Centre of the Earth is an astonishing book for many reasons. It certainly astonished me when I first read it at the age of ten – I couldn't put it down, and I wouldn't talk to anybody until I had finished it. It is one of the first pieces of science fiction ever written and, at the same time, a thoroughly exciting adventure story. It starts, as all good adventures should, with a coded message that has to be deciphered before the journey can begin; it has a surprise ending; and it contains the first-ever mad professor, Otto Lidenbrock. Every other mad professor ever since is simply an imitation of this one. But you have to be patient when you read it. It was written one hundred and forty years ago, which means it is sometimes long-winded and old-fashioned, but I assure you it gives good value in the end.

It is especially interesting to me because Jules Verne based his story on the theories of Humphry Davy, the scientist who investigated the effects of laughing gas and invented the lamps that miners wore fixed to the front of their helmets. Two hundred years ago, Davy lived in a house just around the corner from me. There was a big shed in the garden of this house where Davy did his experiments – I can see it from my window – and local tradition has it that he used to test laughing gas there on his friends, the poets Wordsworth and Coleridge among them, and all of them used to try it out once a week and laugh their heads off. They are knocking down this shed, very noisily, while I'm writing this, in order to build a new house. It occurs to me that Jules Verne might have based his mad professor on the character of Humphry Davy.

Davy had a lot to do with mining and he was convinced, unlike most other scientists, that the centre of the earth was not really made of hot, molten rock. He thought it might simply contain a lot of water. This is the theory that Jules Verne uses. Professor Otto Lidenbrock believes this theory with eccentric fervour and drags Axel, his poor, protesting nephew, off into the depths of the earth, where they do indeed find a lot of water. The great underground ocean is absolutely unforgettable. But if you read carefully, you will see that Jules Verne hedges his bets a little here. The explorers never actually get right to the centre of the earth. You think, So *of course* they never find molten rock! Then you think, Hang *on*! Nobody except mad Professor Lidenbrock has ever gone down there to look! Humphry

Davy could be right after all. Like all good science fiction, this book really makes you *think*.

And here is another astonishing fact. When Jules Verne was a boy, he promised his mother he would never leave home – and he never did. He stayed in France and did all his exploring by reading books. He travelled only in his mind. But such is the power of his imagination that, when the travellers get to Iceland and finally plunge underground, you believe in what they find as if Jules Verne had been there himself and seen it with his own eyes. Jules Verne was an expert mind traveller. Journeying in his head, he wrote this and at least two other adventure stories that are world-famous to this day. Marvellous. Astonishing.

Contents

1

My Uncle Lidenbrock

On 24 May 1863, which was a Sunday, my uncle, Professor Lidenbrock, came rushing back towards his little house, No. 19 Königstrasse, one of the oldest streets in the old quarter of Hamburg.

Martha must have thought she was very behindhand, for the dinner was only just beginning to sizzle on the kitchen stove.

'Well,' I said to myself, 'if my uncle is hungry he'll make a dreadful fuss, for he's the most impatient of men.'

'Professor Lidenbrock here already!' cried poor Martha in astonishment, half opening the dining-room door.

'Yes, Martha; but don't worry if the dinner isn't cooked, because it isn't two o'clock yet. St Michael's clock has only just struck half past one.'

'Then why is Professor Lidenbrock coming home?'

'He'll probably tell us himself.'

'Here he is! I'm off, Mr Axel. You'll get him to see reason, won't you?'

And our good Martha went back to her culinary laboratory.

I was left alone. But as for getting the most irascible of professors to see reason, that was a task beyond a man of my rather undecided character. So I was getting ready to beat a prudent retreat to my little room upstairs, when the street door creaked on its hinges, heavy footsteps shook the wooden staircase, and the master of the house, passing through the dining-room, rushed straight into his study.

But on his way he had found time to fling his stick with the nutcracker head into a corner, his broad-brimmed hat on to the table, and these emphatic words at his nephew:

'Axel, follow me!'

Before I had time to move, the Professor called to me again in an impatient voice:

'Well, haven't you got here yet?'

I rushed into my formidable master's study.

Otto Lidenbrock was not, I must admit, a bad man; but, unless he changes in the most unlikely way, he will end up as a terrible eccentric.

He was a professor at the Johannaeum and gave a course of lectures on mineralogy, during every one of which he lost his temper once or twice. Not that he cared whether his pupils attended regularly, listened attentively, or were successful later: these little matters interested him only very slightly. His teaching was what the German philosophers would call 'subjective': that is to say it was intended for himself and not for others. He was a selfish scholar, a well of science whose pulley creaked when you tried to draw anything out of it. In short, he was a miser. There are quite a few professors like that in Germany.

Unfortunately for him, my uncle had difficulty in speaking fluently, not so much at home as in public, and this is a regrettable defect in an orator. Indeed, in his lectures at the Johannaeum the Professor would often stop short, struggling with a recalcitrant word which refused to slip between his lips, one of those words which resist, swell up, and finally come out in the rather unscientific form of a swear-word. This was what always sent him into a rage.

Now in mineralogy there are a great many barbarous terms, half Greek and half Latin, which are difficult to pronounce and which would take the skin off any poet's lips. I don't want to say a word against that science – far from it – but when one finds oneself in the presence of rhombohedral crystals, retinasphaltic resins, gehlenites, fangasites, molybdenites, tungstates of manganese, and titanite of zirconium, the nimblest tongue may be forgiven for slipping.

This pardonable infirmity of my uncle's was well known in the town and unfair advantage was taken of it; the students waited for the dangerous passages when he lost his temper and then burst out laughing, which is not in good taste, even in Germany. And if there was always a large audience at the Lidenbrock lectures, a great many of those present undoubtedly came with the chief object of amusing themselves at the spectacle of the Professor's rages.

However that may be, my uncle, as I have said before and cannot repeat too often, was a true scholar. Although he sometimes broke his specimens by handling them too roughly, he combined the genius of the geologist with the eye of the mineralogist. With his hammer, his steel pointer, his magnetic needle, his blowpipe, and his bottle of nitric acid, he was a force to be reckoned with. From the fracture, appearance, hardness, fusibility, sound, smell, and taste of any given mineral, he could unhesitatingly class it in its proper place among the six hundred species known to modern science.

The name of Lidenbrock was accordingly mentioned in tones of respect in all colleges and learned societies. Humphry Davy, Humboldt, Captain Franklin, and General Sabine never failed to call on him when passing through Hamburg; and Becquerel, Ebelman, Brewster, Dumas, Milne-Edwards, and Sainte-Claire Deville frequently consulted him about the most difficult problems in Chemistry.

This science was indebted to him for some

remarkable discoveries, and in 1853 a *Treatise on Transcendental Crystallography* by Professor Otto Lidenbrock had appeared at Leipzig, an imposing folio volume with plates, which, however, failed to cover its expenses.

Over and above all this, I should add that my uncle was the curator of the mineralogical museum founded by Mr Struve, the Russian ambassador, a valuable collection known all over Europe.

This, then, was the gentleman who was calling me so impatiently. Picture to yourself a tall, thin man, in excellent health, and with a fair, youthful complexion which took off a good ten of his fifty years. His big eyes were constantly rolling behind huge spectacles; and his long thin nose looked like the blade of a knife. Mischievous students, indeed, asserted that it was magnetized and attracted iron filings. This was sheer calumny: it attracted nothing but snuff, though that in great abundance.

When I have added that my uncle took mathematical strides three feet long, and that as he walked along he kept his fists tightly clenched, a sure sign of an impetuous temperament, you will know him well enough not to hanker after his company.

He lived in his own little house in the Königstrasse, a building which was half brick and half wood, with an indented gable; it overlooked one of those winding canals which intersect in the middle of the oldest quarter of Hamburg, which the great fire of 1842 mercifully spared.

It is true that the old house was not exactly perpendicular, and bulged out a little towards the street; its roof was slightly askew, like the cap over the ear of a Tugendbund student; and the balance of its lines left something to be desired; but, all considering, it stood firm, thanks to an old elm which was solidly embedded in the façade and which in spring used to push its young sprays through the window panes.

My uncle was fairly well off for a German professor. The house belonged to him, both the building and its contents – the latter including his goddaughter Gräuben, a seventeen-year-old native of the Virlande, our good Martha, and myself. In my dual capacity of nephew and orphan I became his laboratory assistant.

I must admit that I took to geology enthusiastically; I had the blood of a mineralogist in my veins and I never felt bored in the company of my precious pebbles.

All in all, life was happy enough in that little house in the Königstrasse, in spite of the master's fits of temper, for although he was rather brusque with me he was fond of me all the same. But the man was incapable of waiting, and was always in a greater hurry than Nature. In April, after he had planted seedlings of mignonette or convolvulus in the earthenware pots in his drawing-room, he would go regularly every morning and pull them by the leaves to make them grow faster.

With such an eccentric character, obedience was the only course to adopt. I therefore rushed into his study.

2

The Strange Parchment

That study of his was a regular museum. Specimens of everything in the mineral world were to be found there, labelled with meticulous exactitude and arranged in the three great classes of inflammable, metallic, and lithoid minerals.

How well I knew them, those knicknacks of mineralogical science! How often, instead of frittering away my time with boys of my own age, I had enjoyed myself dusting those specimens of graphite, anthracite, coal, lignite, and peat! And those examples of bitumen, of resin, of organic salts which had to be protected from the smallest speck of dust! And those metals, from iron to gold, whose relative value was ignored in view of the absolute equality of scientific specimens! And all those stones which would have been enough to rebuild the whole Königstrasse house, and even add a splendid room which would have suited me admirably!

But as I went into the study, my mind was not on these wonders: my thoughts were entirely occupied by my uncle.

He was ensconced in his big Utrecht velvet armchair, and was holding a book which he was considering with the profoundest admiration.

'What a book!' he was saying.

This exclamation reminded me that Professor Lidenbrock was also a bibliomaniac in his spare time; but a book had no value in his eyes unless it was unique or, at the very least, unreadable.

'Well?' he said. 'Can't you see what it is? It's a priceless treasure that I found this morning, rummaging about in that Jew Hevelius's bookshop.'

'Splendid!' I replied, with forced enthusiasm.

After all, why all this excitement about an old quarto volume whose covers seemed to be made of coarse calf, a yellowish book with a faded seal hanging from it?

But for all that the Professor went on uttering admiring exclamations.

'Look,' he said, asking and answering his own questions. 'Isn't it beautiful? Yes, it's splendid! And what a binding! Does it open easily? Yes, and it stays open at any page you like. But does it close well? Yes, for the binding and the leaves form a compact whole, with no gaps or openings anywhere. And look at the back, which doesn't show a single crack after seven hundred years! Now there's a binding Bozerian, Closs, or Purgold would have been proud of!'

While saying all this, my uncle kept opening and shutting the old book. I could do no less than ask him about its contents, although as a matter of fact they did not interest me in the slightest.

'And what is the title of this wonderful work?' I asked, with an eagerness which was too great not to be specious.

'This work,' replied my uncle with increasing excitement, 'is the *Heims Kringla* of Snorro Turleson, the famous Icelandic writer of the twelfth century! It is the chronicle of the Norwegian princes who ruled over Iceland.'

'Really?' I cried, as heartily as I could. 'I suppose this is a translation?'

'What!' roared the Professor. 'What would I be doing with a translation? This is the original work in Icelandic, that magnificent language which is both rich and simple and allows an infinite variety of grammatical combinations and verbal modifications!'

'Like German,' I suggested, not altogether unhappily.

'Yes,' replied my uncle, shrugging his shoulders; 'not to mention the fact that Icelandic has three genders like Greek and declines proper nouns like Latin.'

'Ah!' I said, slightly shaken in my indifference, 'and is the type good?'

'Type! Who said anything about type, you wretched boy? Type, indeed! Ah, you think it's a printed book, do you? It's a manuscript, you idiot, a Runic manuscript.'

'Runic?'

'Yes. Now I suppose you want me to explain wha[...]
means?'

'Of course not,' I replied in an injured voice. But my
uncle took no notice, and told me, against my will, a
good many things I was not particularly interested in
learning.

'The Runes,' he said, 'were letters of an alphabet used in
Iceland in olden times, and legend has it that they were
invented by Odin himself. Look at them, irreverent boy, and
admire these characters sprung from a god's imagination!'

Not knowing what to say, I was going to prostrate
myself before the book – a response which must give
pleasure to gods as well as to kings, for it has the advantage of never causing them any embarrassment – when a
little incident occurred which changed the course of the
conversation. This was the appearance of a dirty piece of
parchment which slipped out of the book and fell on the
floor.

My uncle pounced upon this fragment with
understandable eagerness. An old document, enclosed
perhaps since immemorial time between the pages of an
old book, was bound to have immeasurable value in his
eyes.

'What's this?' he cried.

And at the same time he carefully unfolded on his table
a piece of parchment five inches by three, containing a
few lines of unintelligible characters.

I reproduce them here in exact facsimile. I consider it important to publish these strange signs, for they led Professor Lidenbrock and his nephew to undertake the strangest expedition of the nineteenth century.

The Professor considered this series of characters for a few moments; then, raising his spectacles, he said:

'These are Runic letters; they are absolutely identical with those in Snorro Turleson's manuscript. But what on earth do they mean?'

Since Runic letters struck me as something invented by scholars to mystify the unfortunate world, I was not sorry to see that my uncle could not make head or tail of them. At least that was what I supposed from his fingers, which had begun to twitch terribly.

'And yet it must be old Icelandic!' he muttered between his teeth. And Professor Lidenbrock must have known, for he was reputed to be a regular polyglot. Not that he could speak fluently all the two thousand languages and

four thousand dialects used on this earth, but at lea...
was familiar with a good many of them.

Faced with this difficulty, he was obviously going to lose his temper, and I was steeling myself for a violent scene when the little clock on the mantelpiece struck two.

At that moment Martha opened the study door, saying:

'The soup is ready.'

'To hell with the soup,' cried my uncle, 'and her that made it, and them that drink it!'

Martha took to her heels. I ran after her and, scarcely knowing how I got there, I found myself sitting in my usual place in the dining-room.

I waited for a few minutes. There was no sign of the Professor. It was the first time, to my knowledge, that he had missed his dinner. And what a dinner it was! Parsley soup, a ham omelette seasoned with sorrel, veal with prune sauce, and, for dessert, sugared prawns, the whole accompanied by an excellent Moselle wine.

All this my uncle was going to miss on account of a scrap of old parchment! Naturally, as a devoted nephew, I considered it my duty to eat for him as well as for myself, and I carried out this duty conscientiously.

'I've never known such a thing,' said Martha. 'Professor Lidenbrock not at table!'

'Unbelievable, isn't it?'

'It means that something serious is going to happen!' said the old servant, wagging her head.

In my opinion it meant nothing at all, except perhaps a dreadful scene when my uncle found that his dinner had been eaten.

I had come to my last prawn when a stentorian voice tore me away from the pleasures of dessert. With one bound I went from the dining-room to the study.

3

My Uncle is Baffled

'It's definitely Runic,' said the Professor, frowning. 'But there is a secret to it which I mean to discover, or else . . .

'Sit down there,' he added, extending his fist towards the table, 'and get ready to write.'

In an instant I was ready.

'Now, I am going to dictate to you the letters of our alphabet which correspond to these Icelandic characters. We shall see what that gives us. But by St Michael, be careful not to make a mistake!'

The dictation began, I was as careful as I could be. The letters were called out one after another, and together they formed this incomprehensible succession of words:

m̄.rnlls	esreuel	seecJde
sgtssmf	unteief	niedrke
kt,samn	atrateS	Saodrrn
emtnaeI	nuaect	rrilSa
Atvaar	.nscrc	ieaabs

	eeutul	*frantu*
cc	*oseibo*	*KediiY*

When I had finished, my uncle snatched up the paper
upon which I had been writing and examined it closely
for a long time.

'What does it mean?' he kept repeating mechanically.

Upon my honour I could not have told him. In any case
he was not asking me, and he went on talking to himself.

'It's what they call a cryptogram,' he said, 'in which the
sense is concealed by a deliberate jumbling of the letters,
which would make an intelligible sentence if they were
correctly rearranged. To think that I may have here the
clue to some great discovery!'

For my part I thought there was absolutely nothing
there, but I prudently kept my opinion to myself.

Then the Professor took the book and the parchment,
and compared them. 'They aren't in the same hand-
writing,' he said. 'The cryptogram is of a later date than
the book, and I can see indisputable proof of that right
at the beginning. The first letter is a double *m*, a letter
you would look for in vain in Turleson's book for it was
only added to the Icelandic alphabet in the fourteenth
century. So there are at least two hundred years between
the book and the document.'

That, I admit, struck me as a logical conclusion.

'I am therefore led to think,' continued my uncle, 'that

one of the owners of this book wrote these mysterious letters. But who the devil was that owner? Wouldn't he have written his name somewhere on this manuscript?'

My uncle raised his spectacles, picked up a powerful magnifying glass, and carefully examined the first pages of the book. On the back of the second page, the one bearing the subtitle, he noticed a sort of stain which looked like a blot of ink. However, looking at it closely, he made out a few half-obliterated letters. My uncle realized that this was the interesting point, and he laboured at the stain until, with the help of his magnifying glass, he ended up by distinguishing the following Runic characters, which he read out without hesitation:

ᛚᛆᚿ� ᛋᛆᚴᚿᚢᛋᛋ�

'Arne Saknussemm!' he cried triumphantly. 'Why that's a name, and what is more an Icelandic name, that of a famous alchemist of the sixteenth century!'

I looked at my uncle with a certain admiration. 'Those alchemists,' he went on, 'Avicenna, Bacon, Lully, Paracelsus, were the real scientists, indeed the only scientists, of their time. They made the most astonishing discoveries. Why shouldn't this Saknussemm have concealed some surprising invention behind this incomprehensible cryptogram? That must be it. That *is* it.'

The Professor's imagination took fire at this idea.

'No doubt,' I ventured to reply. 'But what interest could this scientist have had in hiding a wonderful discovery in this way?'

'What indeed? How should I know? Didn't Galileo do the same about Saturn? Anyway, we shall see: I'm going to discover the secret of this document, and I shall neither eat nor sleep until I have guessed it.'

'Oh!' I thought to myself.

'Nor will you, Axel,' he added.

'Good Lord!' I thought, 'it's a good thing I ate two dinners today!'

'First of all,' said my uncle, 'we must find the key to this cipher. That ought not to be difficult.'

At these words I looked up quickly. My uncle went on talking to himself.

'Nothing could be easier. In this document there are 132 letters, namely seventy-nine consonants and fifty-three vowels. This is roughly the proportion found in southern languages, while northern idioms are infinitely richer in consonants. Consequently this is written in a southern language.'

These conclusions struck me as very reasonable.

'But what language is it?'

Here I waited for a display of learning, but instead my uncle showed himself to be a master of analysis.

'This Saknussemm,' he went on, 'was an educated man,

so when he was not writing in his mother tongue, he would naturally write in the language commonly used by educated men in the sixteenth century, namely Latin. If I am wrong, I can go on to try Spanish, French, Italian, Greek, and Hebrew. But the savants of the sixteenth century generally wrote in Latin, so that I am entitled to say, *a priori*, that this is Latin.'

I sat up with a jolt. My memories of Latin rose in revolt at the idea that this string of barbarous words could belong to the sweet language of Virgil.

'Yes, this is Latin,' my uncle continued, 'but Latin in a scrambled form.'

'Well,' I thought to myself, 'if you can unscramble it, my dear uncle, you are a clever man.'

'Let us have a good look at it,' he said, picking up the sheet of paper on which I had written. 'Here is a series of 132 letters in apparent disorder. There are some words consisting of consonants only, like the first, *mm.rnlls*; others, on the other hand, in which vowels predominate, such as the fifth, *unteief*, or the last but one, *oseibo*. Now this arrangement is obviously not deliberate: it has occurred mathematically in obedience to the unknown law which has governed the order of these letters. It seems to me quite certain that the original sentence was written in a regular manner, and afterwards distorted in accordance with a law which we have yet to discover. Whoever possessed the key to this cipher would be able to read it fluently. But what is that key? Axel, have you got it?'

To this question I made no reply, and for a very good reason. My eyes had fallen on a charming picture hanging on the wall, the portrait of Gräuben. My uncle's ward was at Altona at that time, staying with one of her female relations, and her absence made me very sad, for, as I can now confess, the pretty Virlandaise and the Professor's nephew loved each other with all the patience and tranquillity of the German character. We had become engaged, unknown to my uncle, who was too deeply absorbed in his geology to understand such feelings as ours. Gräuben was a lovely blue-eyed blonde, who was rather solemn and serious-minded but loved me none the less for that. For my part, I adored her, and so the picture of my little Virlandaise transferred me in a single instant from the world of realities to that of dreams and memories.

I recalled the faithful companion of my work and my pleasures. Every day she used to help me to arrange my uncle's precious specimens; she and I labelled them together. Oh, Gräuben was an accomplished mineralogist; she could have taught a few things to many a savant. She loved getting to the bottom of abstruse scientific problems. What pleasant hours we had spent studying together, and how often I had envied the lot of those insensible stones which she handled with her charming fingers!

Then, when our recreation time came, we used to go out together, strolling along the shady walks of the Alster and going together to the old tarred windmill which looks so picturesque at the end of the lake. On the way we would chat together, hand in hand, and I would tell her stories which made her laugh. Eventually we would come to the banks of the Elbe, and, after saying good-bye to the swans gliding about among the big water-lilies, we would return to the quay by the steamer.

That was where I had got to in my dream when my uncle, thumping the table with his fist, brought me abruptly back to earth.

'Look here,' he said, 'the first idea which would occur to anybody wanting to mix up the letters in a sentence would be to write the words vertically instead of horizontally.'

'It wouldn't have occurred to me,' I thought.

'Now let's see how that works. Axel, write down any sentence that comes into your head on this scrap of paper; only, instead of arranging the letters in the usual way, one after another, put them in vertical columns, so as to get five or six.'

I understood what he wanted and immediately wrote the following lines of letters:

I	*o*	*m*	*y*	*i*	*r*
l	*u*	*u*	*d*	*t*	*ä*
o	*v*	*c*	*e*	*t*	*u*

v	e	h	a	l	b
e	r	,	r	e	e
y	y	m	l	G	n

'Good!' said the Professor, without reading what I had written. 'Now set out these groups of letters in a horizontal line.'

I obeyed, and obtained the following result:

Iomyir luudtä ovcetu vehalb er,ree yymlGn

'Splendid!' said my uncle, snatching the paper out of my hands. 'This already looks rather like the old document: the vowels and consonants are grouped in the same haphazard way, and there are even capitals and commas in the middle of words, just as there are in Saknussemm's parchment!'

I couldn't help thinking that what he said was extremely ingenious.

'Now,' my uncle went on, looking straight at me, 'to read the sentence which you have just written, and with which I am completely unfamiliar, all I need to do is to take the first letter of each word, then the second letter, and so on.'

And my uncle, to his great surprise, and even more to mine, read out:

'I love you very much, my dear little Gräuben.'

'What's this?' said the Professor.

Yes, without knowing what I was doing, silly, lovesick young man that I was, I had written down that compromising sentence.

'Ah! So you are in love with Gräuben?' said my uncle, in a suitable voice for a guardian.

'Yes! No!' I stammered.

'So you are in love with Gräuben,' he repeated automatically. 'Well, now let's apply my method to the document in question.'

Returning to the consideration of his absorbing theory, my uncle had already forgotten my imprudent words. I say imprudent because the savant's learned head was incapable of understanding matters of the heart. But luckily the important matter of the document carried the day.

As he got ready to carry out his crucial experiment, Professor Lidenbrock's eyes darted flashes of light through his spectacles. His fingers trembled as he picked up the old parchment. He was deeply moved. At last he gave a loud cough, and in a solemn voice, reading out in succession the first letter of each word, then the second, and so on, he dictated the following series to me:

messunkaSenrA.icefdoK.segnittamurtn
ecertserrette,rotaivsadua,ednecsedsadne

lacartniiiluJsiratracSarbmutabiledmek
meretarcsilucoYsleffenSnI

I must admit that when I came to the end I felt very excited; these letters, called out one after another, had conveyed no meaning to my mind, but I expected the Professor to pronounce a magnificent Latin sentence.

To my astonishment, a violent blow from his fist made the table rock on its legs. The ink spurted into the air, and the pen flew out of my hand.

'That can't be it!' exclaimed my uncle. 'It doesn't make sense!'

Then, flying across the study like a cannonball, and descending the stairs like an avalanche, he rushed out into the Königstrasse and disappeared as fast as his legs could carry him.

4
I Find the Key

'Has he gone?' cried Martha, running out of her kitchen as the street door slammed shut, shaking the whole house.

'Yes,' I replied, 'well and truly gone!'

'Well I never! And what about his dinner?' asked the old servant.

'He won't have any.'

'And his supper?'

'He won't have any.'

'What?' cried Martha, clasping her hands.

'No, Martha, he's not going to eat a thing, nor is anybody else in this house. Uncle Lidenbrock is going to starve us all until he has succeeded in deciphering an old scrawl which is absolutely indecipherable.'

'Goodness gracious! You mean we shall have to starve to death?'

I did not dare to admit that, with a man as determined as my uncle, this fate struck me as inevitable.

The old servant, seriously alarmed, went back to her kitchen groaning to herself.

Once I was alone, the idea occurred to me of going to tell the whole story to Gräuben. But how could I leave the house? The Professor might return at any moment. And what if he called me? What if he wanted to go on with this logogryphic riddle which would have baffled even old Oedipus? And if I failed to answer his call, what might happen then?

The wisest thing to do was to remain where I was. As it happened, a mineralogist at Besançon had just sent us a collection of siliceous geodes which had to be classified. I set to work, sorting, labelling, and arranging in their own glass case all these hollow stones, each with a set of little crystals inside it.

But this task did not absorb the whole of my attention. The business of the old document continued to preoccupy me. My head was throbbing and I felt overcome by a vague anxiety. I had a presentiment of some imminent catastrophe.

After an hour's work my geodes were all neatly arranged on their respective shelves. I then dropped into the old Utrecht armchair, my head thrown back and my arms dangling. I lit my long curved pipe, whose bowl was carved in the shape of a reclining naiad, and then amused myself by watching the carbonizing process which was gradually turning my nymph into a negress. Every now and then I pricked up my ears to hear whether anybody was coming upstairs. But no. Where could my uncle be at that moment? I imagined him running along beneath the splendid trees lining the Altona road, gesticulating wildly, dragging his stick along the wall, slashing at the grass, decapitating the thistles, and rousing the lonely storks from their sleep.

Would he return in triumph or in discouragement? Which of the two would get the upper hand, he or the secret? Asking myself these questions, I picked up the sheet of paper covered with the incomprehensible series of letters I had written down, and I murmured over and over again:

'What can it possibly mean?'

I tried grouping these letters together to form words. It was impossible! Whether I put them together in twos, threes, fives, or sixes, the result was still unintelligible. It was no clearer when I noticed that the fourteenth, fifteenth, and sixteenth letters made the English word 'ice'; that the eighty-fourth, eighty-fifth, and eighty-sixth made the word 'sir'; and that in the body of the document, in the second and third lines, there were the Latin words *rota*, *mutabile*, *ira*, *nec*, and *atra*.

'Hang it,' I thought, 'these last words would seem to suggest that my uncle was right about the language the document is written in! And there in the fourth line I can see another Latin word – *luco*, which means a sacred wood.

It's true that in the third line there's the word *tabiled*, which is as Hebrew as it could be, and in the last line the words *mer*, *arc*, and *mère*, which are pure French.'

All this was enough to drive a fellow mad. Four different languages in this ridiculous sentence. What connexion could there possibly be between the words *ice*, *sir*, *anger*, *cruel*, *sacred wood*, *changeable*, *mother*, *bow*, and *sea*? The first and last went together quite well: it was not at all surprising that in a document written in Iceland there should be mention of a sea of ice. But solving the rest of the cryptogram was quite another matter.

As I struggled with this apparently insoluble problem, my brain got heated, my eyes blinked at the sheet of paper, and the hundred and thirty-two letters seemed to flutter around me, like those silver drops which float in the air about you when you get a rush of blood to the head.

I was in the grip of a sort of hallucination; I was stifling; I needed air. Without thinking, I started fanning myself with the sheet of paper so that the back and front came alternately before my eyes.

Imagine my surprise when, in one of these rapid movements, just as the back was turning towards me, I thought I could see some perfectly legible words, Latin words, such as *craterem* and *terrestre*!

Light suddenly dawned upon me; these few clues were enough to give me a glimpse of the truth; I had found the key to the cipher. To understand the document, it was not even necessary to read it through the paper. It could be read out just as it was, just as it had been dictated to me. All the Professor's ingenious theories were correct. He had been right about the arrangement of the letters, and right about the language in which the document was written. He had needed only a little 'something' extra in order to read the Latin sentence from beginning to end, and chance had just given me that 'something'.

You may imagine how excited I was. My eyes misted over, so that I could not see. I had spread the sheet of paper out on the table, so that I only had to glance at it to possess its secret.

At last I succeeded in calming down. I forced myself to walk twice round the room in order to settle my nerves, and then dropped into the huge armchair.

'Now let's see what it says,' I said to myself, after taking a deep breath.

I bent over the table and placed my finger on each letter in succession; and without stopping, without hesitating for a moment, I read out the whole sentence aloud.

But what terror and stupefaction it produced! At first I was absolutely thunderstruck. What! Had what I had just read really happened? Had some man had the audacity to penetrate . . . ?

'Oh, no!' I cried, leaping to my feet. 'My uncle mustn't know about this! It would be the last straw if he got to hear of a journey of this sort. He would want to follow suit, and nothing would stop him, he is such a fanatical geologist. He would set off in spite of everything, and he would take me with him, and we should never come back. Never! Never!'

I was in a state of indescribable agitation.

'No, it shall not be,' I declared, 'and since it is in my power to prevent such an idea from entering my tyrant's head, I shall do so. If he kept turning this document over and over, he too might discover the key. The only thing to do is to destroy it.'

There was a little fire still burning in the hearth. I picked up not only the sheet of paper but also Saknussemm's parchment; and with a trembling hand I was about to fling them both into the fire and destroy the dangerous secret when the study door opened and my uncle appeared.

5
Hunger Defeats Me

I only just had time to put the wretched document back on the table.

Professor Lidenbrock seemed profoundly preoccupied. His all-absorbing idea was not giving him a moment's respite; he had obviously analysed the problem carefully and brought all the resources of his imagination to bear on it during his walk, and now he had come home to apply some new combination.

Sure enough, he sat down in his armchair and, pen in hand, started putting down what looked to me like algebraical equations.

I followed with my eyes his quivering hand, not missing a single movement. Was he going to produce some unexpected result? I trembled, but unnecessarily, for since the only true combination had been found, any other line of investigation was doomed to disappointment.

For three long hours my uncle worked without a word, without raising his head, rubbing out, beginning again, crossing out, and starting again hundreds of times.

I knew perfectly well that if he succeeded in arranging the letters in every possible relative order, the sentence would come out. But I also knew that a mere twenty letters can have 2,432,902,800,176,640,000 different combinations.

Now there were 132 letters in this sentence, and 132 letters produced a number of different combinations running to at least 133 figures, a number almost impossible to enumerate and quite impossible to imagine. I therefore felt sure that there was no danger of my uncle solving the problem by this heroic method.

Meanwhile time went by; night fell; the noises in the street ceased; my uncle, bent over his task, saw nothing, not even Martha opening the door; he heard nothing, not even the good woman's voice asking:

'Are you going to have any supper tonight, Sir?'

So poor Martha had to go away unanswered. As for me, after resisting for a while I was overcome by an invincible drowsiness and I fell asleep on the sofa, while my uncle Lidenbrock went on calculating and rubbing out.

When I awoke the next morning, the indefatigable savant was still at work. His red eyes, his pale complexion, his hair tousled by his feverish hand, and his flushed cheeks revealed what a terrible struggle he was having with the impossible, and what weariness of mind and intellectual turmoil he must have been enduring.

I honestly felt sorry for him. In spite of the reproaches

I felt entitled to level at him, a certain pity took hold of me. The poor man was so possessed by his idea that he had forgotten to lose his temper. All his forces were concentrated on a single point, and, as their usual outlet was closed, there was every reason to fear an explosion at any moment.

With a single word I could have loosened the pressure of that iron vice which was squeezing his brain, but I said nothing.

Yet I was not a cruel fellow by nature. Why, then, did I remain silent in these circumstances? In my uncle's own best interests.

'No, no,' I said to myself, 'I will not speak! I know him – he would want to go, and nothing would stop him. He has a volcanic imagination, and he would risk his life to do something that no other geologist has done. I will remain silent. I will keep the secret which chance has revealed to me. To pass it on would be tantamount to killing Professor Lidenbrock. Let him find it out himself if he can. I have no desire to have his death on my conscience one day.'

Having taken this decision, I folded my arms and waited. But I had reckoned without a little incident which occurred a few hours later.

When Martha wanted to leave the house to go to the market, she found the door locked. The big key was gone. Who had taken it out of the lock? Obviously my uncle must have done so when he had come in the night before from his unexpected walk.

Had he done that on purpose? Or had it just been absent-mindedness on his part? Did he want to submit us to the rigours of hunger? That struck me as going rather too far. Could Martha and I really be the victims of a state of affairs which did not concern us in the slightest? We could indeed, for I remembered a precedent calculated to alarm us. A few years before, when my uncle was working on his great mineralogical classification, he had gone forty-eight hours without eating and the whole household had been obliged to share in that scientific fast. For my part, I had suffered stomach pains which had been anything but amusing for a lad with a healthy appetite.

Now it seemed to me that breakfast was going to fail to appear, like supper the night before. All the same, I decided to be a hero and not give in to the demands of hunger. Martha took the whole thing very much to heart and, poor woman, was greatly distressed. As for me, the impossibility of leaving the house distressed me even more, and for a very good reason, which you can imagine.

My uncle went on working, his imagination far away in the ideal world of combinations; he was living a long way from the earth and quite apart from earthly needs.

About midday, hunger began to have a serious effect on me. Martha, in all innocence, had eaten everything in the larder the night before, so that now there was nothing left in the house. Yet I stood firm. I made this a sort of point of honour.

Two o'clock struck. The situation was becoming ridiculous, indeed unbearable. I began to feel really hungry. I started telling myself that I was exaggerating the importance of the document; that my uncle would not believe it; that he would dismiss it as a joke; that if the worst came to the worst, he could be forcibly restrained; that finally he might find the key to the cipher himself, and in that case I should have fasted in vain.

These arguments struck me as excellent, though the day before I would have rejected them indignantly; I even decided that I had been ridiculous to wait so long, and I resolved to tell all.

I was considering how to broach the subject, in a way which was not too obvious, when the Professor stood up, put on his hat, and got ready to go out.

What! Were we going to let him leave the house and lock us in again? Never!

'Uncle!' I said.

He did not seem to hear me.

'Uncle Lidenbrock!' I said, raising my voice.

'Eh?' he said, like a man suddenly roused from sleep.

'What about that key?'

'What key? The key to the door?'

'No,' I cried, 'the key to the document!'

The Professor looked at me over his spectacles; no

doubt he saw something odd in my expression, for he seized me by the arm, and, incapable of speaking, questioned me with his eyes. Even so, no question was ever put more clearly.

I nodded.

He shook his head with a sort of pity, as if he were dealing with a lunatic.

I nodded more emphatically.

His eyes glistened and his hand tightened menacingly.

This mute conversation in those circumstances would have aroused the interest of the most indifferent onlooker. And the fact is that I had really got to the stage where I no longer dared to speak, I was so afraid that my uncle would smother me in his transports of joy. But he became so insistent that I was finally compelled to answer.

'Yes, that key,' I said. 'By chance . . .'

'What's that you're saying?' he exclaimed with indescribable emotion.

'There,' I said, handing him the sheet of paper on which I had written. 'Read that.'

'But that's meaningless,' he answered, crumpling the paper in his hand.

'Yes, if you start reading at the beginning, but if you read backwards . . .'

Before I had finished the sentence the Professor uttered a cry, or rather more than a cry, a positive roar. Light had suddenly dawned upon him. He was transfigured.

Pouncing on the paper, with misty eyes and a broken voice, he read the whole document, working backwards from the last letter to the first.

It read as follows.

In Sneffels Yoculis craterem kem delibat
umbra Scartaris Julii intra calendas descende,
audas viator, et terrestre centrum attinges.
Kod feci. Arne Saknussemm

Which bad Latin may be translated thus:

Descend into the crater of Sneffells Yokul,
over which the shadow of Scartaris falls
before the kalends of July, bold traveller,
and you will reach the centre of the earth.
I have done this. Arne Saknussemm

On reading this, my uncle gave a jump as if he had unexpectedly received an electric shock. His courage, his joy, his self-assurance were wonderful to behold. He walked up and down; he held his head in both hands; he moved the chairs around; he stacked his books in piles; he juggled, incredible as it may seem, with his precious geodes. At last his nerves calmed down and, like a man exhausted by too lavish an expenditure of vital energy, he sank back into his armchair.

'What time is it?' he asked after a few moments of silence.

'Three o'clock,' I replied.

'Is it really? My dinner has gone down quickly. I'm dying of hunger. Let's have something to eat. After that . . .'

'After that?'

'You can pack my box.'

'What?' I exclaimed.

'And your own,' said the pitiless Professor, going into the dining-room.

6

I Argue in Vain

At these words a shudder went through the whole of my body. However, I controlled myself and even decided to put a good face on things. I knew that only scientific arguments could stop Professor Lidenbrock. Luckily there were plenty of good ones against the practicability of such a journey. To go to the centre of the earth! What a crazy idea! But I kept my dialectics for a suitable opportunity and gave the whole of my attention to the business of eating.

There would be no point in repeating my uncle's curses when he saw the empty table. An explanation was given and Martha set at liberty. She ran to the market, and managed so well that an hour later my hunger had been appeased and I became aware of the situation once more.

During the meal my uncle was almost merry, and indulged in some of those learned jokes which never do anybody any harm. After dessert he beckoned me to follow him into his study.

I obeyed. He sat down at one end of his table, I at the other.

'Axel,' he said in quite a gentle voice, 'you are a very clever young man, and you have done me a great service when, tired of trying, I was going to give up that combination. What mightn't I have tried next? I shall never forget that, my boy, and you shall have your share in the glory we are going to win.'

'Splendid!' I thought. 'He's in a good mood. Now's the time to discuss that glory he mentions.'

'Above all,' my uncle went on, 'I insist on absolute secrecy, you understand? I have plenty of envious rivals in the world of science who would be only too eager to undertake this journey, but they mustn't hear about it until we are back.'

'Do you really think,' I asked, 'that there are many who would be bold enough to risk it?'

'Of course! Who would hesitate at the thought of winning such fame? If this document were made public, a whole army of geologists would rush to follow in Arne Saknussemm's footsteps.'

'I'm not so sure of that, Uncle, for there's nothing to prove that the document is genuine.'

'What! And what about the book we found it in?'

'Oh, I grant you that Saknussemm wrote those lines. But does it follow that he really performed the journey? May not this old parchment be just a hoax?'

I almost regretted making this last, rather foolhardy remark. The Professor bent his shaggy brows, and I was afraid that I had compromised the rest of the conversation. Fortunately I was mistaken. A hint of a smile touched the lips of my solemn companion, and he replied:

'We shall see.'

'Ah!' I said, rather put out. 'But allow me to list all the possible objections to this document.'

'Speak out, my boy, don't be afraid. You are perfectly free to express your opinion. I no longer regard you as my nephew, but as my colleague. So go on.'

'Well, first I should like to ask you what these names Yokul, Sneffels, and Scartaris mean, because I have never heard them before.'

'That is an easy question to answer. As it happens I recently received a map from my friend Augustus Peterman of Leipzig, which could not have arrived at a better time. Take down the third atlas in the second section of the big bookcase, series Z, fourth shelf.'

I stood up, and with the help of these precise instructions soon found the required atlas. My uncle opened it and said:

'Here is one of the best maps of Iceland, Handerson's, and I think it will give us the solution to all your difficulties.'

I bent over the map.

'You can see that there are volcanoes all over the island,'

said the Professor, 'and you will notice that they all bear the name *Yokul*. That word means "glacier" in Icelandic, and at that high latitude most eruptions take place through layers of ice. Hence the term *Yokul* which is applied to all the volcanic mountains in Iceland.'

'I see,' I replied. 'But what is *Sneffels*?'

I was hoping that there would be no answer to this question, but I was disappointed. My uncle went on:

'Follow my finger along the west coast of Iceland. You see Reykjavik, the capital? Good. Well, go up the countless fjords that start from this shore eaten away by the sea, and stop just below the sixty-fifth degree of latitude. What do you see there?'

'A sort of peninsula that looks like a bone with a huge knee-cap at the end of it.'

'Quite a good comparison, my boy. Now can you see anything on that knee-cap?'

'Yes, a mountain which looks as if it has grown out of the sea.'

'Good. Well, that is Sneffels.'

'That?'

'Yes, that. It's a mountain five thousand feet high, one of the most remarkable on the island, and undoubtedly destined to be the most famous in the world if its crater leads to the centre of the globe.'

'But that's impossible!' I said, shrugging my shoulders in disgust at such a ridiculous idea.

'Impossible?' said Professor Lidenbrock in a stern voice. 'And why should it be impossible?'

'Because the crater must be full of lava and burning rocks, and in that case . . .'

'But what if it's an extinct volcano?'

'Extinct?'

'Yes. The number of active volcanoes in the world is now only about three hundred. But there is a far greater number of extinct volcanoes, and Sneffels is one of these. It has had only one eruption known to history, and that was in 1229; after that it gradually calmed down, and at present it is no longer counted among the active volcanoes.'

I could make no reply to such positive statements, and I therefore fell back on the other obscure aspects of the document.

'What does this word *Scartaris* mean?' I asked. 'And where do the kalends of July come into all this?'

My uncle considered for a few moments. I felt a surge of hope, but it was short-lived for soon he answered:

'What is obscure to you is crystal-clear to me. This proves the ingenious care with which Saknussemm described his discovery. Sneffels has several craters, and it was therefore necessary to indicate the one which leads to the centre of the earth. What did the learned Icelander do? He observed that at the approach of the kalends of July, in other words towards the end of June, one of the peaks of the mountain, a peak called Scartaris, cast its shadow as far as the mouth of the crater in question, and he recorded that fact in his document. Nothing could be more precise, and when we reach the summit of Sneffels we shall have no hesitation as to which way to go.'

My uncle certainly had an answer to everything. I saw that I could not shake him as far as the words on the old parchment were concerned. I therefore stopped pressing him on that subject, and since the most important thing was to convince him, I went on to the scientific objections, which in my opinion were much more serious.

'All right,' I said, 'I have to admit that Saknussemm's sentence is quite clear and leaves no room for doubt. I'll even grant that the document seems perfectly genuine. The old savant went to the bottom of Sneffels, he saw the shadow of Scartaris touch the edge of the crater before the kalends of July, he even heard tell in the legendary stories of his day that that crater led to the centre of the earth; but as for his having gone down there and come back alive, no, a hundred times no!'

'And why not?' asked my uncle, in an extremely sarcastic voice.

'Because all the theories of science prove that a feat of that sort is impossible.'

'Oh, so all the theories prove that, do they? What wicked theories they are! And what a nuisance they are going to be!'

I saw that he was making fun of me, but I went on all the same.

'Yes. It is generally recognized that the temperature rises about one degree for every seventy feet below the surface; so that if you admit that ratio to be constant, the radius of the earth being over four thousand miles, the temperature at the centre must be over two million degrees. Consequently all the substances inside the earth must be in a state of incandescent gas, for gold, platinum, and even the hardest rocks cannot resist such a temperature. I therefore have good grounds for asking how it could be possible to penetrate so far.'

'So it's the temperature that worries you, Axel?'

'Of course it is. If we were to go only twenty-five miles down, we should have reached the limit of the earth's crust for the temperature there is over 1,300 degrees.'

'And you are afraid of melting away?'

'I leave you to answer that question,' I retorted rather crossly.

'This is my answer,' said Professor Lidenbrock, taking on his most superior air. 'Neither you nor anybody else knows for certain what is going on inside the earth, seeing that we have penetrated only about one twelve-thousandth part of its radius; what is more, science is eminently perfectible, and each new theory is soon disproved by a newer one. Wasn't it generally believed until Fourier that the temperature of interplanetary space steadily decreased, and don't we know now that the lowest temperature in the ethereal regions is never below forty or fifty degrees below zero? Why shouldn't the same be true of the internal temperature? Why, at a certain depth, shouldn't it reach an impassable limit, instead of rising to the melting-point of the most resistant minerals?'

As my uncle was now putting the question on a hypothetical plane, I had nothing to say in reply.

'Well, let me tell you that some real scientists, including Poisson, have proved that if a temperature of two million degrees existed inside the globe, the fiery gases given off by the melted matter would acquire such an elasticity that the earth's crust would be unable to resist it, and that it would explode like the plates of a bursting boiler.'

'That is Poisson's opinion, Uncle, nothing more.'

'Granted. But it is also the opinion of other distinguished geologists that the interior of the globe is composed of neither gas nor water nor of the heaviest minerals known to us, for in that case the earth would weigh half as much as it does.'

'Oh, you can prove anything with figures.'

'But can you do the same with facts? Isn't it a fact that the number of volcanoes has greatly diminished since the beginning of the world, and may we not conclude that if there is heat in the centre it is decreasing?'

'Uncle, if you are going to enter the region of speculation, I have nothing more to say.'

'But I have something to say, namely that the greatest authorities share my opinion. Do you remember a visit the famous English chemist Humphry Davy paid me in 1825?'

'No, I don't. For the very good reason that I wasn't born until nineteen years later.'

'Well, Humphry Davy came to see me on his way through Hamburg. Among the questions, we spent a long time discussing the hypothesis of the liquid nature of the terrestrial nucleus. We were agreed that this liquidity could not exist, for a reason which science has never been able to refute.'

'What reason is that?' I asked with a certain astonishment.

'Because this liquid mass would be subject, like the sea, to the attraction of the moon, and consequently, twice a day, there would be internal tides which, pushing up the earth's crust, would cause periodical earthquakes.'

'Yet it is obvious,' I said, 'that the surface of the globe has been subjected to the action of fire, and it is reasonable to suppose that the outer crust cooled down first, while the heat took refuge in the centre.'

'You are mistaken there,' replied my uncle. 'The earth was heated by the combustion of its surface and nothing else. Its surface was composed of a great number of metals, such as potassium and sodium, which have the peculiar property of igniting at the mere contact with air and water. These metals caught fire when the atmospheric vapours fell in the form of rain on the soil; and little by little, when the waters penetrated into the fissures of the earth's crust, they started fresh fires together with explosions and eruptions. Hence the large number of volcanoes during the early period of the earth.'

'I must say that's an ingenious theory,' I exclaimed, rather in spite of myself.

'And one which Humphry demonstrated to me, here in this very room, with a simple experiment. He made a small ball largely composed of the metals I mentioned just now, and which was the perfect image of our globe; when he sprayed its surface with a fine rain, it blistered, became oxidized, and formed a miniature mountain; a crater formed at the mountain's summit, and an eruption took place making the whole ball so hot that you couldn't hold it in your hand.'

I began to be shaken by the Professor's arguments, which he put forward, incidentally, with all his usual ardour and enthusiasm.

'As you can see, Axel,' he added, 'the state of the terrestrial nucleus has given rise to a variety of theories among geologists; nothing is less certain than the existence of that internal heat you believe in; my own view is that it doesn't exist, and couldn't possibly exist; but in any case we shall see for ourselves, and like Arne

Saknussemm we shall know what to think about this important question.'

'All right!' I replied, carried away by his enthusiasm. 'We shall see – that is, if it is possible to see anything there.'

'And why shouldn't it be possible? May we not count on electrical phenomena to give us light, and even on the atmosphere, whose pressure may render it luminous as we approach the centre?'

'Yes,' I said, 'that is just possible, I suppose.'

'It is certain,' my uncle retorted triumphantly; 'but silence, you understand, silence about all this, so that nobody has the idea of trying to reach the centre of the earth before us.'

7

Getting Ready

So ended that memorable conversation, leaving me with a sort of fever. I came out of my uncle's study in a daze, and there was not enough air in the streets of Hamburg to set me right again. I therefore made for the banks of the Elbe, where the ferry-steamer links the town with the Harburg railway.

Was I convinced of the truth of what I had just heard? Hadn't I been swayed by Professor Lidenbrock? Was I to take seriously his declared intention to penetrate to the centre of the world? Had I been listening to the mad speculations of a lunatic or to the scientific conclusions of a genius? Where, in all this, did truth stop and error begin?

I drifted about among a thousand contradictory hypotheses, without succeeding in grasping a single one.

Yet I remembered that I had felt convinced, even if my enthusiasm was beginning to cool down; and I would have liked to set off at once, without giving myself time to think. Yes, at that moment I would have had the courage to pack my bag.

But an hour later I must admit that this excitement of mine abated, my nerves relaxed, and from the depths of the earth I rose once more to the surface.

'It's ridiculous!' I exclaimed. 'There's no sense in it! It isn't the sort of proposal to put to a sensible young man. The whole thing must be a mistake. I've slept badly and had a nightmare.'

In the meantime I had followed the bank of the Elbe and gone round the town. After passing the port again I had reached the Altona road. A presentiment was guiding me, which was fully justified, for soon I caught sight of my little Gräuben walking briskly towards Hamburg.

'Gräuben!' I called out to her when I was some distance away.

The girl stopped, rather startled, I imagine, at hearing her name called on the high road. A dozen strides and I was at her side.

'Axel!' she exclaimed in surprise. 'Oh, you have come to meet me. That was nice of you.'

However, when she looked at me Gräuben noticed my worried, anxious expression.

'What's the matter?' she asked, holding out her hand.

'What's the matter, Gräuben?' I echoed.

A couple of minutes and three sentences were sufficient to put my pretty Virlandaise in possession of the facts. For a few moments she remained silent. I don't know whether her heart was beating like mine, but her hand did not tremble in mine. We walked about a hundred yards without speaking.

'Axel!' she said at last.

'Yes, my dear Gräuben?'

'It will be a wonderful journey.'

I gave a start at these words.

'Yes, Axel, a journey worthy of a scientist's nephew. It is a good thing for a man to distinguish himself by some great enterprise.'

'What, Gräuben, you mean you aren't going to advise me against an expedition like that?'

'No, my dear Axel, and I would gladly come with your uncle and you, if it weren't that a girl would only be in the way.'

'You mean that?'

'Yes, I mean it.'

Oh, how hard it is to understand the hearts of girls and women. When they are not the most timid of creatures, they are the bravest. Reason has no part in their lives. This girl was encouraging me to take part in that expedition and would not have been afraid to join it herself! And she was pushing me into it, even though she was in love with me! I was disconcerted, and to tell the truth, ashamed of myself.

'Gräuben,' I said, 'we shall see whether you talk like this tomorrow.'

'Tomorrow, my dear Axel, I shall speak exactly as I have done today.'

Hand in hand, but saying nothing more, Gräuben and I continued on our way. I was tired out by the day's emotions.

'After all,' I thought to myself, 'the kalends of July are still a long way off, and a great many things may happen in the meantime to cure my uncle of his mania for underground exploration.'

Darkness had fallen by the time we reached the house in the Königstrasse. I expected to find the place quiet, my uncle in bed as usual, and Martha giving the dining-room a final flick with her feather duster.

But I had reckoned without the Professor's impatience. I found him shouting and gesticulating in the midst of a crowd of men who were unloading goods on the path. Our old servant was at her wits' end.

'Come along, Axel,' exclaimed my uncle as soon as he saw me, 'hurry up! Your box isn't packed, my papers aren't in order, I can't find the key to my bag, and my gaiters haven't arrived.'

I was thunderstruck. My voice failed me. I could only just murmur the words:

'Are we going, then?'

'Yes, you young idiot, and you go for a walk instead of staying here!'

'We're going?' I repeated in an even feebler voice.

'Yes, first thing the day after tomorrow.'

I could not bear to hear any more, and I fled to my little room.

There was no longer any doubt about it. My uncle had spent the afternoon buying some of the things he needed for his journey, and the path was littered with enough rope ladders, knotted cords, torches, flasks, grappling-irons, alpenstocks, iron-shod sticks, and pickaxes to burden at least a dozen men.

I spent a dreadful night. The next morning I was called early. I had made up my mind not to open the door. But how could I resist the sweet voice which uttered these words:

'My dear Axel?'

I came out of my room, thinking that my haggard features, my pale complexion, and my eyes reddened by lack of sleep would arouse Gräuben's sympathy and change her ideas.

'Ah, my dear Axel,' she said, 'I see that you are feeling better and that a night's rest has done you good.'

'Done me good!' I exclaimed. I rushed to my mirror. Well, the fact was that I did look better than I had expected. I could scarcely believe my eyes.

'Axel,' said Gräuben, 'I have had a long talk with my guardian. He is a bold thinker and a man of great courage, and you must remember that his blood flows in your veins. He has told me about his plans and hopes, and explained why and how he expects to attain his object. He will succeed, I have no doubt of that. Oh, Axel, it is such a wonderful thing to devote oneself to science like that. What glory there is in store for Herr Lidenbrock – and for his companion! When you come back, Axel, you will be a man, his equal, free to speak and act as you wish, and free to . . .'

She stopped short and blushed. Her words revived my spirits. All the same, I still refused to believe in our departure. I took Gräuben along to the Professor's study.

'Uncle,' I said, 'are we really going?'

'Why? Have you any doubts?'

'No,' I said, not wanting to vex him. 'Only I don't see what need there is to hurry.'

'Think of time! Time flying with irreparable speed!'

'But it's only the twenty-sixth of May, and from now until the end of June . . .'

'You ignoramus! Do you think it's as easy as all that to get to Iceland? If you hadn't gone off like a fool, I'd have taken you with me to the Copenhagen office of Liffender & Co. There you'd have seen that there's only one service from Copenhagen to Reykjavik, on the twenty-second of each month.'

'Well?'

'Well, if we waited until the twenty-second of June, we should arrive too late to see the shadow of Scartaris touch the crater of Sneffels. So we have to get to Copenhagen as fast as we can to find some means of transport. Go and pack your things!'

There was no reply to this. I went back to my room, accompanied by Gräuben. It was she who took it upon herself to pack everything I needed in a little portmanteau. She was no more excited than if I had been going on a trip to Lübeck or Heligoland. Her little hands moved about hurriedly. She chatted calmly. She gave me eminently sensible reasons for our expedition. She delighted me, and yet I felt extremely angry with her. Now and then I nearly lost my temper, but she took no notice and went on with her work as methodically as ever.

Finally the last strap round the portmanteau was buckled, and I went downstairs.

All day scientific instruments, firearms, and electrical apparatus had been arriving. Poor Martha did not know where she was.

'Is the Master out of his mind?' she asked me.

I nodded.

'And he's taking you with him?'

I nodded again.

'Where?' she asked.

I pointed towards the centre of the earth.

'Into the cellar?' exclaimed the old servant.

'No,' I said, 'farther down than that.'

Night fell. I had ceased to be conscious of the passage of time.

'I'll see you tomorrow morning,' said my uncle. 'We leave at six sharp.'

At ten o'clock I slumped on to my bed. During the night my fears took hold of me again. I dreamed about abysses all the time. I became delirious. I felt the Professor's strong hand gripping me, dragging me along, pulling me into chasms and quicksands. I kept hurtling into bottomless abysses with the increasing velocity of bodies dropping through space. My life had become an interminable fall.

I awoke at five, worn out with fatigue and emotion. I went down to the dining-room. My uncle was at table, eating a hearty breakfast. I looked at him with horror and disgust. But Gräuben was there, so I said nothing. I could not eat anything.

At half past five there was a rumble of wheels outside. A big carriage had arrived to take us to the station at Altona. Before long it was filled with my uncle's parcels.

'Where's your box?' he asked me.

'It's ready,' I replied in a faltering voice.

'Be quick and bring it down, then, or you'll make us miss the train.'

It was now obviously impossible to fight against my fate. I went back up to my room, and, letting my portmanteau slide down the stairs, I hurried after it.

At that moment my uncle was solemnly handing over the 'reins' of the house to Gräuben. My pretty little

Virlandaise was as calm as ever. She kissed her guardian, but she could not restrain a tear as she touched my cheek with her sweet lips.

'Gräuben!' I exclaimed.

'Go, Axel dear, go,' she said. 'You are leaving your betrothed, but when you come back you will find your wife.'

I pressed her in my arms and then took my seat in the carriage. From the door, Martha and Gräuben waved a final farewell. Then the two horses, at a whistle from the driver, set off at a gallop along the road to Altona.

8

The First Stage

A ltona, which is almost a suburb of Hamburg, is the terminus of the Kiel railway, which was to take us to the shores of the Belts. In less than twenty minutes we were in Holstein.

At half past six the carriage drew up outside the station; all my uncle's bulky parcels and articles of luggage were unloaded, carried in, weighed, labelled, and put in the luggage-van, and at seven o'clock we were sitting opposite each other in our compartment. The whistle sounded and the engine moved off. We were on our way.

Was I resigned? Not yet. However, the cool morning air, and rapidly changing scenery through which the train carried us took my mind off my chief preoccupation.

As for the Professor's thoughts, they were obviously far ahead of the train, which was much too slow for his impatient character. We were alone in the carriage, but neither of us said anything. My uncle examined all his pockets and his travelling-bag with minute care. I saw that he had not forgotten a single one of the documents necessary for the execution of his plans.

One of them was a carefully folded sheet of paper bearing the letter-head of the Danish chancery and signed by Mr Christiansen, the Danish consul at Hamburg and a friend of the Professor's. This was obviously intended to enable us to obtain at Copenhagen a letter of introduction to the Governor of Iceland.

I also noticed the famous document carefully tucked away in the innermost pocket of my uncle's wallet. I cursed it from the bottom of my heart, and turned my attention once more to the countryside. It was a vast succession of uninteresting, monotonous, loamy, and fertile plains – good railway country, and very propitious for those straight lines so dear to railway companies.

But I had no time to tire of this monotony, for three hours after our departure the train stopped at Kiel, a stone's throw from the sea.

As our luggage was registered for Copenhagen, we had no need to bother about it. All the same, the Professor watched it anxiously as it was transferred to the steamer. There it disappeared into the hold.

My uncle, in his haste, had made a mistake over the connexion between train and steamer, so that we had a whole day to spare. The steamer *Ellenora* was not due to sail until nightfall. This resulted in a feverish nine hours, during which the irascible traveller heaped curses on the steamship and railway companies and the governments which allowed such abuses. I had to back him up when he complained to the captain of the *Ellenora* on the subject. He wanted him to get up steam straight away. The captain sent him packing.

At Kiel, as elsewhere, a day goes by somehow or other. By dint of strolling along the grassy shores of the bay on which the little town stands, of roaming through the thick woods which make it look like a nest in a tangle of branches, of admiring the villas, each provided with its little bathing-house, and finally of hurrying along and cursing, we came at last to ten o'clock.

Wreaths of smoke were now rising into the sky from the *Ellenora*'s funnel; the deck was trembling with the throbbing of the boiler; we were on board and the temporary occupants of two berths in the only cabin.

At a quarter past ten the ropes were cast off, and the steamer glided away over the dark waters of the Great Belt.

It was a dark night; there was a smacking breeze and a high sea; a few lights on shore appeared in the darkness; later on, I don't know where, a flashing lighthouse sent out a sparkling light over the waves; this is all that I can remember of that first crossing.

At seven in the morning we landed at Korsör, a little town on the west coast of Zealand. There we changed from the boat to another train, which carried us across a countryside just as flat as the plain of Holstein.

It took us another three hours to reach the Danish capital. My uncle had not slept a wink all night. In his impatience I believe he had been trying to push the train along with his feet.

At last he caught sight of a stretch of water.

'The Sound!' he cried.

On our left there was a huge building which looked like a hospital.

'That's a lunatic asylum,' said one of our travelling companions.

'Good!' I thought. 'That's just the place for us to end our days in!' Although, big as it is, it couldn't be big enough to contain all Professor Lidenbrock's madness!

Finally, at ten in the morning, we alighted at Copenhagen, where the luggage was loaded on to a carriage and taken with us to the Phoenix Hotel in Bredgade. This took half an hour, for the station is outside the city. Then my uncle, after a hasty toilet, carried me off with him. The hotel porter could speak German and English, but the polyglot Professor questioned him in good Danish and it was in good Danish that the man directed him to the Museum of Northern Antiquities.

The curator of this curious establishment, whose marvels would make it possible to reconstruct the country's history by means of its old stone weapons, its cups, and its jewels, was a savant called Professor Thomson, a friend of the Danish consul at Hamburg.

My uncle had a cordial letter of introduction to him. As a general rule, one savant receives another rather coolly. But here this was not the case. Professor Thomson was extremely obliging, and gave a warm welcome to both Professor Lidenbrock and his nephew. I need scarcely say that our secret was kept from the worthy curator of the museum: we were simply disinterested travellers who wished to visit Iceland out of idle curiosity.

Professor Thomson placed himself entirely at our disposal, and we scoured the quays in search of a ship leaving for Iceland.

I hoped against hope that there would be no means of transport whatever, but I was disappointed. A little Danish schooner, the *Valkyrie*, was due to set sail for Reykjavik on 2 June. The captain, Mr Bjarne, happened to be on board. His future passenger was so overwhelmed with joy that he squeezed his hands until the bones almost broke. The good man was somewhat taken aback at this handclasp. To him it seemed a very simple matter to go to Iceland, since that was his trade; but to my uncle it was sublime. The worthy captain took advantage of this enthusiasm to charge us double the usual fare; but we did not trouble our heads over such trifles.

'Come aboard on Tuesday, at seven in the morning,' said Captain Bjarne, after pocketing a respectable number of dollars.

We then thanked Professor Thomson for his help, and returned to the Phoenix Hotel.

'Things are going very well, very well indeed!' said my uncle. 'What a stroke of luck to find that boat ready to sail! Now let's have some breakfast and see the sights of Copenhagen.'

We went to Kongens-Nye-Torw, a square where there were two innocent-looking cannons which could not frighten anybody. Close by, at No. 5, there was a French restaurant where we had an ample breakfast for the modest sum of four marks each.

After that I took a childish pleasure in exploring the city; my uncle let me take him with me, but he saw nothing – neither the insignificant royal palace, nor the pretty seventeenth-century bridge which spans the canal opposite the museum, nor the huge memorial to Thorwaldsen, covered with hideous mural paintings and containing some of the sculptor's works, nor the toy-like castle of Rosenborg in its rather fine park, nor the magnificent Renaissance stock exchange with its spire made of the twisted tails of four bronze dragons, nor the big windmills on the ramparts, whose huge arms filled out in the sea breeze like the sails of a ship.

What delightful walks we should have taken together, my pretty Virlandaise and I, beside the harbour where the two-deckers and the frigates slept peacefully, along the green banks of the strait, and under the shady trees among which the fort is hidden, with its guns poking out their black muzzles between the branches of alder and willow!

But, alas, Gräuben was far away, and I doubted if I would ever see her again.

However, if my uncle remained blind to these delightful scenes, he was very much struck by a certain church spire on the island of Amak, which forms the south-west district of Copenhagen.

I was instructed to make in that direction, and we accordingly embarked on a little steamer which plied on the canals. A few minutes later we reached the dockyard quay.

After walking along a few narrow streets in which convicts wearing grey and yellow trousers were working under the supervision of warders, we arrived at the Vor-Frelsers-Kirk. There seemed to be nothing remarkable about this church, but there was one feature of its tall spire which had attracted the Professor's attention. Starting from the top of the tower, an exterior staircase wound round the spire, circling up into the sky.

'Let's go up,' said my uncle.

'But we may get dizzy,' I retorted.

'All the more reason why we should go up; we have to get used to it.'

'All the same . . .'

'Come along, I tell you. We're wasting time.'

I had to obey. The caretaker, who lived at the other end of the street, let us have the key, and the ascent began.

My uncle went ahead, climbing nimbly. I followed him with a certain trepidation, for I had no head for heights. I possessed neither the equilibrium of an eagle nor its steady nerves.

As long as we were shut inside the interior staircase, all was well; but after 150 steps the air struck me in the face; we had reached the top of the tower. There the aerial staircase began, protected by a thin iron rail and with narrowing steps which seemed to rise into infinite space.

'I can't do it!' I exclaimed.

'You aren't a coward, are you? Come on!' replied the pitiless Professor.

I had to follow him, clinging to the rail. The keen air made me dizzy; I could feel the spire swaying in every gust of wind; my legs began to give way; soon I was climbing on my knees, then on my belly. I shut my eyes, suffering from space-sickness.

At last, with my uncle dragging me up by my collar, I reached the ball at the top of the spire.

'Look,' he said, 'and look hard! You must take lessons in abysses.'

I opened my eyes. I saw the houses looking as if they had been squashed flat by a fall, in the midst of the smoke fog created by their chimneys. Over my head wisps of cloud were passing, and by an optical illusion they seemed to me to be motionless, while the spire, the ball, and I were being carried along at a tremendous speed. Far away on one side there was the green country, and on the other the sea was sparkling under a sheaf of sunbeams. The Sound stretched away to the Point of Elsinore, dotted with a few white sails like seagulls' wings, and in the mist to the east the faintly blurred coast of Sweden was visible. The whole of this vast spectacle spun around beneath my eyes.

None the less I was compelled to get to my feet, stand up straight, and look around. My first lesson in vertigo lasted an hour. When at last I was allowed to come down again and walk on the solid paving-stones in the streets, I could scarcely stand upright.

'We'll do that again tomorrow,' said the Professor.

Sure enough, for five days in succession I repeated this vertiginous exercise; and in spite of myself I made decided progress in the art of 'lofty contemplation'.

9

We Reach Iceland

The day of our departure arrived. The day before, our kind friend Professor Thomson had brought us cordial letters of introduction to Count Trampe, the Governor of Iceland, Mr Pictursson, the Bishop's coadjutor, and Mr Finsen, the mayor of Reykjavik. In return, my uncle shook him warmly by the hand.

On 2 June, at six in the morning, our precious luggage was taken on board the *Valkyrie*, and the captain showed us to our somewhat cramped cabins, under a sort of deckhouse.

'Is the wind favourable?' asked my uncle.

'Couldn't be better,' replied Captain Bjarne. 'It's a sou'-easter. We shall leave the Sound at full speed, with all sails set.'

A few minutes later the schooner, under her foresail, brigantine, topsail, and topgallant sail, got under way and swept through the straits. In an hour the Danish capital seemed to be sinking beneath the waves in the distance, and the *Valkyrie* was skirting the coast of Elsinore. In my nervous frame of mind I fully expected to see the ghost of Hamlet wandering on the famous terrace.

'Sublime madman,' I said, 'you would probably approve of our expedition! You might even come with us to look for the solution of your eternal doubts at the centre of the earth.'

But nothing appeared on the ancient walls. Besides, the castle is much younger than the heroic prince of Denmark. It now serves as a sumptuous lodge for the doorkeeper of the straits of the Sound, through which fifteen thousand ships of all nations pass every year.

The castle of Kronsberg soon disappeared in the mist, as well as the tower of Helsingborg, standing on the Swedish coast, and the schooner bent lightly under the breezes from the Cattegat.

The *Valkyrie* was a splendid ship, but with a sailing-ship you never know what to expect. She was carrying coal, household utensils, pottery, woollen garments, and a cargo of corn to Reykjavik. The crew consisted of only five men, all Danes.

'How long will the passage take?' my uncle asked the captain.

'About ten days,' Captain Bjarne replied, 'provided we don't meet a nor'-wester while we're passing the Faroes.'

'But you aren't liable to suffer a serious delay, are you?'

'No, Herr Lidenbrock, have no fear, we shall arrive in good time.'

Towards the evening the schooner doubled Cape Skager, at the northern point of Denmark, crossed the Skager-rack during the night, skirted the southern point of Norway by Cape Lindness, and entered the North Sea.

Two days later we sighted Peterhead on the coast of Scotland, and the *Valkyrie* turned her head towards the Faroe Islands, passing between the Orkneys and Shetlands.

Soon our schooner encountered the great Atlantic swell; she had to tack against the north wind and reached the Faroes only with some difficulty. On the eighth the captain made out Myganness, the most eastern of these islands, and from that moment set a straight course for Cape Portland, the most southerly point of Iceland.

The voyage passed without incident. I bore the trials of the sea fairly well; my uncle, to his great annoyance and even greater shame, was sick from beginning to end.

He was therefore unable to question Captain Bjarne about Sneffels, the means of communication, and transport facilities; he was obliged to put off these inquiries until his arrival and spent all his time lying in his cabin, whose walls creaked with every pitch of the ship. It must be admitted that his fate was not exactly undeserved.

On the eleventh we passed Cape Portland. The clear weather gave us a good view of Myrdals Jokul, which dominates it. The cape consists of a big hill with steep sides, standing all by itself on the beach.

The *Valkyrie* kept at a fair distance from the coast, continuing westwards through great shoals of whales and sharks. Soon we came in sight of a huge perforated rock, through which the foaming sea was pouring furiously. The Westman Isles seemed to rise from the ocean like a scattering of rocks on a liquid plain. From then on the schooner took a wide berth to clear Cape Reykjaness, which forms the western point of Iceland.

The rough sea prevented my uncle from coming on deck to admire these ragged coasts battered by south-westerly winds.

Forty-eight hours later, coming out of a storm which forced the schooner to scud under bare poles, we sighted to the east the beacon on Cape Skager, where dangerous rocks extend far out to sea. An Icelandic pilot came on board, and three hours later the *Valkyrie* anchored in the Faxa Bay, off Reykjavik.

The Professor at last emerged from his cabin, somewhat pale and haggard, but as enthusiastic as ever and with a satisfied look in his eyes.

The population of the town, immensely interested in the arrival of a ship from which everybody expected something, gathered on the quay.

My uncle was in a hurry to leave his floating prison, not to say his hospital. But before leaving the deck of the schooner he dragged me forward and pointed out to me, to the north of the bay, a high mountain with a double peak, a pair of cones covered with perpetual snow.

'Sneffels!' he cried. 'Sneffels!'

Then, with a gesture reminding me to keep absolute silence, he clambered down into the boat which was waiting for him. I followed him, and soon we were treading Icelandic soil.

The first man we saw was an impressive figure wearing a general's uniform. But he was just a magistrate, the Governor of the island, Baron Trampe in person. The Professor realized at once who he was. He handed the Governor his letters from Copenhagen, and a short conversation in Danish followed, in which I took no part, for a very good reason. But the gist of this first conversation was that Baron Trampe placed himself entirely at Professor Lidenbrock's disposal.

My uncle was also given a kind reception by the mayor, Mr Finsen, whose dress was just as military as the Governor's but whose temperament and office were no less pacific.

As for the Bishop's coadjutor, Mr Picturssen, he was on a pastoral tour in the north just then; for the time being we had to renounce the honour of being presented to him.

But we met a delightful man, Mr Fridriksson, the natural science master at the Reykjavik school, who was extremely helpful. This modest scholar spoke only Icelandic and Latin; he came and offered me his services in the language of Horace, and I felt straight away that we were born to understand each other. In point of fact, he was the only person with whom I could converse at all during my stay in Iceland.

This worthy man made over to us two of the three rooms in his house, and soon we were installed in them with our luggage, the amount of which rather astonished the inhabitants of Reykjavik.

'Well, Axel,' my uncle said to me, 'things are going well, and the worst is over.'

'The worst?' I exclaimed.

'Why, yes. Now we have nothing to do but go down!'

'If that's how you look at it, you are right. But, after all, when we have gone down we shall have to come up again, I imagine?'

'Oh, that doesn't worry me. Come, there's no time to lose. I'm going to the library. There may be a manuscript of Saknussemm's there, and if so I should like to consult it.'

'Then while you are there I'll wander round the town. Don't you want to do the same?'

'Oh, that doesn't appeal to me very much. What's interesting in Iceland isn't above ground but underneath.'

I went out and roamed about at random.

It would have been hard for me to lose my way in the two streets which make up Reykjavik. I therefore had no need to ask for directions, something which easily leads to misunderstanding when the language of gestures is used.

The town stretches along some low, marshy ground between two hills. A huge bed of lava lies on one side of it and slopes gently towards the sea. On the other side extends the vast Faxa Bay, shut in at the north by the enormous Sneffels glacier and of which the *Valkyrie* was the only occupant just then. Usually the English and French fishery protection vessels are anchored in this bay, but at the time they were on duty off the eastern coasts of the island.

The longer of Reykjavik's two streets runs parallel with the shore; here the merchants and shopkeepers live in wooden cabins made of red beams laid horizontally. The other street, more to the west, leads towards a little lake between the Bishop's house and the houses of the other people not involved in trade.

I had soon walked the whole length of these sad, dismal streets; here and there I caught a glimpse of a patch of faded turf, looking like an old woollen carpet worn threadbare by use, or else a sort of kitchen garden, whose sparse vegetables – potatoes, cabbages, and lettuces – would have figured appropriately on a Lilliputian table.

There were also a few sickly looking wallflowers trying to obtain a little sunshine.

About the middle of the non-commercial street, I found the public cemetery, enclosed by a mud wall and with plenty of room in it.

Then, a few yards farther on, I came to the Governor's house, a hovel compared to the town hall of Hamburg, a palace in comparison with the cabins of the Icelandic population.

Between the little lake and the town there stood the church, built in the Protestant style out of calcined stones provided by the volcanoes at their own expense; in high westerly winds it was obvious that the red tiles of its roof would take to the air, to the peril of the congregation.

On a neighbouring hill I saw the national school, where, as I was later informed by our host, the pupils were taught Hebrew, English, French, and Danish, four languages of which, to my shame, I did not know a single word. If I had gone to that school, I should have been the last of its forty pupils, and unworthy to sleep with them in their little double closets where more delicate children would have died of suffocation on the very first night.

In three hours I had seen everything there was to see, not only in the town itself but also in its environs. The view was remarkably dreary. No trees, and indeed scarcely any vegetation. Everywhere the bare bones of volcanic rocks. The Icelanders' huts are made of earth and peat, with their walls sloping inwards so that they look like roofs resting on the ground. But these roofs are fields, and comparatively fertile fields at that. Because of the warmth inside, grass grows on them quite thickly, and at haymaking time it is carefully mown, for otherwise the domestic animals would come and graze on these verdant dwellings.

During my walk I met few people. Returning to the main street, I found the greater part of the population busy drying, salting, and loading cod, their chief export. The men looked robust but clumsy, like fair-haired Germans with pensive eyes, conscious of being somewhat apart from the rest of mankind, poor exiles relegated to this land of ice and whom Nature should have made Eskimoes, seeing that she condemned them to live on the edge of the Arctic Circle. I tried in vain to detect a smile on their lips; now and then their facial muscles contracted in a sort of laugh, but they never smiled.

Their costume consisted of a coarse jersey made of a black wool known in the Scandinavian countries as *vadmel*, a broad-brimmed hat, trousers with a red stripe, and a piece of folded leather by way of footwear.

The women, who had sad, resigned faces, quite pretty but expressionless, were dressed in bodices and skirts of dark *vadmel*; the girls wore a little knitted brown cap over their plaited hair while the married women covered their heads with a coloured handkerchief, with a piece of white linen on top.

After a good walk, I returned to Mr Fridriksson's house, where I found my uncle in company with his host.

10

Our First Dinner in Iceland

Dinner was ready. Professor Lidenbrock did full justice to it, for his compulsory fast on board had turned his stomach into an unfathomable gulf. There was nothing remarkable about the meal itself, which was more Danish than Icelandic; but our host, who was more Icelandic than Danish, reminded me of the hospitable heroes of old. It was obvious that we were more at home than he was himself.

The conversation was in the vernacular, but my uncle put in some German and Mr Fridriksson some Latin so that I should understand. It was chiefly concerned with scientific questions, as befitted a couple of savants, but Professor Lidenbrock was extremely reserved, and with every sentence his eyes enjoined absolute silence on me as to our plans.

First of all Mr Fridriksson asked my uncle how his research at the library had gone.

'Your library!' exclaimed the Professor. 'Why, it consists of nothing but a few odd books on almost empty shelves.'

'What!' replied Mr Fridriksson. 'But we have eight thousand volumes, many of them valuable and rare, both works in the old Scandinavian language and all the latest books which Copenhagen sends us every year.'

'How do you make out that there are eight thousand volumes? As far as I could see . . .'

'Oh, Professor Lidenbrock, they are all over the country. On our old icy island people are fond of study. There isn't a single farmer or fisherman who can't read and doesn't read. We believe that books, instead of mouldering behind an iron grating, far from inquisitive gazes, should be worn out under the eyes of a great many readers. Consequently these volumes are passed from one person to another, and often return to their shelves only after an absence of a year or two.'

'And in the meantime,' said my uncle rather crossly, 'foreigners . . .'

'What can you expect? Foreigners have their own libraries at home, and, after all, the important thing is that our peasants should be educated. As I have already said, the love of study is in our blood. In 1816, for instance, we founded a literary society which has done very well; foreign savants pride themselves on belonging to it; and it publishes books to educate our compatriots and does great services to the country. If you would agree to be one of our corresponding members, Professor Lidenbrock, you would give us the greatest pleasure.'

My uncle, who already belonged to about a hundred learned societies, accepted with a good grace which obviously touched Mr Fridriksson.

'Now,' he went on, 'will you be kind enough to tell me what books you hoped to find in our library, and I may perhaps be able to tell you something about them?'

I looked at my uncle. He hesitated before replying. This question went to the heart of his plans. However, after a moment's reflection he decided to speak.

'Mr Fridriksson,' he said, 'I wanted to know whether, among your old books, you had those of Arne Saknussemm.'

'Arne Saknussemm!' replied the Reykjavik teacher. 'You mean the sixteenth-century savant who was at one and the same time a great naturalist, a great alchemist, and a great traveller?'

'Exactly.'

'One of the glories of Icelandic literature and science?'

'Just so.'

'A most illustrious man?'

'I grant you that.'

'And whose courage matched his genius?'

'I see that you know him well.'

My uncle was clearly delighted to hear his hero spoken of in this way. His eyes were fixed on Mr Fridriksson.

'Well,' he asked, 'what about his works?'

'Oh, his works . . . We haven't got them.'

'What – not in Iceland?'

'They aren't to be found in Iceland or anywhere else.'

'Why is that?'

'Because Arne Saknussemm was persecuted for heresy and in 1573 his works were burnt by the common hangman at Copenhagen.'

'Excellent! Splendid!' cried my uncle, to the horror of the Icelandic schoolmaster.

'I beg your pardon?' he said.

'Yes, that explains everything. It all ties up. It's all quite clear. Now I see why Saknussemm, put on the Index and forced to hide the discoveries due to his genius, was obliged to hide his secret in an incomprehensible cryptogram . . .'

'What secret?' asked Mr Fridriksson, his interest aroused.

'A secret which . . . whose . . .' stammered my uncle.

'Have you some secret document in your possession?' asked our host.

'No . . . I was just making a supposition, a pure supposition.'

'I see,' replied Mr Fridriksson, who was kind enough not to press the point when he saw the Professor's embarrassment. 'I hope,' he added, 'you won't leave our island without seeing some of its mineralogical wealth.'

'No, indeed,' replied my uncle; 'but I have arrived rather late in the day. I presume other savants have been here before me?'

'Yes, Professor Lidenbrock. The researches carried out by Messrs Olafsen and Povelsen on the King's instructions, Troil's field-work, the scientific mission of Messrs Gaimard and Robert based on the French corvette *La Recherche*, and the recent observations made by the scientists from the frigate *La Reine Hortense* have greatly added to our knowledge of Iceland. But, believe me, there is still plenty to do.'

'Do you think so?' asked my uncle with an innocent air, trying to hide the gleam in his eyes.

'Oh, yes. There are so many mountains, glaciers, and volcanoes to be studied, about which hardly anything is known. Why, to go no farther, look at that mountain you can see on the horizon. That is Sneffels.'

'Ah!' said my uncle. 'Sneffels.'

'Yes, one of the most interesting volcanoes, with a crater which is seldom visited.'

'Is it extinct?'

'Oh, yes. It has been extinct for the past five hundred years.'

'Well,' my uncle went on, frantically crossing his legs to keep himself from jumping into the air, 'I think I should like to begin my geological studies with that Seffel . . . Fessel . . . What do you call it?'

'Sneffels,' replied the worthy Mr Fridriksson.

This part of the conversation had been in Latin, so I had understood it all. I could scarcely conceal my amusement at seeing my uncle's attempts to suppress his obvious elation; he kept trying to assume an innocent expression which looked more like a diabolical grin.

'Yes,' he said, 'what you say gives me an idea. We shall try to climb that mountain and perhaps even study its crater.'

'I am very sorry,' said Mr Fridriksson, 'that my duties don't allow me to leave the town; otherwise I would have accompanied you with both pleasure and profit to myself.'

'Oh, no! Oh, no!' my uncle replied hurriedly. 'We wouldn't dream of disturbing anybody, Mr Fridriksson. Thank you very much all the same. The company of a learned man such as yourself would have been extremely useful, but your professional duties . . .'

I only hope that our host, in the innocence of his Icelandic soul, did not understand my uncle's heavy irony.

'Professor Lidenbrock,' he said, 'I thoroughly approve of your decision to begin with that volcano. You will garner a rich harvest of interesting observations there. But tell me, how do you expect to get to the Sneffels peninsula?'

'By sea, by crossing the bay. That's the shortest route.'

'No doubt it is; but it's impossible to take it.'

'Why?'

'Because we haven't got a single rowing-boat at Reykjavik.'

'The devil you haven't!'

'You will have to go by land, following the coastline. It will take longer, but it will be more interesting.'

'Good. I'll see about getting a guide.'

'I have one I can offer you.'

'A reliable, intelligent man?'

'Yes, a man who lives on the peninsula. He's an eider hunter and an able fellow. I'm sure you'll be pleased with him. He speaks perfect Danish too.'

'When can I see him?'

'Tomorrow, if you like.'

'Why not today?'

'Because he won't be here till tomorrow.'

'Tomorrow then,' said my uncle with a sigh.

This momentous conversation ended a few minutes later with the German professor expressing his warmest thanks to his Icelandic colleague. In the course of this dinner my uncle had learnt some important things, including the story of Saknussemm, the reason for the mysterious nature of his document, the fact that his host would not be accompanying him on his expedition, and the information that the very next day he would have a guide at his disposal.

11

Our Guide Hans

In the evening I went for a short walk on the beach, returning early to go to bed on my plank bed, where I slept soundly all night.

When I awoke I heard my uncle talking volubly in the next room. I got up straight away and quickly joined him.

He was chatting in Danish with a big, strapping fellow, who was obviously uncommonly strong. His eyes, set in a large, ingenuous face, were a dreamy blue and struck me as very intelligent. Long hair, which would have been called red even in England, fell over his athletic shoulders. This Icelander was supple in his movements, but he did not move his arms very much, like a man who knew or cared nothing of the language of gestures. Everything about him indicated a perfectly calm temperament, not indolent but peaceful. You could see at a glance that he asked nothing of anybody, that he worked as it suited him, and that nothing in this world could astonish or disturb his philosophy of life.

I gathered more about his character from the way in

which he listened to the Professor's excited verbiage. He stood there with his arms folded, motionless in the face of my uncle's wild gesticulations; to express the negative, his head turned from left to right; for the affirmative it bent forward – and that so slightly that his long hair barely moved. He carried economy of movement to the point of avarice.

Certainly I should never have guessed from looking at this man that he was a hunter; admittedly he would not frighten the game, but how could he ever get near it?

The mystery was explained when Mr Fridriksson told me that this calm person only hunted the eider, a bird whose plumage constitutes the chief wealth of the island. This plumage is known, in fact, as eiderdown, and no great expenditure of movement is required to obtain it.

In early summer the female, a sort of pretty duck, goes and builds her nest among the rocks of the fjords with which the coast is fringed. After building this nest she lines it with fine feathers which she plucks from her belly. Then the hunter, or rather the trader, arrives and takes the nest, and the female starts her work all over again. This goes on as long as she has any down left. When she has stripped herself bare, the male takes his turn to pluck himself. But as his feathers are hard and coarse and have no commercial value, the hunter does not bother to take his nest. The female accordingly lays her eggs, the young hatch out, and the next year the harvesting of the eiderdown begins again.

Now, as the eider does not pick steep cliffs on which to build her nest, but rather those smooth, terraced rocks which slope into the sea, the Icelandic hunter can pursue his occupation without undue exertion. He is a farmer who has no need to sow or cut his harvest, but simply has to gather it in.

This grave, phlegmatic, silent individual was called Hans Bjelke, and he came recommended by Mr Fridriksson. He was to be our guide.

His ways formed a great contrast with my uncle's but they got on very well together. Neither of them worried about terms: the one was ready to accept what he was offered, the other to offer what he was asked. Never was a bargain more easily concluded.

Under this agreement Hans undertook to guide us to the village of Stapi, on the south shore of the Sneffels peninsula, at the very foot of the volcano. The distance by land was about twenty-two miles, which my uncle reckoned we could cover in two days. But when he discovered that the Danish mile was eight thousand yards long he was obliged to revise his calculations and allow seven or eight days for the journey.

We were to have four horses – one each for my uncle and myself, and two for our luggage. Hans, as was his custom, was to go on foot. He knew that part of the coast perfectly, and he promised to take us the shortest way.

His engagement with my uncle did not come to an end with our arrival at Stapi: he was to continue in his service for the whole period of his scientific researches, in return for three rix-dollars a week, but it was expressly stipulated that this sum should be paid to the guide every Saturday evening, a condition which he regarded as a *sine qua non* of the engagement.

The start was fixed for 16 June. My uncle wanted to pay the hunter a sum in advance, but he refused with a single word.

'*Efter*,' he said.

'After,' said the Professor, for my edification.

Once the agreement had been concluded, Hans promptly withdrew.

'A splendid fellow,' exclaimed my uncle, 'but he little knows what a wonderful part he is going to play in the future!'

'So he's coming with us to . . .'

'Yes, Axel, to the centre of the earth.'

Forty-eight hours remained until our departure; to my great regret I had to spend them on our preparations. All our ingenuity was devoted to packing every article to the best advantage: instruments here, arms there, tools in this package, provisions in that – four sets of parcels in all.

The instruments consisted of:

1. An Eigel Centigrade thermometer, reading up to 150°, which seemed to me either too high or too low. Too high if the temperature of the air was to rise so far, for in that case we should be baked to death. Too low if it was to take the temperature of hot springs or other melted matter.

2. A manometer of compressed air, to indicate pressures higher than that of the atmosphere at sea-level. An ordinary barometer would not have answered the purpose, as the atmospheric pressure would increase in proportion to the depth of our descent underground.

3. A chronometer made by the younger Boisonnas of Geneva, and set to the meridian of Hamburg.

4. Two compasses, one for inclination, the other for declination.

5. A night glass.

6. Two Ruhmkorff coils which, by means of an electric current, provided a safe, handy, and portable light.

The arms consisted of two rifles made by Purdley More & Co., and two Colt revolvers. Why were we taking arms? We had no need to fear savages or wild beasts, or so at least I supposed. But my uncle seemed to be just as attached to his arsenal as he was to his instruments, and particularly to a large quantity of gun cotton, which is unaffected by damp and has a greater explosive force than ordinary gunpowder.

The tools consisted of two mattocks, two pickaxes, a

silk rope ladder, three iron-shod staves, an axe, a hammer, a dozen iron wedges and spikes, and some long knotted cords. All this made a big package, for the ladder was three hundred feet long.

Lastly there were the provisions – not a big package, but one that I found reassuring, for I knew that it contained enough meat extract and biscuits to last us six months. Gin was the only liquid, and there was no water at all, but we had some flasks and my uncle counted on finding springs from which we could fill them. The fears I had expressed as to the quality and temperature of these springs, and indeed as to their existence, had been totally disregarded.

To complete the exact inventory of our travelling accessories, I ought to add that we had a medicine chest containing blunt scissors, splints for fractures, a piece of tape of unbleached linen, bandages and compresses, lint, and a basin for bleeding – all rather terrifying objects – as well as a set of bottles of dextrine, medical alcohol, liquid acetate of lead, ether, vinegar, and ammonia – drugs which did nothing to reassure me. Finally we had all the necessary chemicals for the Ruhmkorff lamps.

My uncle had been careful not to forget tobacco, gunpowder, and touchwood, nor a leather belt which he wore next to his skin and which contained a goodly sum of gold, silver, and notes. Six pairs of stout boots, water-proofed with a mixture of tar and indiarubber, were packed with the tools.

'Clothed, shod, and equipped like this,' said my uncle, 'there's no reason why we shouldn't go a very long way.'

The whole of the fourteenth was spent packing all these various articles. In the evening we dined with Baron Trampe, in company with the mayor of Reykjavik and Dr Hyaltalin, the leading medical man in the place. Mr Fridriksson was not there; I later learnt that he and the Governor were at loggerheads over some administrative question and avoided meeting each other. I was therefore unable to understand a single word that was spoken in the course of this semi-official dinner. I only noticed that my uncle talked all the time.

The next day, the fifteenth, we completed our preparations. Our host delighted the Professor by presenting him with a map of Iceland infinitely superior to that of Handerson. It was a map made by Mr Olaf Nikolas Olsen, on a scale of 1: 480,000, on the basis of geological studies by Mr Scheel Frisac and a topographical survey by Mr Bjorn Gumlavgson. Published by the Icelandic Literary Society, it was a precious document for a mineralogist.

Our last evening was spent in friendly conversation with Mr Fridriksson, to whom I had taken a great liking; the talk was followed, in my case at least, by a restless night.

At five in the morning the neighing of four horses pawing the ground under my window woke me. I dressed quickly and went down into the street. There Hans was loading the last of our luggage, almost without moving a limb but with remarkable skill. My uncle was giving more advice than help, and the guide seemed to be paying very little attention to his instructions.

At six o'clock everything was ready. Mr Fridriksson shook hands with us. My uncle thanked him warmly in Icelandic for his kind hospitality. For my part I elaborated a cordial farewell in my best Latin. Then we mounted our horses, and with his final farewell Mr Fridriksson called out to me a line of Virgil which seemed eminently applicable to the uncertain travellers that we were:

'Et quacumque viam dederit fortuna sequamur.'

12

Slow Progress

We had set off under a cloudy but settled sky. There was no danger either of tiring heat or of heavy rain. It was perfect tourist weather.

The pleasure of riding on horseback through unknown country put me in a good mood for the start of our journey. I gave myself up to the happiness of the tourist, compounded of desires and freedom, and began to make the best of the expedition.

'Besides,' I said to myself, 'where's the risk in travelling through a most interesting country, climbing a remarkable mountain, and at the worst going down into an extinct crater. Obviously that's all that Saknussemm did. As for the existence of a passage leading to the centre of the world, that's pure imagination and absolutely impossible. So let's get all the pleasure we can out of this expedition without worrying about it.'

I had scarcely finished this reasoning before we had left Reykjavik behind.

Hans walked ahead, at a quick, even, and untiring

pace. The two baggage-horses followed him of their own accord, and behind them came my uncle and me, looking not too ridiculous on our small but hardy animals.

Iceland is one of the largest islands in Europe. It has a surface of fourteen thousand square miles, but has a population of only sixty thousand. The geographers have divided it into four quarters, and we had to cross diagonally the south-west quarter, known as the Sudvestr Fjordungr.

On leaving Reykjavik, Hans had immediately taken a path along the coast. We rode between meagre pastures which were having all the trouble in the world to look green; yellow came to them more easily. The rugged summits of the trachyte hills on the horizon were blurred by the mist in the east; now and then a few patches of snow, concentrating the diffused light, glittered on the slopes of the distant mountains; certain peaks, rising more sheerly than the others, pierced the grey clouds and reappeared above shifting vapours, like reefs emerging in the sky.

Often these chains of barren rocks would stretch out towards the sea, encroaching on the pasturage; but there was always enough room left to pass. Besides, our horses instinctively chose the best way without ever slackening their pace. My uncle was cheated even of the satisfaction of urging his mount on with voice or whip: he had no excuse for losing his patience. I could not help smiling at seeing him, such a tall man, on his little horse, and, as his long legs almost touched the ground, he looked like a centaur with six legs.

'Good horse! Good horse!' he kept saying. 'You will see, Axel, that there is no animal more intelligent than the Icelandic horse. Snow, storms, impassable roads, rocks, glaciers – nothing can stop him. He is brave, steady, and reliable. He never stumbles, never shies. If there's a river or a fjord to cross – and there'll be plenty, I can tell you that – you will see him plunge straight into the water as if he were amphibious and swim across to the opposite bank. But we mustn't hurry him; just let him alone and we shall do our thirty miles a day.'

'*We* may, but what about the guide?'

'Oh, I'm not worried about him. People like that can walk miles without even noticing it. This man moves about so little that he can't get tired. Besides, if need be I can always let him have my horse. I shall soon get cramp if I don't have a little exercise. My arms are all right, but I mustn't forget about my legs.'

Meanwhile we were making rapid progress. The country was already almost a desert. Here and there we saw an isolated farm, a lonely *boer*, made of wood, earth, or blocks of lava, and looking like a beggar by the wayside. These dilapidated huts gave the impression of asking the passer-by for charity, and we almost felt inclined to give them alms. In this region there were no roads or paths, and the vegetation, however slowly it grew, soon obliterated all trace of the rare travellers.

Yet this part of the province, not far from the capital, was regarded as one of the inhabited and cultivated portions of Iceland. What then must the other parts be like, if they were more deserted than this desert? After travelling half a mile, we had not seen a single farmer standing at the door of his cottage, nor a single shepherd minding a flock less wild than himself; nothing but a few cows and sheep left to their own devices. What then could we expect to see in the regions convulsed by eruptions and born of volcanic explosions and subterranean disturbances?

We were destined to see them later on; but, consulting Olsen's map, I saw that we were avoiding them by following the winding coastline. The great plutonic movement was in fact largely confined to the interior of the island; there the horizontal layers of superimposed rocks, known as *trapps* in the Scandinavian languages, the beds of trachyte, the eruptions of basalt, tuff, and all the volcanic conglomerates, and the streams of molten lava and porphyry have created a land of supernatural horror. I had no idea at that time of the sight which awaited us on the Sneffels peninsula, where this debris of a Nature in eruption forms a scene of frightful chaos.

Two hours after leaving Reykjavik we reached the little town or *aolkirkja* ('principal church') of Gufunes. There was nothing remarkable about the place. It consisted of only a few houses, and would scarcely be regarded as a hamlet in Germany.

Here Hans stopped for half an hour; he shared our frugal breakfast, answering my uncle's questions about the road with yes or no, and when asked where he proposed to spend the night he said simply:

'Gardär.'

I consulted the map to see where Gardär was. I saw a village of that name on the banks of the Hvalfjord, eighteen miles from Reykjavik. I showed it to my uncle.

'Only eighteen miles!' he said. 'Four miles out of a hundred! What a miserable little walk!'

He began to say something to the guide, who, without answering, took his place at the head of the horses and set off again.

Three hours later, still treading on the pale grass of the pastureland, we rounded the Kollafjord, a detour which was less trouble than crossing that inlet. Soon we entered a *pingstaoer* or parish called Ejulberg, from whose steeple twelve o'clock would have struck if Icelandic churches had been rich enough to possess clocks; but they are like their parishioners, who have no watches and manage very well without.

There the horses were baited; then, taking a narrow path between a chain of hills and the sea, they carried us straight to the *aolkirkja* of Brantär, and a mile farther on to the *annexia* or chapel of ease of Sauboer, on the south bank of the Hvalfjord.

It was now four o'clock, and we had travelled four Icelandic miles or twenty English miles.

The fjord was at least two miles wide at this point; the waves broke with a roar on the sharp rocks, and the whole inlet was confined between steep walls of rock three thousand feet high and remarkable for its brown strata separated by beds of reddish tuff. However intelligent our horses might be, I did not look forward to crossing an arm of the sea on the back of a quadruped.

'If they are really intelligent,' I said, 'they won't try to cross. In any case I intend to be intelligent for them.'

But my uncle refused to wait. He spurred his horse on towards the shore. The animal sniffed at the nearest wave and stopped short. My uncle, who had instincts of his own, urged it on, only to meet with a fresh refusal from the animal, which shook its head. There followed oaths and blows with the whip, whereupon the horse reared up and tried to throw its rider. Finally it bent its knees, escaped from under the Professor's legs, and left him standing on two boulders on the shore, like the Colossus of Rhodes.

'Confounded animal!' cried the rider, suddenly transformed into a pedestrian, and as shamefaced as a cavalry officer transferred to the infantry.

'*Farja*,' said the guide, touching him on the shoulder.

'What! A ferry?'

'*Der*,' replied Hans, pointing to a boat.

'Then why didn't you say so? Well, let's go.'

'*Tidvatten*,' said the guide.

'What is he saying?' I asked.

'He says the tide,' said my uncle, translating the Danish word for my benefit.

'Perhaps he means that we have to wait for the tide?'

'*Förbida?*' asked my uncle.

'*Ja*,' replied Hans.

My uncle stamped his foot, while the horses made their way towards the ferry.

I quite understood the need to wait for a particular state of the tide before undertaking the passage of the fjord, that in which the sea is at its highest level. Then the ebb and flow have no perceptible effect, and the ferry is in no danger of being carried either to the head of the fjord or out to sea.

That favourable moment arrived only at six in the evening, when my uncle and I, the guide, two ferrymen, and the four horses took our places in a rather fragile-looking sort of flat boat. Accustomed as I was to the steam ferry-boats on the Elbe, I found the oars of the two boatmen a poor means of propulsion. It took us over an hour to cross the fjord; but at least the passage was accomplished without any mishaps.

Half an hour later we reached the *aolkirkja* of Gardär.

13

Icelandic Hospitality

It should have been dark, but at the sixty-fifth parallel there was nothing surprising about the length of the polar day; in Iceland, during June and July, the sun never sets.

All the same, the temperature had fallen. I was cold, and above all hungry. The *boer* which opened its doors to receive us was a welcome sight.

It was a peasant's house, but in point of hospitality it was equal to a king's palace. On our arrival, the master came and shook hands with us, and without more ado beckoned to us to follow him.

It would indeed have been impossible to walk beside him. A long, dark, narrow passage led into the house, which was built of roughly squared beams, and gave access to each of the four rooms: the kitchen, the weaving shop, the *badstofa* or family bedroom, and the visitors' room, which was the best of all. My uncle, whose height had not been taken into consideration when the house was built, inevitably bumped his head several times against the beams of the ceiling.

We were shown into our room, a large apartment with a floor of beaten earth and a window whose panes were sheep's membranes of limited transparency. The beds consisted of dry hay heaped into two wooden frames painted red and decorated with Icelandic sayings. I had not expected so much comfort; the only drawback was that the house was pervaded with a strong smell of dried fish, pickled meat, and sour milk, which made a disagreeable impression on my nose.

When we had taken off our travelling wraps we heard our host's voice inviting us into the kitchen, the only room where a fire was lighted, even in the severest cold.

My uncle lost no time in obeying this friendly injunction, and I followed him.

The kitchen fireplace was of a primitive model: in the middle of the room there was a stone to serve as a hearth, and in the roof a hole to let out the smoke. This kitchen also served as a dining-room.

When we came in, the host, as if he had not seen us before, greeted us with the word '*Saellvertu*', which means 'Be happy', and came and kissed us on the cheek.

After him his wife pronounced the same word, accompanied by the same ceremonial; then the two of them, placing their right hands on their hearts, gave a low bow.

I hasten to add that this Icelandic lady was the mother of nineteen children, who, big and little alike, were all swarming about in the midst of the wreaths of smoke with which the fire was filling the room. Every few moments I noticed a little fair-haired head with a somewhat melancholy expression appearing out of this cloud. It made me think of a circle of unwashed angels.

My uncle and I were very friendly to this brood, and soon there were three or four of the children on our shoulders, as many on our knees, and the rest between our legs. Those who could talk kept saying '*Saellvertu*' in every conceivable tone of voice, while those who could not shouted all the louder.

This concert was brought to a close by the announcement that supper was ready. At that moment our guide returned from feeding the horses – that is, from taking the thrifty course of turning them loose to graze; the poor animals had to be content with cropping the scanty moss on the rocks and some not very nourishing seaweed; the next day they would not fail to return of their own accord to resume work.

'*Saellvertu*,' said Hans.

Then quietly, automatically, without one kiss being any warmer than another, he kissed the host, the hostess, and their nineteen children.

When this ceremony was over we sat down, twenty-four in number, and therefore literally one on top of the other. The luckiest had only two children on their knees.

However, silence fell on these little people at the arrival

of the soup, and the taciturnity natural to Icelanders, even in childhood, resumed its sway. The host served out to us a soup made from lichen and by no means unpleasant, then a huge piece of dried fish swimming in sour butter which was twenty years old and therefore, according to Icelandic ideas of gastronomy, vastly preferable to fresh butter. With this there was some *skyr*, a sort of clotted milk, accompanied with biscuits and seasoned with the juice of juniper berries; and to drink we had a thin milk mixed with water, which they call *blanda*. Whether this strange food was wholesome or not, I am not in a position to judge; all I can say is that I was hungry, and that at dessert I drank a thick buckwheat broth down to the last spoonful.

As soon as the meal was over, the children disappeared, and their elders gathered round the hearth, where there was a fire of peat, briar, cow-dung, and dry fish-bones. Then, after this 'warming-up', the various groups retired to their respective rooms. The hostess, as was customary, offered to take off our stockings and trousers; but on meeting with the most graceful of refusals on our part, did not insist, and I was at last able to snuggle down in my bed of hay.

At five o'clock the next morning we took leave of the Icelandic peasant, my uncle persuading him with some difficulty to accept a suitable remuneration; and Hans gave the signal for departure.

A hundred yards from Gardär, the ground began to change in character; the soil became marshy and the going more difficult. On the right, the chain of mountains stretched away indefinitely like a huge system of natural fortifications, whose counterscarp we were following; often we were confronted with streams which we had to ford, taking care not to wet our baggage.

The solitude became more and more profound; but sometimes we seemed to see a human silhouette fleeing in the distance, and when a bend in the road brought us unexpectedly close to one of these spectres, I experienced a sudden disgust at the sight of a swollen head with shining skin and no hair, and a body revealing repulsive sores through the rents in its miserable rags.

The poor creature did not come and hold out his deformed hand; on the contrary, he fled, but not before Hans had greeted him with the customary '*Saellvertu*'.

'*Spetelsk*,' he explained.

'A leper!' my uncle repeated. And this word by itself produced a repulsive effect. This horrible disease of leprosy is quite common in Iceland; it is not contagious but hereditary, so these wretched creatures are forbidden to marry.

These sights were not calculated to offset the depressing effect of the landscape, which was becoming profoundly dismal; the last tufts of grass were dying under our feet. There was not a tree to be seen, apart from a few thickets of dwarf birches which looked more like brushwood. Nor were there any animals, except a few horses for which their owners had no food, and which were roaming wild over the dreary plains. Now and then we saw a hawk soaring among the grey clouds and then darting away towards southern climes. I surrendered myself to the melancholy inseparable from this wild scenery, and my memory carried me back to my native land.

Soon we had to cross several little fjords and then a real gulf; the tide, which was high just then, allowed us to cross without waiting and to reach the hamlet of Alftanes, a mile farther on.

That evening, after fording two rivers full of trout and pike, the Alfa and the Heta, we were obliged to spend the night in a deserted hovel worthy to be haunted by all the goblins in Scandinavian mythology; the Ice King had certainly taken up his abode there, and all the night he showed us what he could do.

The next day was uneventful: the same marshy ground, the same uniformity, the same dismal landscape. But by nightfall we had covered half the distance we had to go, and we slept in the *annexia* of Krösolbt.

On 19 June, for about a mile, that is an Icelandic mile, we walked on a floor of lava; this sort of surface is called *hraun* in those parts; the wrinkles in the lava looked like cables, sometimes stretched out, sometimes coiled up; a huge solidified torrent came down from the neighbouring mountains, testifying to the former violence of these now extinct volcanoes. Even now the vapour from a few hot springs could be seen here and there.

We had no time to examine these phenomena; we had to press on. Soon our horses had marshy ground under their feet again, with little lakes every now and then. We were then heading west, having rounded the great bay of Faxa, and the two white peaks of Sneffels appeared in the clouds less than five miles away.

The horses were making good progress, unimpeded by the difficulties of the terrain. For my part, I was beginning to feel very tired, but my uncle remained as fresh and upright as on the first day; I could not help admiring him as much as the guide, who regarded this expedition as a mere excursion.

On Saturday, 20 June, at six in the evening, we reached Büdir, a village on the sea-shore, where the guide claimed his promised wages. My uncle settled with him. It was Hans's own family, that is his uncles and cousins, who offered us hospitality here; we were well received, and, without wishing to impose on the kindness of these good folk, I would gladly have stayed with them to recover from the fatigue. But my uncle, who had no fatigue to recover from, would not hear of it, and the next morning we had to straddle our faithful animals once more.

The ground revealed the proximity of the mountain, whose granite roots protruded from the soil like those of an old oak. We were skirting the huge base of the volcano. The Professor never took his eyes off it, gesticulating as if he were challenging it and saying:

'So that is the giant I am going to defeat!'

Finally, after four hours' walking, the horses stopped of their own accord at the door of the parsonage at Stapi.

14

A Final Argument

Stapi is a village of about thirty huts, built on lava in the rays of sunshine reflected by the volcano. It lies in the bed of a little fjord, shut in by a basalt wall of the strangest appearance.

As is well known, basalt is a brown rock of igneous origin. It assumes regular shapes arranged in the most surprising patterns. Here nature has done her work geometrically, with set-square, compasses, and plumbline. If elsewhere her art consists in flinging huge masses together in disorder, unfinished cones and imperfect pyramids in a weird jumble of lines, here, wishing to set an example of regularity and anticipating the earliest architects, she has created an order of severe simplicity, unsurpassed by either the splendours of Babylon or the wonders of Greece.

I had of course heard of the Giant's Causeway in Ireland, and of Fingal's Cave in one of the Hebrides, but I had never yet set eyes on a basaltic formation. At Stapi this phenomenon was to be seen in all its beauty.

The wall shutting in the fjord, like the whole coast of the peninsula, consisted of a series of vertical columns thirty feet high. These straight, perfectly proportioned pillars supported an architrave of horizontal columns which projected so as to form half an arch over the sea. At intervals, under this natural roof, the eye was caught by beautiful vaulted openings, through which the waves came foaming in. A few fragments of basalt columns, torn from their place by the fury of the ocean, lay on the ground like the remains of an ancient temple, ruins which had remained eternally young and over which the centuries had passed without leaving any trace.

Such was our last halting-place on earth. Hans had brought us here with great skill, and it reassured me a little to think that he was going to stay with us.

On arriving at the door of the rector's house, a simple low-built cabin, no more imposing or more comfortable than its neighbours, I saw a man shoeing a horse, with a hammer in his hand and a leather apron round his waist.

'*Saellvertu*,' said the guide.

'*God dag*,' answered the blacksmith in perfect Danish.

'*Kyrkoherde*,' said Hans, turning to my uncle.

'The rector!' repeated the latter. 'It seems, Axel, that this good man is the rector.'

Meanwhile our guide was explaining the situation to the *kyrkoherde*, who, stopping his work for a moment, uttered a sort of cry which is doubtless used between horses and horse-dealers. Immediately a tall, shrewish-looking woman came out of the hut. If she was not six feet tall, she was certainly not far short of it.

I was afraid that she might offer the travellers the usual Icelandic kiss, but she did nothing of the sort, and indeed was none too gracious in inviting us into her house.

The guest-room struck me as the worst in the whole rectory, small, dirty, and evil-smelling. But we had to make the best of it. The rector did not seem to go in for traditional hospitality – far from it. Before the day was over, I saw that we were dealing with a blacksmith, a fisherman, a hunter, a joiner, but not in any respect with a minister of the Lord. Admittedly it was a weekday, and perhaps he was different on Sunday.

I have no desire to say anything against these poor ecclesiastics, who, after all, have a wretched life. They receive a ridiculously small pittance from the Danish Government, and from their parish they get a quarter of the tithe, which does not amount to as much as sixty marks or four pounds a year. Hence the need to work for their living; but after fishing, hunting, and shoeing horses for a while, one eventually gets into the habit of talking and behaving like hunters, fishermen, and other rather uncultivated people; and that same evening I noticed that sobriety was not one of our host's virtues.

My uncle soon saw what sort of man he had to deal

with; instead of a good and learned man, he was faced with a coarse, vulgar peasant. He therefore decided to begin his great expedition straight away and to leave this inhospitable parsonage. He ignored his own tiredness and resolved to spend a few days on the mountain.

The preparations for our departure were accordingly made the very day after our arrival at Stapi. Hans hired the services of three Icelanders to take the place of the horses in carrying our things; but it was made clear that, as soon as we arrived at the crater, these natives were to turn back and leave us to our own devices.

My uncle was now obliged to explain to the guide that he intended to explore the interior of the volcano as far as he could go.

Hans simply nodded his head. To go there or anywhere else, to plunge into the bowels of his island or to cross its surface, was all one to him. As for me, I had been distracted by the incidents on our journey and had to some extent forgotten the future, but now fear gripped me once again. But what could I do? The place to oppose Professor Lidenbrock would have been Hamburg, not the foot of Sneffels.

One idea worried me more than all the rest – a terrifying idea calculated to shake firmer nerves than mine.

'Let me see,' I said to myself, 'we are going to climb Sneffels. Good. We are going to descend into the crater.

Good. Others have done the same and lived to tell the tale. But that isn't all. If we find a passage leading into the bowels of the earth, if that confounded Saknussemm spoke the truth, we are going to lose our way among the subterranean galleries of the volcano. Now there is no proof that Sneffels is extinct. How can we be sure that an eruption isn't brewing at this very moment? Just because the monster has been asleep since 1229, does it follow that it can never wake up again? And if it does wake up, what will become of us?'

This was a matter requiring serious thought, and serious thought I gave it. I could not sleep without dreaming of eruptions; and the more I thought about it, the less the idea of playing the part of a volcanic cinder appealed to me.

Finally I could not bear it any longer, and I decided to state my case to my uncle as cleverly as I could, in the form of a completely impossible hypothesis.

I went to see him and told him of my fears, drawing back to give him room for the expected explosion.

'I've been thinking about that,' he replied simply.

What did he mean by these words? Was he actually going to listen to reason? Was he thinking of giving up his project? This was too good to be true.

After a few moments' silence, during which I did not dare to ask him any questions, he went on:

'I've been thinking about that. Ever since we arrived at

Stapi, I've been pondering over the important question you have just put to me, for we mustn't be imprudent.'

'No, indeed!' I said emphatically.

'Sneffels has been silent for six hundred years, but it may speak again. Now eruptions are always preceded by certain well-known phenomena. I have therefore questioned the local inhabitants and examined the ground, and I can assure you, Axel, that there will be no eruption.' This emphatic declaration left me speechless and amazed.

'You don't believe me?' said my uncle. 'Well, then, follow me.'

I obeyed without a word. Leaving the parsonage, the Professor took a straight path which, through an opening in the basaltic wall, led away from the sea. Soon we were in the open country, if one can give that name to a vast expanse of volcanic debris. The land looked as if it had been crushed under a rain of huge rocks of trap, basalt, granite, and every kind of igneous material.

Here and there I could see white exhalations rising into the air; these vapours, known as *reykir* in Icelandic, were coming from the hot springs, and their force revealed the volcanic activity underground. This seemed to me to justify my fears, so I was disappointed when my uncle said to me:

'You see all these vapours, Axel? Well, they prove that we have nothing to fear from the volcano.'

'I don't see how they prove anything of the sort,' I said.

'Listen,' the Professor went on. 'At the approach of an eruption these vapours become twice as active and then disappear completely while the eruption is in progress, for the imprisoned gases, once the pressure has been relieved, escape by way of the crater instead of through the fissures in the ground. So if these vapours remain in their usual state, if their activity doesn't increase, and if the wind and rain don't give place to a still and heavy atmosphere, then you may be sure that there is no eruption in the offing.'

'But . . .'

'Enough. When science has spoken, it behoves us to be silent.'

I returned to the parsonage utterly crestfallen. My uncle had beaten me with his scientific arguments. All the same, I had one hope left, and this was that when we reached the bottom of the crater we should find no passage, and that in spite of all the Saknussemms in the world it would be impossible to go any deeper.

I had a terrible nightmare that night, in which I was in the depths of a volcano, from which I was shot into interplanetary space in the shape of an eruptive rock.

The next day, 23 June, Hans was waiting for us with his companions laden with the provisions, tools, and instruments. Two iron-shod sticks, two rifles, and two cartridge-belts had been set aside for my uncle and myself.

Hans, as a cautious man, had added to our baggage a leather bottle full of water, which, together with our flasks, assured us of a week's water.

It was nine in the morning. The rector and his tall shrew of a wife were waiting at the door. We imagined that they wanted to bid us a kind farewell. But this farewell took the unexpected form of a heavy bill, in which everything was charged for, even the poisonous air we had breathed in the pastoral house. This worthy couple were holding us to ransom like any Swiss inn-keeper, and putting a high price on their dubious hospitality.

My uncle paid without quibbling; a man setting off for the centre of the earth does not haggle over a few rix-dollars.

Once this matter had been settled Hans gave the signal for departure, and a few moments later we had left Stapi.

15
The Summit of Sneffels

Sneffels is five thousand feet high. Its double summit forms the limit of a belt of trachyte which stands apart from the contour-system of the island. From our starting-point we could not see its two peaks against the greyish background of the sky. All that I could see was a huge skull-cap of snow on the giant's brow.

We walked in single file, led by the guide, who took narrow paths where two people could not have gone abreast. Conversation therefore became more or less impossible.

After passing the basaltic wall of the fjord of Stapi, we came first of all to a fibrous peat bog, the remains of the former vegetation of the peninsula's marshes. The vast quantity of this as yet unused fuel would be sufficient to warm the whole population of Iceland for a century; this huge bog, judging by the depth of certain ravines, was often seventy feet deep, and revealed successive layers of carbonized remains of vegetation separated by thinner seams of tufaceous pumice.

As befitted Professor Lidenbrock's nephew, and in spite of my worries, I could not help observing with interest the mineralogical curiosities displayed in this huge natural history museum, and at the same time I recapitulated in my mind the whole geological history of Iceland.

This fascinating island had obviously risen from the depths of the sea at a comparatively recent date. Indeed, perhaps it was still rising imperceptibly. If this was so, its origins could only be attributed to the action of subterranean fires, and in that case Sir Humphry Davy's theory, Saknussemm's document, and my uncle's ideas all went up in smoke. This hypothesis led me to make a close examination of the nature of the ground, and I soon became aware of the succession of phenomena which had given it birth.

Iceland, which is absolutely devoid of alluvial soil, is entirely composed of volcanic tufa, that is to say an agglomeration of porous rocks and stones. Before the existence of the volcanoes it consisted of trap rocks, slowly raised above sea-level by the action of central forces. The internal fires had not yet broken through.

Later on, however, a wide chasm formed diagonally across the island from south-west to north-east, through which the trachytic paste gradually emerged. At this stage the phenomenon took place without any violence; the amount expelled was enormous, and the melted matter thrown up from the bowels of the earth spread out slowly in vast sheets or hillocked masses. This was the period when the felspars, syenites, and porphyrics appeared.

But thanks to this spread the thickness of the island increased enormously, and consequently its power of resistance. It is easy to imagine what a vast quantity of gases accumulated beneath its surface when, after the cooling of the trachytic crust, it ceased to offer any outlet. A moment therefore inevitably came when the explosive force of these gases was such that they raised the heavy crust and provided themselves with openings in the shape of tall chimneys. Hence the volcano formed by the raising of the crust, and then the crater suddenly pierced at the summit of the volcano.

The eruptive phenomena were then followed by the volcanic phenomena. First of all, through the newly formed outlets there escaped the ejected basalt of which the plain we were then crossing offered such wonderful examples. We were walking over those massive, dark-grey rocks which the cooling process had moulded into hexagonal prisms. In the distance we could see a great number of flattened cones which had once been so many fiery openings.

After the basaltic eruption had spent itself, the volcano, its power increased by the extinction of the lesser craters, provided an outlet for the lava, ashes, and cinders whose long screes I could see stretching down the sides of the mountain like flowing tresses.

Such was the succession of phenomena which created Iceland; all of them arose from the action of the internal fires, and to suppose that the mass inside did not still exist in a permanent state of liquid incandescence was folly. But the supreme folly was the idea of trying to reach the centre of the earth . . .

I consequently felt somewhat reassured about the result of our undertaking as we advanced to the assault of Sneffels.

The way was becoming increasingly difficult; the ground was rising; pieces of rock kept breaking off and the greatest care was needed to avoid dangerous falls.

Hans walked on as calmly as if he were on level ground; sometimes he disappeared behind the huge blocks, and for a moment was lost from sight; then a shrill whistle from his lips would tell us which way to go. Often, too, he would stop, pick up a few stones, and arrange them in a recognizable pattern, so as to provide landmarks to guide us on our return journey. This was a wise precaution in itself, but one which future events were to render useless.

Three hours' tiring march had brought us only to the base of the mountain. There Hans called a halt, and a frugal breakfast was shared out. My uncle ate hurriedly to get on faster. But since this halt was meant for rest as well as for food, he had to await the pleasure of the guide, who gave the signal for departure an hour later. The three

Icelanders, who were just as taciturn as their comrade the guide, did not say a word and ate very little.

We now began scaling the slopes of Sneffels. Its snow-covered summit, by an optical illusion not uncommon in mountainous country, seemed to me to be very close, and yet how many hours it took to reach it! The stones, which were not held together by either earth or grass, kept rolling down to the plain with the speed of an avalanche.

At some places the slopes of the mountain formed an angle of at least thirty-six degrees with the horizon; it was impossible to climb them, and we had to skirt these stony cliffs, an operation which was anything but easy. At such places we helped each other with our sticks.

I must say that my uncle kept as close to me as he could; he never lost sight of me, and on many an occasion his arm provided me with a firm support. As for himself, he must have had an innate sense of balance for he never stumbled. The Icelanders, although heavily burdened, climbed with the agility of born mountaineers.

Judging by the height of the summit of Sneffels, it seemed to me impossible to reach it from our side, unless the slope became less steep. Fortunately, after an hour of tremendous exertion and difficult feats, in the midst of the vast expanse of snow covering the crest of the volcano, a sort of staircase unexpectedly appeared, which greatly simplified our ascent. It was formed by one of those torrents of stones thrown up by the eruptions and called *stina* by the Icelanders. If this torrent had not been arrested in its fall by the form of the mountain-sides it would have gone on into the sea and formed new islands.

Such as it was, it served us well. The slopes grew steeper still, but these stone steps enabled us to climb them easily, and indeed so rapidly that, having stayed behind for a moment while my companions continued their ascent, I saw them already reduced by distance to microscopic dimensions.

By seven in the evening we had ascended the two thousand steps of this staircase, and we found ourselves on a sort of bulge in the mountain, a kind of bed on which the actual cone of the crater rested.

The sea stretched away three thousand two hundred feet below. We had passed the perpetual snow-line, which is not very high in Iceland on account of the constant humidity of the climate. It was bitterly cold, and the wind was blowing hard. I was exhausted. The Professor saw that my legs were failing me, and, in spite of his impatience, he decided to stop. He accordingly signalled to the guide, but Hans shook his head and said:

'*Ofvanför.*'

'It seems that we have to go higher,' said my uncle.

Then he asked Hans for his reason.

'*Mistour,*' replied the guide.

'*Ja, mistour,*' repeated one of the Icelanders in a rather frightened voice.

'What does that word mean?' I asked anxiously.

'Look,' said my uncle.

I looked down in the direction of the plain. A huge column of powdered pumice-stone, sand, and dust was rising into the air, twisting about like a waterspout; the wind was driving it against that side of Sneffels to which we were clinging, and this opaque screen between ourselves and the sun was casting a great shadow over the mountain. If this column were to bend towards us, we should inevitably be caught up in its eddies. This phenomenon, which is not uncommon when the wind blows from the glaciers, is called *mistour* in Icelandic.

'*Hastigt! Hastigt!*' cried our guide.

Without knowing Danish, I understood that we had to follow Hans as fast as we could. The guide started skirting the cone of the crater, but diagonally so as to make our ascent easier. Soon the dust-storm fell upon the mountain, which trembled at the shock; the stones caught up in the eddies of the wind rained down as in an eruption. Fortunately we were now on the opposite side and sheltered from any danger. But for our guide's precaution, however, our mangled bodies, pounded to dust, would have fallen a long way off like the remains of some unknown meteor.

Yet Hans thought it unwise to spend the night on the

side of the cone. We continued our zigzag climb; the fifteen hundred feet which remained to be covered took us nearly five hours; what with all the tacking and counter-marching we did, the distance must have been at least seven miles. I could not stand it any longer; I was weak from cold and hunger, and the rarefied air was not enough for my lungs.

At last, at eleven o'clock at night, in complete darkness, we reached the summit of Sneffels; and before taking shelter inside the crater, I had time to see the midnight sun, at the lowest point of its course, casting its pale rays on the island sleeping at my feet.

16

Inside the Crater

Supper was rapidly devoured, and the little party settled down for the night as best they could. The bed was hard, the shelter not very substantial, and the situation rather unpleasant, at five thousand feet above sea-level. Yet I slept remarkably soundly that night, one of the best I had had for a long time. I did not even have any dreams.

The next day we awoke half frozen by the sharp air, but in bright sunshine. I got up from my granite bed and went to enjoy the magnificent spectacle which lay before me.

I was standing on the summit of one of Sneffel's peaks, the one to the south. From that point the view extended over the greater part of the island. By an optical effect common to all great heights, the shores seemed higher than the central part. It was as if one of Helbesmer's relief-maps were spread out at my feet. I could see deep valleys criss-crossing in all directions, precipices hollowed out like wells, lakes reduced to ponds, and rivers turned into streams. On my right were countless glaciers and innumerable peaks, some plumed with faint wreaths of smoke. The undulations of this infinite succession of mountains, whose patches of snow looked like foam, reminded one of the surface of a stormy sea. If I turned towards the west, there the ocean stretched out in all its magnificence, like a continuation of those foaming summits. The eye could scarcely tell where the land ended and the waves began.

I lost myself in that wonderful ecstasy produced by great peaks, this time without any giddiness, for I was beginning to grow accustomed at last to this sort of sublime contemplation. My dazzled gaze bathed in the transparent rays of the sun. I forgot who I was and where I was, living the life of the elves and sylphs of Scandinavian mythology. In fact, I was intoxicated by the pleasure of altitude, oblivious of the abysses into which my fate was shortly going to plunge me. But I was brought back to an awareness of reality by the arrival of Hans and the Professor, who joined me on the summit of the peak.

My uncle, turning to the west, pointed out to me a light vapour, a mist, or a semblance of land which rose above the horizon of the sea.

'Greenland,' he said.

'Greenland?' I exclaimed.

'Yes, we are only about a hundred miles away; and during thaws Polar bears are carried here from Greenland on ice-floes. But never mind that. We are at the top of

Sneffels, and here are two peaks, one to the south, the other to the north. Hans will tell us what the Icelanders call the one on which we are standing now.'

The question having been put, the guide replied:

'Scartaris.'

My uncle shot a triumphant glance at me.

'Now for the crater!' he cried.

The crater of Sneffels was in the shape of an inverted cone with an opening about a mile across. Its depth I estimated at about two thousand feet. One may imagine the condition of a reservoir of this capacity when filled with thunder and flames. The bottom of the funnel did not measure more than five hundred feet in circumference, so that the fairly gentle slope made it easy to reach its lower part. I was involuntarily reminded of a huge, funnel-shaped blunderbuss, and the comparison alarmed me.

'To go down into a blunderbuss,' I thought, 'when it may be loaded, and may go off at the slightest touch, is sheer lunacy.'

But there was no going back. Hans, with an air of indifference, set off in front again, and I followed him without a word.

To make the descent easier, Hans wound his way down the cone in long ellipses. We had to walk among the erupted rocks, some of which, shaken out of their sockets, went bouncing down to the bottom of the abyss. Their fall awoke reverberating echoes which were strangely sonorous.

In some parts of the cone there were glaciers. Here Hans advanced only with extreme caution, sounding his way with his iron stick to discover crevasses. At certain doubtful points we had to fasten ourselves together with a long rope, so that if anyone unexpectedly lost his footing he would be held up by his companions. This was a prudent precaution, but it did not exclude all danger.

In spite, however, of all the difficulties of the descent on slopes with which the guide was unfamiliar, it was accomplished without accident, except for the loss of a coil of rope which slipped from the hands of one of the Icelanders and took the shortest way to the bottom of the abyss.

By noon we had arrived. I raised my head and saw above me the upper aperture of the cone, framing a greatly reduced but almost perfectly circular patch of sky. At one point only the peak of Scartaris stood out, rising into space.

At the bottom of the crater there were three chimneys, through which, in the time of its eruptions, Sneffels had expelled its lava and steam from its central furnace. Each of these furnaces was about a hundred feet in diameter. They yawned open at our feet. I had not the courage to look into them, but Professor Lidenbrock had already made a rapid survey of all three; he was panting for breath, running from one to the other, gesticulating and muttering unintelligible words. Hans and his companions, sitting on blocks of lava, watched him running about and obviously regarded him as a lunatic.

Suddenly my uncle gave a shout. I thought that he had lost his footing and had fallen into one of the three chimneys. But no – I saw him with his arms outstretched and his legs wide apart in front of a granite rock which stood in the centre of the crater like a huge pedestal placed there for a statue of Pluto. His attitude was one of amazement, but amazement soon gave way to delirious joy.

'Axel! Axel!' he cried. 'Come here! Come here!'

I ran over to him. Neither Hans nor the Icelanders stirred a muscle.

'Look,' said the Professor.

And, sharing his amazement, if not his joy, I read on the western face of the block, in Runic characters half worn away by time, this accursed name:

$$\text{ᚱᛌᚾᛐ ᛋᛁᛦᛌᚾᛌᛌᛐᚷ}$$

'Arne Saknussemm!' cried my uncle. 'Have you any doubts *now*?'

I made no reply, and returned in consternation to my

lava seat, overwhelmed by this piece of evidence.

How long I remained plunged in thought I cannot say. All I know is that when I raised my head I saw only my uncle and Hans at the bottom of the crater. The Icelanders had been dismissed, and they were now descending the outer slopes of Sneffels on their way back to Stapi.

Hans was sleeping peacefully at the foot of a rock, in a stream of lava where he had made himself an improvised bed, while my uncle was circling around the bottom of the crater like a wild beast caught in a trapper's pit. I had neither the desire nor the strength to get up, and following the guide's example I abandoned myself to an uneasy slumber, constantly imagining that I could hear noises or feel tremors in the sides of the mountain.

This was how the first night inside the crater went by.

The next day a grey, cloudy, heavy sky settled over the summit of the cone. I noticed this not so much from the darkness inside the crater as from the anger which took hold of my uncle.

I understood the reason for this, and hope dawned again in my heart. Let me explain.

Of the three ways open to us beneath our feet, only one had been taken by Saknussemm. According to the Icelandic scholar, it could be recognized by the circumstance mentioned in the cryptogram, namely that the shadow of Scartaris touched its edge during the last days of June. That sharp peak could in fact be regarded as the gnomon of a sun-dial, whose shadow on a given day pointed out the way to the centre of the earth.

Now, if the sun failed to shine there would be no shadow and consequently no guide. It was 25 June. If the sky would only remain cloudy for six days, the expedition would have to be postponed for another year.

I will not attempt to describe Professor Lidenbrock's helpless anger. The day wore on and no shadow appeared on the bottom of the crater, Hans did not stir from his place even though he must have wondered what we were waiting for – if he ever wondered anything. My uncle did not speak to me once. His gaze, perpetually directed towards the sky, was lost in its grey and misty depths.

On the twenty-sixth there was still no sign. Sleet fell all day. Hans built a hut with blocks of lava. I derived a certain pleasure from studying the countless little waterfalls running down the sides of the cone, making a deafening sound which was amplified by each and every stone.

My uncle could no longer contain himself. The situation was enough to irritate a more patient man than himself, for it was tantamount to sinking within sight of land.

But heaven always mingles great joys with great vexations, and it held in store for Professor Lidenbrock a satisfaction to match his desperate anxiety.

The next day the sky was still overcast; but on Sunday,

28 June, the last day but two of the month, a change in the weather came with the change of the moon. The sun poured its rays into the crater. Every hillock, every rock, every stone, every roughness, had its share of the torrent of light and promptly cast its shadow over the ground. Among them all, that of Scartaris stood out like a sharp edge and started turning imperceptibly with the sun.

My uncle turned with it.

At midday, in the shortest period of its course, it gently touched the edge of the central chimney.

'It's there!' cried the Professor. 'It's there! Now for the centre of the earth!' he added in Danish.

I looked at Hans.

'Forut!' said the guide calmly.

'Forward!' replied my uncle.

It was thirteen minutes past one.

17
Our Real Journey Begins

The real journey was beginning. So far our labours had been greater than our difficulties; now the latter were literally to spring up at every step.

I had not yet looked down into the bottomless pit into which I was about to plunge, but now the time had come. I could either resign myself to the whole business or refuse to take part in it. But I was ashamed to draw back in the presence of the guide. Hans was treating the adventure so calmly, so unconcernedly, with such a total disregard for any possible danger that I blushed at the idea of being less courageous than he was. If I had been alone I would have brought out all my old arguments, but in the presence of the guide I remained silent. My mind conjured up the memory of my pretty Virlandaise, and I walked across to the central chimney.

I have already said that it was a hundred feet in diameter, or three hundred feet in circumference. I leaned over a projecting rock and looked down. My hair stood on end. The fascination of the void took hold of me. I felt my centre of gravity moving, and vertigo rising to my head like intoxication. There is nothing more overwhelming than this attraction of the abyss. I was on the point of falling when a hand pulled me back; it was that of Hans. It was obvious that I had not taken enough 'lessons in abysses' on the Frelsers-Kirk in Copenhagen.

Even so, however brief my examination of the chimney had been, I had seen how it was shaped. Its almost perpendicular walls were covered with countless projections which would facilitate our descent. But, if the staircase was there all right, the banisters were missing. A rope fastened to the edge of the opening might help us on our way down, but how could we unfasten it when we arrived at the other end?

My uncle used a very simple method to get over this difficulty. He uncoiled a rope about as thick as a thumb and four hundred feet long; first he let down half of it, then looped it over a projecting block of lava and threw the other half down. Each of us could then descend by holding on to both halves of the rope, which would not be able to unwind; when we were two hundred feet down, nothing would be easier than to regain possession of the whole rope by letting go of one end and pulling on the other. Then this process would be repeated *ad infinitum*.

'Now,' said my uncle, after completing these preparations,

'let us see about the baggage; we're going to divide it into three packages, and each of us will strap one on to his back. I'm talking about the fragile objects only.'

The Professor obviously did not include us under that heading.

'Hans,' he went on, 'will take charge of the tools and some of the provisions. You, Axel, will take another third of the provisions, together with the arms; and I will take the rest of the provisions, and the delicate instruments.'

'But,' I said, 'who's going to take the clothes down, and this pile of ropes and ladders?'

'They will go down by themselves.'

'What do you mean?' I asked.

'You'll see.'

My uncle was fond of resorting to drastic measures, and never hesitated. On his instructions, Hans tied all the non-fragile articles in a single bundle, roped them together securely, and threw them bodily down the chimney.

I heard the loud rushing sound produced by the displacement of the layers of air. My uncle, leaning over the abyss, followed the descent of his baggage with a satisfied air, and only stood up when it had disappeared from sight.

'Good,' he said. 'Our turn now.'

Now I ask any honest man if it was possible to hear these words without a shudder!

The Professor fastened the package of instruments on his back, Hans took the one containing the tools, and I the one with the arms. The descent began in the following order: Hans, my uncle, and me. It took place in profound silence, disturbed only by the fall of loose stones hurtling into the abyss.

I let myself fall, so to speak, frantically clutching the double rope with one hand and steadying myself with the other by means of my iron-shod stick. A single thought dominated my mind – the fear that the rock from which I was hanging might give way. The rope struck me as very fragile to bear the weight of three persons. I used it as little as possible, performing miracles of equilibrium on the lava projections which my feet tried to grip as if they were hands.

Whenever one of these slippery steps shook under Hans's feet, he would say in his quiet voice,

'Gif akt!'

'Be careful!' repeated my uncle.

After half an hour we had reached the surface of a rock which was firmly attached to the wall of the chimney.

Hans pulled one end of the rope; the other rose into the air and, after passing round the projecting rock at the top of the chimney, came down, bringing with it a dangerous sort of rain, or rather hail, of stones and pieces of lava.

Leaning over the edge of our narrow ledge, I observed that the bottom of the hole was still invisible.

The manoeuvre with the rope was begun again, and half an hour later we had descended another two hundred feet.

I doubt whether, during this descent, even the most enthusiastic geologist would have tried to study the nature of the surrounding rocks. For my part, I know that I did not trouble my head about them: it was all one to me whether they were Pliocene, Miocene, Eocene, Cretaceous, Jurassic, Triassic, Permian, Carboniferous, Devonian, Silurian, or Primitive. But the Professor was probably making observations or taking notes, for at one of our halts he said to me:

'The farther I go, the more confident I feel. The order of these volcanic formations fully confirms Davy's theory. We are in the middle of the primordial stratum, in which the chemical operation took place of metals catching fire at the contact of air and water. I absolutely reject the idea of central heat. In any case, we shall soon see.'

His conclusion was always the same. Small wonder that I felt no desire to argue. My silence was taken for agreement, and the descent began again.

After three hours I still could not see the bottom of the chimney. When I raised my head I saw its opening growing perceptibly smaller. Its walls sloped slightly and were therefore drawing closer to each other. It was gradually getting darker.

Still we kept on descending. It seemed to me that the falling stones were making a duller sound on impact, and that they were reaching the bottom of the abyss sooner.

As I had taken care to keep an exact account of our manoeuvres with the rope, I could calculate precisely what depth we had reached and how much time had gone by.

We had now repeated the operation fourteen times, and each descent took half an hour. That made seven hours, plus fourteen quarters of an hour for rest, or three and a half hours. Altogether ten and a half hours. We had started at one o'clock, so it must now be eleven. As for the depth we had reached, these fourteen operations with a rope two hundred feet long made it 2,800 feet.

At that moment Hans called out:

'Halt!'

I stopped short just as I was going to hit my uncle's head with my feet.

'We have arrived,' he said.

'Where?' I asked, slipping down beside him.

'At the bottom of the perpendicular chimney.'

'Isn't there any other way out, then?'

'Yes, I can just make out a sort of corridor slanting

away to the right. We'll see about that tomorrow. Let's have our supper first and then sleep.'

It was not yet completely dark. We opened the bag of provisions, ate our meal, and settled down as best we could on a bed of stones and pieces of lava.

When, lying on my back, I opened my eyes, I saw a bright point of light at the end of the three-thousand-foot tube, which acted like a gigantic telescope.

It was a star which did not appear to sparkle, and which, according to my calculations, must have been B *Ursa minor*.

Then I fell into a deep sleep.

18

Ten Thousand Feet Below Sea-Level

At eight in the morning a ray of daylight woke us up. The countless facets of the lava walls caught it as it passed and scattered it like a shower of sparks. This light was bright enough to enable us to distinguish surrounding objects.

'Well, Axel, what do you think about all this? Have you ever spent a more peaceful night in our little house in the Königstrasse? No carts rumbling past, no hawkers crying their wares, no boatmen shouting!'

'Oh, it's certainly quiet enough at the bottom of this well, but this very quietness is rather alarming.'

'Come now!' cried my uncle. 'If you are frightened already what will you be like later on? So far we haven't gone so much as an inch into the bowels of the earth.'

'What do you mean?'

'I mean that we have only reached the bottom of the island. This long vertical tube, which begins at the crater of Sneffels, ends roughly at sea-level.'

'Are you sure about that?'

'Certain. Look at the barometer.'

Sure enough, the mercury, which had gradually risen in the instrument as we had descended, had stopped at twenty-nine inches.

'You see,' the Professor went on, 'as yet we have only the pressure of one atmosphere, and I am looking forward to the time when we shall have to substitute the manometer for the barometer.'

This instrument would in fact become useless as soon as the weight of the atmosphere exceeded its pressure at sea-level.

'But,' I said, 'won't this constantly increasing pressure be very painful for us?'

'No. We shall descend slowly, and our lungs will get used to breathing a denser atmosphere. Aeronauts suffer from a lack of air when they go high up, and we for our part may have too much. But of the two alternatives, this is the one I prefer. Don't let us lose a moment. Where is the bundle which came down here before us?'

I then remembered that we had looked for it in vain the previous evening. My uncle questioned Hans, who, after gazing around with the keen eyes of a hunter, replied:

'Der huppe!'

'Up there.'

True enough, the bundle was caught on a projection about a hundred feet above us. Straight away the agile

Icelander climbed up like a cat, and in a few minutes the bundle was returned to us.

'Now,' said my uncle, 'let us have breakfast, bearing in mind that we may have a long journey in front of us.'

We washed down our biscuits and meat with a few mouthfuls of water mixed with gin.

Once breakfast was over, my uncle took out of his pocket a little notebook intended for scientific observations. He consulted his various instruments one after another, and recorded the following data:

Monday, 29 June

Chronometer:	8.17 a.m.
Barometer:	29 inches 7 lines.
Thermometer:	6°C.
Direction:	E.S.E.

This last observation, indicated by the compass, referred to the dark gallery my uncle had pointed out to me.

'Now, Axel,' exclaimed the Professor in an enthusiastic voice, 'we are really going to plunge into the bowels of the earth. This then is the precise moment at which our journey begins.'

With these words my uncle took in one hand the Ruhmkorff coil hanging from his neck, and with the other he connected it to the filament in the lamp. A reasonably bright light immediately dispelled the darkness of the gallery.

Hans was carrying the other apparatus, which was also set in activity. This ingenious use of electricity would enable us to go on for a long time by creating an artificial daylight, even in the midst of the most inflammable gases.

'Forward!' cried my uncle.

Each of us shouldered his bundle. With my uncle leading the way, Hans coming second, pushing the package of ropes and clothes in front of him, and me third, we entered the gallery.

Just as I was plunging into this dark passage, I raised my head and caught a last glimpse, through the long tube, of that Icelandic sky which I was never to see again.

The lava, in the last eruption of 1229, had forced its way along this tunnel. It still lined the walls with a thick, shining coat, intensifying the electric light a hundredfold by reflection.

Our only difficulty as we made our way along the gallery consisted in not slipping too fast down a slope of about forty-five degrees; fortunately certain irregularities and blisters acted as steps, and we had nothing to do but descend, letting our baggage slide in front of us at the end of a long rope.

But the substance which formed steps under our feet

had become stalactites on the walls. The lava, which was porous at certain points, had formed little round blisters; crystals of opaque quartz, studded with limpid tears of glass and hanging from the ceiling like chandeliers, seemed to light up as we passed. It was as if the genii of the abyss were illuminating their palace to welcome their guests from the surface.

'It's magnificent!' I cried spontaneously. 'What a sight, Uncle! Don't you admire those shades of lava imperceptibly passing from reddish brown to bright yellow? And those crystals which look like lighted globes?'

'Ah, so you're beginning to appreciate all this, are you, Axel?' replied my uncle. 'So you consider this splendid, do you? Well, you'll see even finer sights, I hope. Now, quick march!'

He might more appropriately have said: 'Quick slide!' for we were doing nothing but letting ourselves slip effortlessly down steep slopes. This was Virgil's *facilis descensus Averni* with a vengeance. The compass, which I consulted frequently, pointed steadily south-east. This lava stream deviated neither to the right nor to the left: it had all the inflexibility of the straight line.

Yet there was no considerable rise in temperature. This seemed to confirm Davy's theories, and more than once I consulted the thermometer with surprise. Two hours after our departure, it had only reached 10°, an increase of 4°. This led me to think that our descent was more horizontal than vertical. As for the exact depth reached, that was easy to ascertain: every now and then the Professor measured the angles of deviation and inclination, but he kept the results to himself.

About eight in the evening he called a halt. Hans promptly sat down, and we fastened the lamps to projections in the lava. We were in a sort of cave where there was no lack of air: on the contrary, we could feel breezes. What atmospheric disturbance was causing them? This was a question I made no attempt to answer just then. Hunger and fatigue made me incapable of reasoning. A descent lasting seven hours without a break cannot be made without considerable expenditure of strength, and I was utterly exhausted. The word 'halt' was therefore music to my ears. Hans spread out some food on a block of lava and we all ate hungrily. One thing worried me, however: our stock of water was half finished. My uncle was counting on replenishing it from underground springs, but so far we had seen no sign of any. I could not refrain from pointing this out to him.

'Does this absence of springs surprise you?' he asked.

'More than that – it worries me. We have only enough water left for five days.'

'Don't worry, Axel. I assure you that we shall find water, indeed more than we want.'

'When?'

'When we have got through this bed of lava. How do you imagine that springs could break through these walls?'

'But this stream of lava may go down a long way. It seems to me that we haven't got very far vertically.'

'Why do you suppose that?'

'Because if we had got a long way inside the earth's crust, it would be much hotter.'

'According to your theory,' replied my uncle. 'But what does the thermometer say?'

'Hardly 15°, which means a rise of only 9° since we set off.'

'And what do you conclude from that?'

'According to the most precise observations, the rise of temperature underground is one degree for every hundred feet. But certain local conditions may modify this figure. Thus at Yakoutsk in Siberia it has been observed that the increase of one degree occurred every thirty-six feet. This difference obviously depends on the conductibility of the rocks. What is more, in the neighbourhood of an extinct volcano, and through gneiss, it has been observed that the rise of temperature is one degree only for 125 feet. Let us take this last estimate, which is the most favourable of all, and calculate.'

'Calculate away, my boy.'

'Nothing could be easier,' I said, putting down some figures in my notebook. 'Nine times 125 feet gives a depth of 1,125 feet.'

'Absolutely correct.'

'Well?'

'Well, according to my observations we have reached a depth of ten thousand feet below sea-level.'

'Impossible!'

'Perfectly possible, or else figures aren't figures any more!'

The Professor's calculations were correct. We had already gone six thousand feet beyond the greatest depth hitherto reached by man, as in the mines of Kitzbühel in the Tyrol and Württemberg in Bohemia.

The temperature, which ought to have been 81° here was barely 15°. Which gave me furiously to think.

19

Upwards Again

The next day, 30 June, at six in the morning, we began the descent again.

We were still following the lava gallery, a real natural ramp, as gently sloping as those inclined planes which can still be found in place of the staircase in some old houses. This went on until 12.17, at which moment we came up with Hans, who had just stopped.

'Ah!' exclaimed my uncle. 'We have come to the end of the chimney.'

I looked around me. We were at the intersection of two roads, both of them dark and narrow. Which ought we to take? This was a difficult question to decide.

My uncle, however, did not wish to appear to hesitate before either me or the guide; he pointed to the eastern tunnel, and soon all three of us were inside it.

In any case, any hesitation before this choice of roads would have lasted indefinitely, for there was no indication to guide our choice. We had to trust entirely to chance.

The slope of this new gallery was very slight, and its

section extremely variable. Sometimes a succession of arches appeared before us like the aisles of a Gothic cathedral; here the architects of the Middle Ages might have studied all the forms of that religious architecture which developed from the pointed arch. A mile farther on, we would have to bend our heads under low arches of the Romanesque type, resting on thick pillars half embedded in the walls. In some places this arrangement gave place to low substructures which looked like bearers' workings, and we had to crawl along through narrow tunnels.

The temperature remained at a perfectly bearable level. I could not help thinking of what it must have been when the lava vomited by Sneffels had rushed along this route, now so quiet. I imagined the torrents of fire breaking against every corner in the gallery and the accumulation of the superheated gases in this confined space.

'I only hope,' I thought, 'that the old volcano doesn't take it into his head to start that sort of thing now.'

I refrained from communicating these fears to Uncle Lidenbrock, who would not have understood. His one idea was to go on, and he walked, slid, even tumbled with a determination which one could not help admiring.

At six in the evening, after a fairly easy day's walk, we had gone five miles south, but barely a quarter of a mile in depth.

My uncle called a halt for rest. We ate without much conversation, and went to sleep without much reflection.

Our arrangements for the night were very simple; a travelling-rug each, in which we rolled ourselves, was our only bedding. We had no cause to fear either cold or intrusive visits. Travellers who plunge into the deserts of Africa or the forests of the New World are obliged to watch over each other during the night hours. But here there was absolute solitude and complete safety, with no wild beasts or savages to fear.

We awoke the next day fresh and in good spirits, and resumed our journey, following the path of the lava as before. It was impossible to recognize the nature of the rocks through which it passed. The tunnel, instead of plunging downwards into the bowels of the earth, was tending to become horizontal, and it even seemed to me to be rising slightly. About ten in the morning this rise became so marked and consequently so tiring that I was obliged to slow down.

'What's the matter, Axel?' the Professor asked impatiently.

'I'm tired out,' I replied.

'What, after three hours' walk over such easy ground?'

'It may be easy, but it's tiring all the same.'

'What, when we've nothing to do but go down?'

'I beg your pardon, but you mean go up.'

'Up?' said my uncle, shrugging his shoulders.

'Yes, up. The slope changed half an hour ago, and if we keep on like this, we shall certainly return to the surface in Iceland.'

The Professor shook his head with the air of a man who does not want to be convinced. I tried to continue the conversation, but he did not reply and gave the signal to go on. I saw that his silence was nothing but concentrated ill-humour.

However, I bravely shouldered my burden again and hurried after Hans, who was following my uncle. I was anxious not to be left behind and my chief preoccupation was not to lose sight of my companions. I shuddered at the thought of losing my way in this maze.

Besides, if the upward path was becoming increasingly tiring, I consoled myself with the thought that it was bringing me nearer to the surface. This was a hope which every step confirmed, and I rejoiced at the thought of seeing my little Gräuben again.

At noon a change occurred in the walls of the gallery. I noticed this by a decrease in the amount of light reflected by the sides. The coating of lava had given place to solid rock, arranged in sloping and often vertical strata. We were passing through rocks of the transitional period, the Silurian Period.

'It's all quite clear!' I exclaimed. 'In the second period the water deposits formed these schists, limestones, and shales! We are turning our backs on the granite mass! We are like people from Hamburg taking the Hanover road to go to Lübeck!'

I ought to have kept these remarks to myself, but my geological temperament got the better of my prudence and Uncle Lidenbrock heard my exclamations.

'What is it?' he asked.

'Look!' I replied, pointing to the succession of shales and limestones, and the first signs of slate.

'Well?'

'We have come to the rocks of the period when the first plants and animals appeared.'

'Oh! Do you think so?'

'Have a good look yourself.'

I made the Professor move his lamp over the walls of the gallery, expecting him to show some sign of surprise. But he did not say a word, and simply walked on.

Had he understood me or not? Was he refusing, out of avuncular or scientific vanity, to admit that he had made a mistake in choosing the eastern tunnel? Or was he determined to explore this passage to the end? It was obvious that we had left the lava route, and that this path could not possibly lead to the furnace of Sneffels.

All the same, I wondered whether I might not be attributing too much importance to this change in the rock, and making a mistake myself. Were we really choosing these layers of rock superimposed on the granite foundation?

'If I am right,' I thought, 'I am bound to find some

remains of primitive plants, and then there will be no denying the evidence of our eyes. I must keep my eyes skinned.'

I had not gone a hundred yards before I found incontrovertible proof. This was scarcely surprising, for in the Silurian epoch, the seas contained over fifteen hundred vegetable and animal species. My feet, which had grown accustomed to the hard lava floor, suddenly began stirring up a dust composed of the debris of plants and shells. On the walls there were distinct impressions of rock weeds and club mosses. Professor Lidenbrock must have recognized them, but he shut his eyes, I imagine, and pressed on at an unvarying pace.

This was carrying stubbornness too far, and I could not stand it any longer. I picked up a perfectly preserved shell which had belonged to an animal rather similar to the present-day woodlouse; then, catching up with my uncle, I said:

'Look at this!'

'Well,' he said calmly, 'it's the shell of a crustacean of the extinct species of the trilobites, that's all.'

'But don't you conclude . . . ?'

'What you conclude yourself? Yes, I do. We have left the granite mass and the lava route. I may have made a mistake, but I cannot be sure of that until we reach the end of this gallery.'

'That is the right course to adopt, Uncle, and I would

approve wholeheartedly if we weren't threatened by an ever-increasing danger.'

'And what is that?'

'A shortage of water.'

'Well, Axel, we must ration ourselves.'

20

A Dead End

It was indeed essential for us to ration ourselves. Our stock of water could not last more than three days, as I realized that evening at supper-time. And unfortunately we had little hope of finding a spring in these Silurian layers.

The whole of the next day the gallery unfolded its endless series of arches before us. We walked on almost without a word, as if Hans's silence had infected us.

The path was not rising now, at least not perceptibly. Sometimes it even seemed to slope downwards. But this tendency, which was very slight in any case, could not reassure the Professor, for there was no change in the nature of the beds, and the transitional characteristics were more and more obvious.

The schist, limestone, and old red sandstone sparkled magnificently in the electric light. We might have imagined that we were passing through an open trench in Devonshire, which has given its name to this sort of ground. Specimens of magnificent marbles lined the walls, some of agate-grey capriciously streaked with white veins, others of crimson, and yet others of a yellow splashed with red; while farther on there were dark-coloured griottes relieved by the lighter hues of limestone.

Most of these marbles bore impressions of primitive organisms. Creation had obviously made considerable progress since the previous day. Instead of the rudimentary trilobites, I noticed remains of a more advanced order of creatures, including ganoid fishes and some of those saurians in which palaeontologists have detected the earliest reptile forms. The Devonian seas were inhabited by a vast number of creatures of this species, and deposited them in thousands on the newly formed rocks.

It was becoming obvious that we were climbing the ladder of animal life on which man occupies the highest rung. But Professor Lidenbrock seemed to be taking no notice.

He was waiting for one of two things to happen: either for a vertical shaft to appear at his feet, down which he might continue his descent, or for an obstacle to arise which would force us to turn back. But evening came without either expectation having been realized.

On the Friday, after a night during which I began to feel the pangs of thirst, our little band set off again along the winding passages of the gallery.

After ten hours' walking, I observed that the reflection of our lamps from the walls was greatly diminishing.

Marble, schist, limestone, and sandstone were giving place to a dark, lustreless lining.

At one point, where the tunnel was becoming very narrow, I leaned against the left-hand wall. When I took my hand away, it was quite black. I looked more closely and saw that we were surrounded by coal.

'A coal-mine!' I exclaimed.

'A mine without any miners,' replied my uncle.

'Oh! Who knows?'

'*I* know,' retorted the Professor curtly. 'I am positive that this gallery driven through these beds of coal is not the work of man. But whether it is or it isn't is all one to me. It's time to eat. Let's have supper.'

Hans prepared some food. I ate scarcely anything, but drank the few drops of water which comprised my ration. Half the guide's flask was all that remained to slake the thirst of three men.

After their meal, my two companions stretched out on their rugs and found in sleep a remedy for their fatigue. But I could not sleep, and counted the hours until morning.

At six o'clock on the Saturday morning we set off again. Twenty minutes later we reached a vast cavern, and I then realized that this mine could not have been dug by the hand of man; if it had, the ceiling would have been shored up, whereas in fact it seemed as if only a miracle of equilibrium were holding it up.

This cavern was a hundred feet wide and a hundred and fifty high. The ground had been torn apart by a subterranean disturbance. Yielding to some powerful jolt, it had broken asunder, leaving this huge hollow into which human beings were now penetrating for the first time.

The whole history of the coal period was written on these dark walls, and a geologist could easily follow all its various phases. The beds of coal were separated by compact strata of sandstone or clay, and gave the impression of being crushed by the upper layers.

At that age of the world which preceded the Secondary Period, the earth was covered with vast stretches of vegetation, the product of the dual action of tropical heat and constant moisture. A misty atmosphere enveloped the earth, screening it from the rays of the sun.

Hence the conclusion that the high temperature then prevailing was not due to the sun, which may not even have been ready yet to play the brilliant part it now acts. There were no 'climates', as yet, and a torrid heat, equal at the equator and at both poles, was spread over the whole surface of the globe. This heat came from the interior of the earth.

Despite Professor Lidenbrock's theories, a violent fire was blazing in the bowels of the sphere, and its action extended as far as the outer layers of the earth's crust. The plants, deprived of the beneficent rays of the sun, produced neither flowers nor scent, but their roots drew vigorous life from the burning soil of this early period.

There were few trees, only herbaceous plants – tall grasses, ferns, lycopods, sigillarias, and asterophyllites, belonging to families which are now rare but at that time contained thousands of species.

Now it is to this exuberant vegetation that the coal measures owe their origin. The as yet elastic crust of the earth obeyed the movements of the liquid mass underneath. Countless fissures and depressions resulted, and the plants, sinking beneath the surface of the waters, gradually formed huge accumulations.

Then natural chemistry came into action; in the depths of the seas the vegetable masses were turned into peat to begin with, and then, under the influence of the gases and the heat of fermentation, were completely mineralized.

Thus were formed those huge beds of coal which, despite their size, the industrial nations will exhaust within three centuries unless they limit their consumption.

These reflections occurred to me while I was considering the mineral wealth accumulated in this particular portion of the earth.

'These beds,' I told myself, 'will probably never be worked. The exploitation of such deep, out-of-the-way mines would be far too costly. Besides, why should anyone attempt it when there is still plenty of coal just under the surface in a great many countries? So these beds will doubtless remain as they are now, intact, until the last trump.'

Meanwhile we were pressing on, and I was probably the only one who was forgetting the length of the journey in my absorption in geological considerations. The temperature remained more or less what it had been during our passage through the lava and the schist, but my sense of smell detected a strong odour of protocarburet of hydrogen. I immediately recognized the presence in this gallery of a considerable quantity of that dangerous gas which miners call firedamp, and the explosion of which has caused so many dreadful catastrophes.

Luckily our light was provided by Ruhmkorff's ingenious apparatus. If we had had the misfortune and imprudence to explore this gallery with torches, a terrible explosion would have put an end to the expedition by annihilating the explorers.

This journey through the coal-mine lasted till evening, with my uncle scarcely able to restrain his impatience at the horizontal nature of the path. The darkness, which was always complete twenty yards ahead, prevented us from estimating the length of the gallery; and I was beginning to think it would never come to an end when, all of a sudden, at six o'clock, a wall unexpectedly appeared before us. To the right, to the left, above and below, there was no way through. We had come to a dead end.

'Well, so much the better!' cried my uncle. 'Now at least we know where we stand. We are not on Saknussemm's road, and there's nothing we can do but turn back. Let us take a night's rest, and in less than three days we shall be back at the place where the paths fork.'

'Yes,' I said, 'if we have the strength!'

'And why shouldn't we?'

'Because tomorrow we shall have no water left.'

'And no courage either?' asked the Professor, giving me a stern look.

I did not dare to reply.

21

The New Columbus

The next day we started early in the morning. We had
to hurry, because we were three days' walk from the
fork.

I will not dwell on the hardships we suffered on this
return journey. My uncle bore them with the anger of a
man conscious of being in the wrong; Hans with the
resignation of his calm nature; and I, I must admit, with
loud complaints. I lacked the spirit to stand up to this
bad luck.

As I had foreseen, our water gave out completely at
the end of our first day's march. After that we had
nothing to drink but gin, but this infernal liquor burnt
my throat and I could not even bear the sight of it. I
found the heat stifling and was paralysed with fatigue.
More than once I nearly fell in a dead faint. Then the
others would stop, and my uncle or the Icelander would
do his best to revive me. But I could see that the former
was already suffering acutely from extreme fatigue and
the tortures of thirst.

At last, on Tuesday, 7 July, crawling on our hands and knees, we arrived half-dead at the junction of the two galleries. There I dropped like a lifeless mass, stretched out on the lava floor. It was ten in the morning.

Hans and my uncle, sitting with their backs against the wall, tried to nibble a few pieces of biscuit. Long moans escaped from my swollen lips. I fell into a deep sleep.

After a while my uncle came over to me and raised me in his arms.

'Poor child!' he murmured in tones of genuine pity.

I was touched by these words, not being accustomed to displays of affection by the stern Professor. I seized his trembling hands in mine. He let me hold them and looked at me with tears in his eyes.

Then I saw him take the flask hanging at his side. To my amazement he put it to my lips.

'Drink,' he said.

Had I heard right? Was my uncle out of his mind? I looked at him stupidly, incapable of understanding.

'Drink,' he said again.

And raising his flask, he poured the contents into my mouth.

Oh, what bliss I knew at that moment! A mouthful of water slaked my burning thirst – just one mouthful, but it was enough to recall the life which was ebbing away from me.

I thanked my uncle with clasped hands.

'Yes,' he said, 'a mouthful of water – but it's the last, you understand, the very last. I had kept it carefully at the bottom of my flask, resisting a score of times the terrible temptation to drink it. But no, Axel, I kept it for you.'

'Dear Uncle!' I murmured, with my eyes full of tears.

'Yes, poor boy, I knew that as soon as you reached this fork you would drop half-dead, and I kept these last drops of water to revive you.'

'Thank you! Thank you!' I cried.

Although my thirst had only been partially quenched, I had recovered a little of my strength. The muscles of my throat, which had been contracted till then, relaxed, and my lips were less inflamed. I found that I could speak.

'Look,' I said, 'there's only one thing left for us to do; we have no water, so we must go back.'

While I was saying this, my uncle avoided looking at me; he hung his head, and his gaze shifted away from mine.

'We must go back,' I exclaimed: 'we must return to Sneffels. May God give us the strength to climb up to the top of the crater again!'

'Go back!' said my uncle, as if he were answering himself rather than me.

'Yes, go back, and without losing a single minute.'

A rather long silence followed.

'So, Axel,' the Professor went on in a strange tone of

voice, 'those few drops of water didn't restore your courage and energy?'

'Courage?'

'You seem just as downhearted as before, and you still express nothing but despair.'

What sort of man was I dealing with, and what plans was that fearless mind of his hatching now?

'What, you don't want to go back?'

'And give up this expedition, just when success seems assured? Never!'

'Then we must resign ourselves to dying?'

'No, Axel, no. You must go back. I don't want you to die. Hans will go with you. Leave me here alone.'

'Leave you here!'

'Leave me, I tell you. I have begun this journey, and I mean to finish it, or never return. Go back, Axel, go back!'

My uncle was in a state of extreme excitement. His voice, which had been gentle and affectionate for a moment, had become hard and threatening again. He was fighting with sombre determination against the impossible and I could not bear to abandon him at the bottom of this abyss, but on the other hand the instinct of self-preservation urged me to leave him.

The guide followed this scene with his usual unconcern. Yet he understood what was going on between his two companions. Our gestures were sufficient in themselves to show the different courses which each of us was trying to urge upon the other; but Hans seemed uninterested in this question which concerned his very existence, ready to set off if he was given the signal for departure or to stay if his master so wished it.

How I longed at that moment to be able to make him understand me! My words, my groans, my tone of voice would have got the better of that cold temperament. Those dangers which the guide seemed incapable of understanding I would have made real and intelligible to him. Together we might have convinced the stubborn Professor; if necessary we would have forced him to regain the heights of Sneffels.

I went over to Hans and laid my hand on his. He did not budge. I pointed along the passage leading back to the crater. He remained motionless. My anguished expression and panting breath revealed my sufferings. The Icelander gently shook his head, and calmly pointing to my uncle, he said:

'Master.'

'Master?' I cried. 'No, you madman, he isn't the master of your life! We must go back! We must take him with us! Do you hear me? Do you understand?'

I had seized Hans by the arm and was trying to force him to get up. While I was struggling with him my uncle intervened.

'Calm down, Axel,' he said. 'You will get nothing out of

that stolid servant. So listen to the proposal I want to put to you.'

I folded my arms and looked my uncle straight in the face.

'The lack of water,' he said, 'is the only obstacle in our way. In the eastern gallery, made of lava, schist, and coal, we haven't found a single drop of moisture. We may be more fortunate if we follow the western tunnel.'

I shook my head with an air of total incredulity.

'Hear me out,' the Professor went on, forcing his voice. 'While you were lying here motionless, I went and examined the course of that gallery. It plunges straight into the bowels of the earth, and in a few hours it will bring us to the granite mass. There we are bound to find abundant springs. The nature of the rock makes that certain, and instinct joins with logic to support my conviction. Now this is the proposal I want to put to you. When Columbus asked his crews for three days more to reach land, those crews, sick and terrified though they were, granted his request – and he discovered the New World. I am the Columbus of these subterranean regions, and I am asking you for only one day more. If, after one day, I have not found the water we need, I swear to you that we will return to the surface.'

In spite of my irritation I was touched by these words and by the effort it must have cost my uncle to make such a promise.

'Well,' I said, 'do as you wish, and may God reward your superhuman energy. You have only a few hours left in which to tempt Fate. Let us be on our way!'

22

I Collapse

The descent began again, this time by the new gallery. Hans went first as usual. We had not gone a hundred yards before the Professor, passing his lamp along the walls, cried:

'These are primitive rocks! Now we are on the right track! Forward!'

When in its early days the earth was slowly cooling down, the shrinking process produced dislocations, fissures, hollows, and chasms. The passage along which we were walking was a fissure of this sort, through which molten granite had once poured. Its countless windings formed an inextricable labyrinth through the primeval mass.

The farther down we went, the more clearly the succession of beds forming the primitive terrane appeared. Geologists regard this primitive terrane as the foundation of the mineral crust of the earth, and they have established that it consists of three different layers, schist, gneiss, and mica schist, resting on that unshakeable rock called granite.

Never had mineralogists found themselves in such wonderful conditions for studying nature *in situ*. What the boring-machine, an insensible clumsy machine, could not bring to the surface of the inner texture of the globe, we were going to be able to study with our own eyes and touch with our own hands.

Through the beds of schist, which were tinged with splendid shades of green, there wound metallic threads of copper and manganese, with occasional traces of platinum and gold. My mind lingered for a while on these riches buried in the bowels of the earth, hidden for ever from the covetous eyes of mankind. These treasures had been buried so deep by the convulsions of primeval times that neither the pickaxe nor the mattock would ever be able to extract them from their tomb.

The schists were followed by layers of gneiss, remarkable for the regularity and parallelism of its strata, and then by the mica schists, disposed in large flakes which attracted the eye by the sparkle of the white mica.

The beams from our lamps, reflected by the tiny facets of the rocky mass, criss-crossed in all directions so that I felt as if I were walking through a hollow diamond inside which the rays were shattering against each other in countless coruscations.

About six o'clock this festival of light abated to a noticeable extent and almost ceased. The walls took on a crystallized but sombre appearance; the mica combined with feldspar and quartz to form the rock of rocks, the hardest of all, which carries the weight of the four terranes without being crushed. We were immured in a huge prison of granite.

It was now eight in the evening, and there was still no sign of water. I was suffering agonies of thirst. My uncle strode on, refusing to stop and listening for the murmur of some spring. But there was nothing to be heard.

Finally my legs began to fail me. I bore my torments as best I could so as not to force my uncle to stop. That would have driven him to despair, for the day was drawing to a close – the last day that belonged to him.

At last my strength gave out completely. I gave a cry and fell.

'Help! I'm dying!'

My uncle turned back. He gazed at me with his arms folded and then muttered: 'It's all over!'

The last thing I saw was a frightening gesture of rage before I closed my eyes.

When I opened them again, I saw my two companions motionless and rolled up in their rugs. Were they asleep? For my part, I could not get a moment's sleep. I was suffering too much, most of all at the thought that there was no remedy. My uncle's last words – 'It's all over!' – echoed in my ears, for in my present state of weakness there could be no hope of returning to the surface.

We had nearly four miles of the earth's crust above us, and this mass seemed to be bearing down with all its weight on my shoulders. I felt crushed, and I exhausted myself in violent attempts to turn over on my granite bed.

A few hours went by. A profound silence, like that of the grave, reigned around us. No sound could reach us through these walls, the thinnest of which was five miles thick.

Yet in the midst of my drowsiness I thought I heard a noise. It was growing dark in the tunnel and as I gazed hard it seemed to me that I could see the Icelander disappearing with the lamp in his hand.

Why was he leaving us? Was he abandoning us to our fate? My uncle was asleep. I tried to give a shout, but my voice could not break through my parched lips. It was now completely dark and the last sounds had just died away in the distance.

'Hans has abandoned us!' I cried. 'Hans! Hans!'

I shouted these words within me: they went no farther. Yet after the first moment of panic, I felt ashamed of my suspicions of a man whose conduct so far had been above reproach. His departure could not be desertion, for instead of going up the gallery he was descending it. Treachery would have taken him up, not down. This reasoning allayed my fears to some extent, and I turned to other thoughts. Only some serious motive would have led that quiet man to forfeit his sleep. Was he on the track of some discovery? Had he, in the silence of the night, heard some murmur which my ears had failed to detect?

23

We Find Water

For a whole hour my delirious brain passed in review all the reasons which might have roused the quiet huntsman to action. The most fantastic ideas got tangled up in my mind. I thought that I was going mad.

But at last I heard the sound of footsteps in the depths of the abyss. Hans was coming up again. A flickering light began to glimmer on the walls, and then came round the nearest bend in the corridor. Hans appeared.

He went up to my uncle, put his hand on his shoulder, and gently woke him. My uncle got up.

'What is it?' he asked.

'*Vatten,*' replied the guide.

It would seem that intense suffering can turn anybody into a polyglot. I did not know a single word of Danish, yet I instinctively understood the word our guide had uttered.

'Water! Water!' I cried, clapping my hands and gesticulating like a madman.

'Water!' repeated my uncle. '*Hvar?*' he asked the Icelander.

'*Nedat,*' replied Hans.

Where? Down below! I could understand everything. I seized the guide's hands and squeezed them, while he gazed calmly at me.

We got ready quickly and were soon making our way down a corridor with a slope of one in three. Half an hour later we had gone a mile and a quarter, and were two thousand feet farther down.

At that moment I distinctly heard an unfamiliar sound travelling through the granite walls, a sort of dull rumbling, like distant thunder. During this first half-hour of our walk, seeing no sign of the promised spring, my fears had been reawakened, but now my uncle explained the origin of the noise I could hear.

'Hans was not mistaken,' he said. 'What you can hear is the roar of a torrent.'

'A torrent?' I exclaimed.

'There's no doubt about it. A subterranean river is flowing around us.'

We hurried on, spurred on by hope. I no longer felt tired: this murmur of running water had already refreshed me. The torrent, which for some time had been over our heads, was now roaring and leaping along inside the left-hand wall. I kept passing my hand over the rock, hoping to find traces of moisture or damp, but in vain.

Another half-hour went by, and another mile and a quarter was covered.

It now became clear that the guide had gone no further

during his absence. Guided by an instinct peculiar to mountaineers and water-diviners, he had as it were felt this torrent through the rock, but he had certainly not seen any of the precious liquid or quenched his thirst with it.

Soon indeed it became clear that, if we went on, we should be getting farther away from the stream, the noise of which was becoming fainter.

We turned back. Hans stopped at the exact spot where the torrent seemed closest to us. I sat near the wall, where I could hear the water rushing past me with extreme violence about two feet away. But a granite wall still separated us from it.

Without thinking, without asking myself whether there might not be some way of obtaining this water, I gave way to a feeling of despair.

Hans looked at me, and I thought I saw a smile appear on his lips.

He stood up and took the lamp. I followed him. He went up to the wall while I watched him. He pressed his ear against the dry stone and moved it slowly to and fro, listening intently. I realized that he was trying to find the exact spot where the noise of the torrent was loudest. He found that spot three feet up from the floor.

I was tremendously excited, though I scarcely dared to guess what the guide intended to do. But I understood and clasped my hands and hugged him when I saw him seize his pickaxe and attack the rock.

'We are saved,' I cried.

'Yes,' said my uncle, in a state of frantic excitement. 'Hans is right! What a splendid fellow he is! We wouldn't have thought of that!'

He was right; this solution, simple though it was, would never have occurred to us. Admittedly nothing could be more dangerous than to take a pickaxe to this underpinning of the world. What if the wall caved in and crushed us? What if the torrent, bursting through the rock, carried us away? These dangers were very real, but at that moment no fears of rock-falls or floods could hold us back, and our thirst was so intense that we would have dug into the very bed of the ocean to allay it.

Hans set about his task, which neither my uncle nor I could have performed: we should simply have struck splinters from the rock in our impatience. The guide, on the contrary, was calm and self-possessed, wearing the rock away with a succession of light blows and producing an opening six inches wide. I could hear the sound of the water growing, and I imagined I could already feel the refreshing liquid on my lips.

Soon the pickaxe had penetrated two feet into the granite wall. Hans had been at work for over an hour and I was writhing about with impatience. My uncle wanted to join in himself; I had some difficulty in holding him back, and indeed he had just taken hold of his pickaxe when a sudden hissing was heard. A jet of water shot out of the hole and broke against the opposite wall.

Hans, almost thrown off his balance by the shock, could not repress a cry of pain. I understood why when, plunging my hands into the jet, I in my turn gave a loud cry. The spring was scalding hot.

'This water is boiling!' I cried.

'Well, it will cool down,' replied my uncle.

The corridor was filling with steam, while a stream was forming and running away down its subterranean windings. Soon we were able to take our first draught.

What pleasure it gave us! What incomparable ecstasy! What was this water, and where did it come from? We did not care: it was water, and, although it was still warm, it brought back the life which had been on the point of departing. I drank without stopping, without so much as tasting.

It was only after a minute's bliss that I exclaimed:

'Why there's iron in it!'

'Nothing better for the digestion,' retorted my uncle. 'It obviously has a high mineral content. This expedition of ours will be just as good for us as a stay at Spa or Toeplitz!'

'Oh, how delicious it is!'

'I should think so, six miles underground! It has an inky flavour which is not unpleasant. What a splendid source of strength Hans has found us here! I propose we should give his name to this health-giving stream.'

'Agreed!' I cried.

And the name of 'Hansbach' was promptly bestowed on it.

Hans did not give himself any airs as a result. After refreshing himself in moderation, he settled down in a corner in his usual quiet fashion.

'Now,' I said, 'we mustn't let this water run away.'

'Why not?' asked my uncle. 'I imagine the spring is inexhaustible.'

'All the same, let's fill the water-bottle and the flasks, and then try to stop up the opening.'

My advice was followed. With fragments of granite and pieces of tow, Hans tried to plug the hole he had made in the wall. This was anything but easy. He only succeeded in scalding his hands; the pressure was too great, and all his efforts were fruitless.

'It's obvious,' I said, 'that the upper reaches of this watercourse are very high up, judging by the force of the jet.'

'There's no doubt about that,' replied my uncle. 'If this column of water is 32,000 feet high, its pressure is equal to that of a thousand atmospheres. But I've got an idea.'

'What?'

'Why should we be so anxious to stop up this opening?'

'Because . . .'

For the life of me I could not think of a reason.

'When our flasks are empty, can we be sure of being able to refill them?'

'No, it's quite true that we can't.'

'Well then, let's allow this water to run on! It will run downwards as a matter of course, and will guide us as well as refresh us on our way.'

'What a splendid idea!' I exclaimed. 'And with this stream to help us, there's no reason why our expedition shouldn't be successful.'

'Ah, so you're coming round to my way of thinking, my boy!' said the Professor, laughing.

'I'm not just coming round – I've come!'

'Wait a moment, though. Let's begin by getting a few hours' rest.'

I had completely forgotten that it was night. The chronometer reminded me of that fact, and soon all three of us, adequately restored and refreshed, fell into a sound sleep.

24

Under the Sea

The next day, we had already forgotten all our past sufferings. At first I was surprised at not feeling thirsty any more, and for a moment I wondered why this was. The murmuring stream running at my feet gave me the answer.

We had breakfast and drank some of this excellent ferruginous water. I felt wonderfully cheered and resolved to go a long way. Why shouldn't a man as determined as my uncle attain his object, when he was accompanied by a guide as industrious as Hans and a nephew as devoted as myself? Such were the splendid ideas which occurred to me. If anyone had suggested that I should return to the summit of Sneffels, I would have refused with the utmost indignation.

Fortunately, all that we had to do was descend.

'Let us start!' I cried, awakening with my shout the oldest echoes in the world.

We set off again at eight on Thursday morning. The winding granite tunnel had all sorts of unexpected bends and seemed as tortuous as a maze, but its general direction was consistently south-east. My uncle kept consulting his compass very attentively, to keep account of the way we had come.

The gallery was almost horizontal, with a slope of one in forty at the most. The murmuring stream ran gently at our feet; I thought of it as a sort of familiar spirit guiding us underground, and now and then I stroked the warm naiad whose singing accompanied our steps. Good humour has always taken a mythological form with me.

As for my uncle, he kept inveighing against the horizontal nature of the path, as an enthusiast for verticals. Our route seemed to be stretching away into infinity, and instead of sliding down the terrestrial radius, as he put it, we were travelling along the hypotenuse. But we had no choice, and as long as we were approaching the centre, however gradually, we could not grumble. Besides, every now and then the slope became steeper, our naiad tumbled down it with a moan, and we went deeper with her.

On the whole, however, that day and the next we made considerable progress horizontally but comparatively little vertically.

In the evening of Friday, 10 July, according to our calculations, we were seventy-five miles south-west of Reykjavik and seven miles down.

Then, all of a sudden, a frightening shaft opened at our

feet. My uncle could not help clapping his hands for joy when he saw how steep it was.

'Now we shall make progress,' he cried, 'and without much effort, because the projections of the rock make a regular staircase!'

The ropes were fastened by Hans so as to guard against all possibility of accident, and the descent continued. I can scarcely describe it as perilous, for I was already familiar with this sort of operation.

This shaft was a narrow crack in the granite mass, of the kind geologists call a 'fault', and it had obviously been caused by the contraction of the earth's crust while it was cooling. If it had once been a passage for the eruptive matter thrown up by Sneffels, I could not understand why that matter had left no trace. We were descending a sort of spiral staircase which looked as if it had been made by the hand of man.

Every quarter of an hour we had to pause to take a rest and relieve our leg muscles.

We would sit down on some projecting rock with our legs dangling, chatting while we ate and drinking from the stream. Needless to say, in this fault the Hansbach had become a cascade and lost some of its volume as a result: but it still provided more than enough water to satisfy our thirst. Besides, when the slope became gentler it would be sure to resume its peaceful course. At the moment it reminded me of my worthy uncle, with his fits of impatience and anger, while on gentler slopes it was more like our calm Icelandic guide.

On 11 and 12 July we followed the spirals of this fault, penetrating another five miles deeper into the earth's crust, or about thirteen miles below sea-level. But on the thirteenth, about midday, the fault took a much gentler slope, of about forty-five degrees, in a south-easterly direction. The path then became easy and absolutely monotonous. This was inevitable, for the journey could scarcely be enlivened by changes in the landscape.

On Wednesday the fifteenth we were eighteen miles underground and about 125 miles from Sneffels. Although we were a little tired, our health was perfectly satisfactory and the medicine-chest was still untouched.

My uncle took hourly readings of the compass, the chronometer, the manometer, and thermometer – those which he has published in the scientific report on his journey. It was therefore a simple matter for him to establish his whereabouts. When he told me that we had travelled 125 miles horizontally, I could not help giving an exclamation of surprise.

'What is it?' he asked.

'Nothing, I was just thinking.'

'Thinking what, my boy?'

'That if your calculations are correct, we are no longer under Iceland.'

'Do you think so?'

'We can easily make sure.'

I took some measurements with my compass on the map.

'I was right,' I said. 'We have passed Cape Portland, and these 125 miles to the south-east have brought us under the sea.'

'Under the sea,' repeated my uncle, rubbing his hands with delight.

'So the ocean is over our heads!' I exclaimed.

'Why, of course, Axel. What could be more natural? Aren't there coal-mines at Newcastle which extend a long way under the sea?'

The Professor might consider this situation to be perfectly natural, but I felt a little uneasy at the thought of that mass of water over my head. Yet it really made very little difference whether it was the plains and mountains of Iceland that we had over us or the waves of the Atlantic, provided that the granite underpinning held good. In any case, I rapidly became accustomed to the idea, for the gallery, now running straight, now winding about, as capricious in its slopes as in its detours, but constantly heading south-east and always going deeper, soon took us to very great depths indeed.

Four days later, on Saturday, 18 July, we arrived in the evening at a sort of huge grotto; my uncle gave Hans his weekly wages of three rix-dollars, and it was decided that the next day should be a day of rest.

25
A Day of Rest

I consequently awoke on Sunday morning without the usual preoccupation with an early start. And although we were in the deepest of abysses, this was still extremely pleasant. Besides, we had grown accustomed to this troglodyte existence of ours. I hardly gave a thought now to sun, stars, and moon, trees, houses, and towns, all those terrestrial superfluities which men who live on the surface of the earth have come to regard as necessities. Living as fossils, we did not give a jot for these useless wonders.

The grotto formed a huge hall, over whose granite floor flowed our faithful stream. At this distance from its source, its water had only the temperature of its surroundings and could be drunk straight away.

After breakfast the Professor decided to spend a few hours putting his daily notes in order.

'First of all,' he said, 'I am going to work out our exact position. On our return I want to be able to draw a map of our journey, a sort of vertical section of the globe, which will show the course of our expedition.'

'That will be very interesting, Uncle, but are your observations sufficiently precise to enable you to do this?'

'Yes. I have kept a careful account of every angle and incline. I am sure I have made no mistakes. First let us see where we are. Take the compass and tell me the direction it indicates.'

I examined the instrument carefully and replied:

'East by south.'

'Good!' said the Professor, noting this down and making some rapid calculations. 'I estimate that we have come 213 miles from our starting-point.'

'So we are travelling under the Atlantic?'

'Exactly.'

'And at this very moment a storm may be raging above us, and ships may be being tossed about by the waves?'

'That may well be the case.'

'And whales may be lashing the roof of our prison with their tails?'

'Don't worry, Axel, they won't succeed in shaking it. But let's go back to our calculations. We are 213 miles south-east of Sneffels, and from my notes I estimate that we are at a depth of 48 miles.'

'But that is the limit which scientists set to the thickness of the earth's crust!'

'I don't deny it.'

'And here, according to the law of increasing temperature, there ought to be a heat of 1,500° Centigrade.'

'*Ought* to be, my boy.'

'And all this granite ought to be melting.'

'Well, you can see for yourself that it isn't, and that the facts, as so often happens, disprove the theory.'

'I am obliged to agree, but I can't help feeling surprised.'

'What does the thermometer say?'

'27.6°.'

'Therefore the scientists are wrong by 1,472.4°. Therefore the theory of a proportional increase in temperature is wrong. Therefore Humphry Davy was right. Therefore I was right in believing him. What have you got to say to that?'

'Nothing.'

In fact there were a lot of things I could have said. I did not accept Davy's theory in any respect, and I still clung to the theory of central heat, even though I could not feel the effects of that heat. I preferred to think, in fact, that this chimney of an extinct volcano, covered with a refractory coating of lava, did not allow the heat to pass through its walls.

But without stopping to prepare new arguments, I confined myself to taking the situation as it was.

'Uncle,' I said, 'admitting that your calculations are correct, will you allow me to draw a vigorous conclusion from them?'

'Conclude away, my boy.'

'At the latitude of Iceland, where we are now, the radius of the earth is about 4,749 miles, isn't it?'

'4,750.'

'Let's say 4,800 in round figures. And out of 4,800 miles we have done forty-eight?'

'As you say.'

'And this at a cost of 213 miles diagonally?'

'Exactly.'

'In about twenty days?'

'In twenty days.'

'Well, forty-eight miles are one hundredth of the earth's radius. If we keep on like that, it will take us two thousand days, or nearly five and a half years, to reach the centre!'

The Professor made no reply.

'Not counting the fact that if we go two hundred miles horizontally for every forty vertically, we shall come out at some point on the earth's circumference long before we reach the centre.'

'To blazes with your calculations!' retorted my uncle angrily. 'To blazes with your hypotheses! What are they based on? How do you know that this corridor doesn't go straight to our destination? Besides, there's a precedent for what I'm doing. Another man has done it, and where he has succeeded I shall succeed too.'

'I hope so, but after all, I'm entitled . . .'

'You're entitled to hold your tongue, Axel, instead of talking nonsense like that.'

I saw that my uncle was about to be metamorphosed into the fearsome Professor, and I made no reply.

'Now,' he went on, 'look at the manometer. What does it say?'

'It indicates a considerable pressure.'

'Good. You can see that by descending gradually, and accustoming ourselves little by little to the density of this atmosphere, we have avoided any sort of inconvenience.'

'Except for slight ear-ache.'

'That's nothing, and you can get rid of it by breathing quickly, to equalize the pressure inside your lungs with that outside.'

'Yes, of course,' I replied, determined to say nothing more which might annoy my uncle. 'It's even a positive pleasure to live in this dense atmosphere. Have you noticed how clearly you can hear everything down here?'

'I have. A deaf man would soon come to hear perfectly in these conditions.'

'But won't this density increase?'

'Yes, in accordance with a rather uncertain law. It is true that the weight of matter will diminish as fast as we descend. You know that it is at the surface of the globe that weight is most perceptible, and that at the centre of the earth objects weigh nothing at all.'

'I know that; but tell me, won't this air we are

breathing end up by acquiring the same density as water?'

'Probably, under a pressure of 710 atmospheres.'

'And lower down?'

'Lower down the density will increase even further.'

'Then how shall we continue our descent?'

'We shall have to fill our pockets with stones.'

'You have an answer for everything, Uncle.'

I did not dare to go any further into the region of theory, for I would have come across another insurmountable difficulty which would have infuriated the Professor.

All the same it was obvious that the air, under a pressure which might reach that of thousands of atmospheres, would end up by solidifying, and then, even if our bodies had survived as long as that, we should have to stop, in spite of all the reasoning in the world.

But I did not put forward this argument. My uncle would have met it with his inevitable Saknussemm, a precedent which carried no weight with me, for even admitting that the learned Icelander's journey had really taken place, there remained one very simple question to be asked: since neither the barometer nor the manometer had been invented by the sixteenth century, how had Saknussemm been able to tell when he had reached the centre of the earth?

But I kept this objection to myself, and waited for events to take their course.

The rest of the day was spent in calculations and conversation. I was always in agreement with Professor Lidenbrock, and I envied the stolid indifference of Hans, who, without bothering his head about cause and effect, went blindly wherever Fate led him.

26

Alone

It must be admitted that so far things had gone fairly well, and I had little cause to complain. If our difficulties became no worse, there was no reason why we should not attain our object. And what glory would be ours then! I had quite seriously begun reasoning like the Professor, possibly on account of the strange environment in which I found myself.

For a few days steeper slopes, some even alarmingly close to the perpendicular, took us deep into the inner mass. Some days we advanced between four and five miles nearer to the centre. These were dangerous descents, in which Hans's skill and wonderful self-possession were invaluable to us. That calm Icelander helped us with almost incredible devotion and simplicity, and thanks to him we got out of a good many difficult situations which would have been too much for just the two of us.

On the other hand his silence became more profound with every day that passed, and I do believe that it even began infecting us. External objects have a decided effect on the brain. Anyone shut up between four walls ends up by losing the power to associate words and ideas. How many prisoners in solitary confinement have become dull-witted, if not actually insane, for want of exercise for their thinking faculties!

During the fortnight following our last conversation, no incident worth recording took place. I can recall only one serious event which occurred about this time, but then I have good reason to remember it and indeed could never forget even the smallest detail.

By 7 August our successive descents had brought us to a depth of seventy-five miles; in other words we had seventy-five miles of rock, ocean, continents, and towns over our heads. We must then have been about five hundred miles from Iceland.

That day the tunnel was going down a very gentle slope. I was walking in front; my uncle had one of the Ruhmkorff lamps and I had the other, which I was using to examine the beds of granite.

Suddenly, turning round, I found that I was alone.

'Well,' I thought, 'I've been walking too fast, or else Hans and my uncle have stopped somewhere. I must go back and join them. Luckily it isn't a steep slope.'

I turned back and walked for a quarter of an hour. I gazed around, but saw nobody. I called out, but got no reply; my voice was lost among the cavernous echoes.

I began to feel uneasy, and a shiver ran down my spine.

'Keep calm,' I said aloud to myself. 'I am sure to find my companions again. There's only one path, after all. Seeing that I was in front, I must go back.'

For half an hour I climbed the slope. I listened to hear if anyone was calling me, for in that dense atmosphere a voice could carry a long way. But an extraordinary silence reigned in the long gallery.

I stopped. I could not bring myself to believe that I was alone. I might have gone a little astray, but I could not be lost. And people who go astray always find their way again.

'Come,' I said to myself; 'since there's only one path, and since they are following it, I am bound to find them again. All I have to do is to keep on climbing. Unless, of course, not seeing me, and forgetting that I was in front, they have turned back too. But even then I shall catch up with them if I hurry. That's obvious.'

I repeated these last words like a man who is only half-convinced. Besides, putting even these simple ideas together took me quite a long time.

Then a doubt seized me. Had I really been in front of the others? Yes, that was certain. Hans had been following me, ahead of my uncle. I could even remember him stopping for a little while to adjust the bundle on his shoulders. It must have been at that very moment that I had gone ahead.

'Besides,' I thought, 'I have a guarantee against losing my way, an unbreakable thread to guide me through this labyrinth, and that is my faithful stream. I have only to follow its course backwards, and I am sure to find my companions.'

This conclusion revived my spirits, and I decided to set off again without a moment's delay. I blessed my uncle's foresight in preventing Hans from stopping up the hole he had made in the granite wall. This beneficent spring, after having quenched our thirst on the way, was now going to be my guide through the winding galleries inside the earth's crust.

Before continuing my climb, I thought a wash would do me good and I bent down to plunge my head in the Hansbach.

To my horror and amazement I found that I was standing on rough, dry granite. The stream was no longer flowing at my feet!

27
Lost and Panic-Stricken

To describe my despair at that moment would be impossible, for there is no word for it in any human language. I was buried alive, with the prospect of dying from the tortures of hunger and thirst.

Mechanically I passed my burning hands over the granite floor. How hard and dry the rock seemed to me!

But how had I come to leave the course of the stream? For there was no denying that it was no longer there. Now I understood the reason for that strange silence when I had listened for the last time to hear if I could make out any sound from my companions. At the moment when I had set foot on the wrong path, I had obviously failed to notice the absence of the stream. Clearly there had been a fork in the gallery just then, and I had taken one route while the Hansbach, obeying the caprices of another slope, had led my companions off into unknown depths.

How was I to return? There was no trace of any footsteps, for my feet left no mark on the granite floor. I racked my brains for a solution to this apparently insoluble problem. My position could be summed up in a single word: lost!

Yes, lost at a depth which struck me as immeasurable. Those seventy-five miles of rock seemed to weigh on my shoulders with a terrifying pressure. I felt crushed.

I tried to turn my thoughts to things on the surface of the earth, but I was hard put to it to succeed. Hamburg, the house in the Königstrasse, my poor Gräuben, all that world underneath which I had lost my bearings passed rapidly before my terrified memory. I saw again in a vivid hallucination all the incidents of our journey, the sea-crossing, Iceland, Mr Fridriksson, and Sneffels. I told myself that if, in the position in which I found myself, I still retained even the shadow of a hope, that would be a sign of madness, and that the best thing I could do was to despair.

After all, what human power could possibly open up those huge arches of rock curving over my head and take me back to the surface? Who could put my feet on the right path and reunite me with my companions?

'Oh, Uncle!' I exclaimed in a despairing voice.

This was the only word of reproach which came to my lips, for I knew how much the poor man must be suffering while he in his turn was looking for me.

When I saw that I was beyond all human aid, and incapable of doing anything for myself, I thought of appealing to heaven for help. Memories of my childhood, and especially of my mother, whom I had known only in my earliest years, came back to me, and I knelt in fervent prayer, unworthy though I was of being heard by the God to whom I was appealing so late.

This recourse to Providence calmed me slightly, and I was able to concentrate all my mental faculties on my situation.

My flask was full and I had food for three days; but I could not remain alone longer than that. Should I go up or down? Up, of course, as far as I could go. Like that I was bound to reach the point where I had left the stream, at that baleful fork in the road. Then, with the stream at my feet, I might still be able to regain the summit of Sneffels.

Why hadn't I thought of that sooner? Here was obviously a chance of reaching safety. The most urgent necessity was therefore to find the Hansbach again.

I stood up, and, leaning on my iron-shod stick, I started walking back up the gallery. The slope was rather steep. I walked along hopefully and unhesitatingly, knowing that I had no choice.

For half an hour I met with no obstacle. I tried to recognize my way by the shape of the tunnel, the projection of certain rocks, the arrangement of the bends. But no distinguishing feature caught my attention, and soon I discovered that this gallery could not bring me back to the fork, for it came to a dead end. I bumped into an impenetrable wall and fell on the rock floor.

I cannot describe the terror and despair which seized upon me then. I lay there aghast. My last hope had just been shattered against that granite wall.

Lost in that labyrinth whose winding passages crisscrossed in all directions, I could not hope to find a way out: I was doomed to die the most horrible of deaths. Strange to relate, it occurred to me that if my fossilized remains were found one day, their presence seventy-five miles below the surface would lead to some earnest scientific speculations!

I tried to speak aloud, but only hoarse sounds passed between my dry lips and I lay there panting for breath.

In the midst of this anguish a new terror took hold of me. My lamp had been damaged in my fall. I had no means of repairing it, and its light was failing and would soon go out.

I watched the glow from the electric current gradually fading in the filament of the lamp. A procession of moving shadows passed along the darkening walls. I no longer dared to blink my eyes for fear of losing the slightest glimmer of this fleeting light. Every moment it seemed to me that it was about to vanish and that darkness was closing in on me.

Finally a last gleam flickered in the lamp. I watched it anxiously, concentrating the full power of my eyes on it, as on the last sensation of light which they were ever to experience, until at last it went out and I was plunged into unfathomable darkness.

A terrible cry burst from my lips. On earth, even on the darkest night, light never entirely abdicates its rights. It may be subtle and diffuse, but however little there may be the eye finally perceives it. Here there was none. The total darkness made me a blind man in the full meaning of the word.

At this point I lost my head. I stood up with my arms stretched out before me, trying to feel my way. I started dashing haphazardly through that inextricable maze, going downwards all the time, running through the earth's crust like an inhabitant of the subterranean galleries, crying, shouting, yelling, bruising myself on the jagged rocks, falling and getting up again, trying to drink the blood which was running down my face, and constantly expecting to run into some wall and dash my head to pieces.

I shall never know where this mad flight took me. After several hours, doubtless utterly exhausted, I fell headlong on the floor and fainted.

28

I Hear Voices

When I regained consciousness, my face was wet with tears. I cannot say how long I had been unconscious, for I no longer had any means of telling the time. Never had any human being been so isolated or forsaken as I was then.

After my fall I had lost a great deal of blood, and could feel that I was covered with it. How sorry I felt that I was not dead, and that that ordeal still lay ahead of me! I did not want to think any more, and, overwhelmed by pain, I rolled myself across to the foot of the opposite wall.

I was just about to lose consciousness again, and hoping for complete annihilation, when a loud noise struck my ears. It was like a roll of thunder, and I could hear the sound-waves gradually fading away in the distant depths of the abyss.

Where could this noise come from? From some subterranean phenomenon, I imagined, such as an explosion of gas or the fall of some great pillar of the globe.

I went on listening, in case the noise was repeated. A quarter of an hour went by. Silence reigned in the gallery. I could not hear even the beating of my heart.

All of a sudden my ear, which happened to be resting against the wall, appeared to catch the sound of words – vague, indistinguishable, and remote, but none the less words. I gave a start.

'It's a hallucination!' I thought.

But no – listening more attentively, I definitely heard a murmur of voices, though I was too weak to make out what they were saying. Yet somebody was speaking, I was sure of that.

For a moment I was afraid that the words might be my own, brought back to me by an echo. Perhaps I had cried out without knowing. I closed my lips tightly and laid my ear against the wall again.

'Yes, somebody is definitely speaking!'

Even when I dragged myself a few feet farther along the wall, I could still hear distinctly. I managed to make out certain vague, strange, incomprehensible words, which reached me as if they had been uttered in a whisper. The word *forlorad* was repeated several times, in a sorrowful tone of voice.

What did it mean? Who was speaking? Obviously either my uncle or Hans. But if I could hear them, they could hear me.

'Help!' I cried with all my might. 'Help!'

I listened, straining my ears for some reply from the darkness, a shout, even a sigh. There was nothing to be heard. A few minutes went by. A whole world of ideas came crowding into my mind. It occurred to me that perhaps my weakened voice was unable to carry to my companions.

'For it's they,' I said to myself. 'What other men could be seventy-five miles underground?'

I listened again. Moving my ear about over the wall, I found a place where the voices seemed to sound most clearly. The word *forlorad* reached me again, followed by that roll of thunder which had roused me from my lethargy.

'No,' I said, 'no. It isn't through the rock that those voices are reaching me. The wall is solid granite, and the loudest explosion couldn't come through it. This noise is coming along the gallery itself, by some peculiar acoustic effect.'

I listened once more, and this time I distinctly heard my name. It was my uncle who had pronounced it. He was talking to the guide, and *forlorad* was a Danish word!

Then everything became clear to me. To make myself heard, I had to speak along the wall, which would conduct the sound of my voice just as a wire conducts electricity.

But there was no time to lose. If my companion moved even a few steps away, the acoustic effect would be destroyed. I therefore drew close to the wall and, speaking as clearly as possible, said:

'Uncle Lidenbrock!'

I waited in extreme anxiety. Sound does not travel very fast, and a dense atmosphere does not increase its speed, but only its intensity. A few seconds, which seemed like centuries, went by, and at last these words reached me:

'Axel! Axel! Is that you?'

'Yes, yes!' I replied.

'Where are you, my boy?'

'Lost, in absolute darkness.'

'But your lamp?'

'It has gone out.'

'And the stream?'

'Disappeared.'

'Axel, my poor boy, cheer up!'

'Wait a moment, I'm exhausted. I haven't the strength to reply. But speak to me!'

'Courage,' my uncle went on. 'Don't speak, but just listen to me. We've been up and down the gallery looking for you, all in vain. Oh, I've wept for you, my boy! Finally, thinking you were still somewhere on the Hansbach, we came back downstream, firing our guns. Now, though our voices can meet, that is just an acoustic effect, and our hands cannot touch. But don't despair, Axel. It is already something to be able to hear each other.'

In the meantime I had been thinking, and a little hope, faint as yet, returned to me. First of all there was something I had to know. I put my lips close to the wall and said:

'Uncle!'

'Yes, my boy?' came the reply a few seconds later.

'To begin with we must know how far apart we are.'

'That's easy.'

'You have your chronometer?'

'Yes.'

'Well, take it and say my name, noting the exact second when you speak. I will repeat it as soon as I hear it, and you will again note the exact second at which my reply reaches you.'

'Right; and half the time taken between my call and your reply will be the time my voice takes to reach you.'

'That's it, Uncle.'

'Are you ready?'

'Yes.'

'Well, get ready. I'm going to call your name.'

I put my ear to the wall, and as soon as the name 'Axel' reached me, I immediately replied: 'Axel,' then waited.

'Forty seconds,' said my uncle. 'Forty seconds went by between the two words, so sound takes twenty seconds to cover the distance between us. Now at 1,020 feet a second, that makes 20,400 feet, or just under four miles.'

'Four miles!' I murmured.

'Oh, that's not an impossible distance, Axel.'

'But should I go up or down?'

'Down – and I'll tell you why. We are in a huge cavern, with a great many galleries leading into it. The one you are in is sure to bring you here, because all these cracks and fissures seem to radiate from the cavern we are in. So get up and start walking. Drag yourself along if need be, slide down the steep slopes, and you find our arms ready to welcome you at the end. Now on your way, my boy, on your way!'

These words cheered me up.

'Good-bye, Uncle,' I cried. 'I'm leaving now. We shan't be able to talk to one another after I've left this place. So good-bye.'

'*Au revoir*, Axel, *au revoir!*'

These were the last words I heard. This astonishing

conversation, conducted through the earth over a distance of nearly four miles, ended on this note of hope. I offered up my thanks to God, for He had led me through those huge dark spaces to what was perhaps the only spot where my companions' voices could have reached me.

This amazing acoustic effect is easy to explain on scientific grounds: it was due to the shape of the gallery and the conducting power of the rock. There are a good many examples of this propagation of sounds which cannot be heard in the intervening space. The phenomenon has been observed in various places, including the Whispering Gallery at St Paul's in London, and especially in those curious caves near Syracuse in Sicily, of which the most remarkable in this respect is called the Ear of Dionysius.

These instances came to my mind, and I realized that since my uncle's voice had reached me, there could be no obstacle between us. Following the course taken by the sound, I was bound to arrive at its starting-point, provided my strength did not fail me.

I therefore got up and set off, dragging myself along rather than walking. The slope was quite steep, and I let myself slide.

Soon the speed of my descent increased at an alarming rate, until it began to be more of a fall. I no longer had the strength to stop myself.

All of a sudden the ground disappeared from under my feet. I felt myself falling down a vertical shaft and bouncing off the projections on the walls. My head hit a sharp rock and I lost consciousness.

29

Saved

When I came to, I was in semi-darkness, stretched out on some thick rugs. My uncle was watching my face for some sign of life. At my first sigh he took my hand, and when I opened my eyes he gave a cry of joy.

'He's alive! He's alive!' he cried.

'Yes,' I answered feebly.

'My dear boy,' said my uncle, clasping me in his arms, 'you are saved!'

I was deeply touched by the affectionate tone in which he uttered these words, and even more by the gesture which accompanied them. But it required an occasion such as this to bring out the Professor's real tenderness.

At that moment Hans came up, and I think I may safely say that there was joy in his eyes when he saw my uncle holding my hand.

'*God dag*,' he said.

'Good day, Hans, good day,' I murmured. 'And now, Uncle, tell me where we are.'

'Tomorrow, Axel, tomorrow. Just now you are too weak. I have bandaged your head with compresses which must not be disturbed; so sleep now, and tomorrow I will tell you everything.'

'But at least tell me what time it is, and what day.'

'It's eleven o'clock at night, and today is Sunday the ninth of August. I forbid you to ask me any more questions until the tenth.'

I was indeed very weak, and my eyes shut of their own accord. I needed a good night's rest, and I therefore let myself drop off to sleep, with the thought that I had been alone for three days.

The next morning, on awakening, I looked round me. My bed, made up of all our travelling-rugs, was installed in a delightful grotto, adorned with magnificent stalagmites and carpeted with fine sand. It was half-light. There was no torch or lamp burning, yet certain inexplicable gleams of light were filtering in through a narrow opening in the grotto. I could also hear a vague, mysterious murmur, something like the sound of waves breaking on a shore, and now and then a noise like the whistling of wind.

I wondered whether I was really awake, whether I was dreaming, whether my brain had been cracked in my fall and I was hearing purely imaginary noises. But neither my eyes nor my ears could be deceived to this extent.

'That really is a ray of daylight,' I thought, 'slipping in through that cleft in the rocks! That really is the murmur of the waves and the whistling of the wind! Am I utterly mistaken, or have we returned to the surface of the earth? Has my uncle given up the expedition or brought it to a successful conclusion?'

I was asking myself these unanswerable questions when the Professor appeared.

'Good morning, Axel,' he said gaily. 'I'm ready to wager that you are feeling better!'

'I am indeed,' I said, sitting up on the rugs.

'That isn't surprising, because you have slept well. Hans and I took turns in watching over you, and we could see you visibly recovering.'

'I certainly feel in fine shape, and I'm ready to prove it by making short work of anything you give me in the way of breakfast.'

'Oh, you shall have something to eat, my boy. The fever has left you. Hans rubbed your wounds with some secret Icelandic ointment, and they have healed up wonderfully. He really is a splendid fellow!'

While he was talking, my uncle prepared some food for me which I wolfed down, in spite of his advice to eat slowly. Meanwhile I plied him with questions which he answered straight away.

I then learnt that my providential fall had brought me to the end of an almost perpendicular shaft; and as I had landed in the midst of a torrent of stones, the smallest of which would have been enough to kill me, it looked as if a loose portion of the rock had come down with me. This frightening vehicle had carried me, bleeding and unconscious, right into my uncle's arms.

'It really is a miracle,' he told me, 'that you weren't killed a hundred times over. For heaven's sake don't let us get separated again, or we might be parted for good.'

Not get separated again? Then the expedition wasn't over? I opened my eyes wide in astonishment, and this immediately brought the question:

'What's the matter, Axel?'

'I want to ask you something. You say that I'm safe and sound?'

'Yes.'

'And none of my limbs is broken.'

'Not a single one.'

'And my head?'

'Apart from a few bruises, your head is perfectly all right, and set firmly on your shoulders.'

'Well, I'm afraid that my brain is affected.'

'Your brain affected?'

'Yes. We haven't returned to the surface, have we?'

'No, certainly not.'

'Then I must be mad, because I can see daylight, and I can hear the wind blowing and the sea breaking on the shore.'

'Oh, is that all?'

'Won't you explain?'

'I can't explain anything, because it's inexplicable; but you shall see for yourself, and then you'll realize that geologists have still a lot to learn.'

'Then let's go out!' I cried, sitting up.

'No, Axel! The open air might be bad for you.'

'The open air?'

'Yes, the wind is rather strong. I don't want you to risk going out in it.'

'But I tell you I feel perfectly well.'

'Have a little patience, my boy. A relapse would cause us a lot of trouble, and we have no time to lose, for the voyage may be a long one.'

'The voyage?'

'Yes . . . Rest today, and tomorrow we'll set sail.'

'Set sail?'

I sat up with a start. Set sail? Did that mean there was a river, a lake, or sea outside? Was there a ship waiting for us, anchored in some underground harbour?

My curiosity was aroused to fever-pitch, and my uncle tried in vain to restrain me. When he saw that my impatience was likely to do me more harm than the satisfaction of my curiosity, he gave way.

I dressed quickly. As an extra precaution I wrapped one of the rugs around me and then I left the grotto.

30

An Underground Sea

At first I saw nothing. My eyes, which had grown unaccustomed to light, abruptly closed. When I managed to open them again, I was more astounded than delighted.

'The sea!' I cried.

'Yes,' said my uncle, 'the Lidenbrock Sea – for I don't imagine that any other explorer is likely to dispute my claim to having discovered it and my right to call it by my name!'

A vast sheet of water, the beginning of a lake or an ocean, stretched away out of sight. The deeply indented shore offered the waves a beach of fine golden sand, strewn with those little shells which were inhabited by the first living creatures. The waves broke on this shore with that sonorous murmur peculiar to huge enclosed spaces. A light foam was whipped up by a moderate wind, and some of the spray was blown into my face. From this gently sloping beach, about two hundred yards from the waves, a line of huge cliffs curved upwards to incredible heights.

Some of them, crossing the beach with their sharp spurs, formed capes and promontories which had been eaten away by the teeth of the surf. Farther on, their massive outline could be seen clearly defined against the misty backcloth of the horizon.

It was a real sea, with the capricious contour of earthly shores, but utterly deserted and horribly wild in appearance.

If my eyes could range far out over this sea, it was because a very special kind of light revealed its every detail. It was not the light of the sun, with its dazzling shafts of brilliance and the splendour of its rays; nor was it the pale, vague glow of the moon, which is just a cold reflection. No, the power of this light, its tremulous diffusion, its clear bright whiteness, its coolness, and its superiority as a source of illumination to moonlight, clearly indicated an electric origin. It was like an aurora borealis, a continuous cosmic phenomenon, filling a cavern big enough to contain an ocean.

The vault over my head, the sky if you like, seemed to be composed of huge clouds, shifting and changing vapours which, as a result of condensation, must at certain times fall in torrents of rain. But just then 'the weather was fine'. The electric light was producing some astonishing effects on the higher clouds. Their lower spirals were in deep shadow, and often, between two separate strata, a ray of remarkable brightness would shine down at us. But it was nothing like sunlight, seeing that there was no warmth in it. The general effect was supremely melancholy and sad. Instead of a sky shining with stars, I could feel that above those clouds there was a granite vault which oppressed me with its weight, and that space, vast though it was, would not have been large enough for the orbit of the humblest of satellites.

Then I remembered the theory of an English captain, who compared the earth to a huge hollow sphere, inside which the air remained luminous as a result of its pressure, while two stars, Pluto and Proserpina, moved about on their mysterious orbits. Could he have been telling the truth?

We were indeed imprisoned inside a huge cavern. It was impossible to gauge its width, since the shore stretched away on either side as far as the eye could see, or its length, for our gaze was soon halted by a somewhat indefinite horizon. As for its height, it must have been several miles. The eye could not see where this ceiling rested on its granite buttresses, but there were clouds hanging in the atmosphere, at a height which I put at 12,000 feet, a greater altitude than that of the terrestrial clouds, and doubtless due to the great density of the air.

Obviously the word 'cavern' cannot give any idea of the vast dimensions of this huge space. But human words are totally inadequate for anyone who ventures into the abysses of the earth.

Besides I did not know what geological theory could explain the existence of such a huge excavation. Could the cooling of the earth have produced it? I knew of certain famous caves, from the descriptions of them given by travellers, but none of them had anything like the dimensions of this one.

If the grotto of Gauchara, in Colombia, had not given up the secret of its depth to Humboldt, who had explored it to a depth of 2,500 feet, it probably did not go much farther down. The huge Mammoth Cave in Kentucky was admittedly gigantic in its proportions, since its ceiling rose five hundred feet above the level of an unfathomable lake, and travellers had gone twenty-five miles along it without coming to the end. But what were these cavities compared with the one which I was now admiring, with its cloudy sky, its electric light, and a vast sea contained in its depths? My imagination felt powerless before such immensity.

I gazed at these marvels in silence, unable to find words to express my feelings. I felt as if I were on some distant planet, Uranus or Neptune, witnessing phenomena quite foreign to my 'terrestrial' nature. New words were required for such new sensations, and my imagination failed to supply them. I gazed, I thought, I admired, with a stupefaction not unmixed with fear.

The unexpected nature of this sight had brought back the flush of health to my cheeks: I was treating myself with astonishment and bringing about a cure by means of this novel therapeutic system; besides, the keen, dense air was reinvigorating me by supplying extra oxygen to my lungs.

It will be easily appreciated that, after an imprisonment of over forty days in a narrow gallery, it was sheer bliss to breathe this moist, salty air; so I had no reason to regret having left my dark grotto. My uncle, who was already familiar with these wonders, had ceased to marvel at them.

'Do you feel strong enough to walk about a little?' he asked me.

'Yes,' I replied, 'and I should like nothing better.'

'Then take my arm, Axel, and let us follow the windings of the shore.'

I eagerly accepted, and we began to skirt this new ocean. On the left steep rocks, piled one upon another, formed a prodigiously impressive heap of titanic proportions. Down their sides flowed countless cascades, which fell in loud, limpid sheets of water. A few light clouds of steam, passing from one rock to another, indicated the presence of hot springs; and streams flowed gently towards the common basin, murmuring delightfully as they descended the slopes.

Among these streams I recognized our faithful companion, the Hansbach, which flowed quietly into the sea as if it had done nothing else since the beginning of the world.

'We shall miss it in the future,' I said with a sigh.

'Nonsense!' said the Professor. 'What does it matter whether we have that stream or another with us?'

I thought this reply rather ungrateful.

But at that moment my attention was drawn by an unexpected sight. Five hundred yards away, at the end of a steep promontory, a tall, dense forest appeared. It consisted of trees of medium height, shaped like parasols, with sharp geometrical outlines; the wind seemed to have no effect on their foliage, and in the midst of the gusts they remained motionless like a group of petrified cedars.

I quickened my step, anxious to put a name to these strange objects. Were they outside the 200,000 species of vegetables already known, and had they to be accorded a special place among the lacustrian flora? No; when we arrived under their shade, my surprise turned to admiration. I found myself, in fact, confronted with products of the earth, but on a gigantic scale. My uncle promptly called them by their name.

'It's just a forest of mushrooms,' he said.

And he was right. It may be imagined how big these plants which love heat and moisture had grown. I knew that the *Lycopodon giganteum*, according to Bulliard, attains a circumference of eight or nine feet, but here there were white mushrooms thirty or forty feet high, with heads of an equal diameter. There were thousands of them; the light could not manage to penetrate between them, and complete darkness reigned between those domes, crowded together as closely as the round roofs of an African city.

Yet I wanted to go farther, though it was mortally cold under those fleshy vaults. For half an hour we wandered about those damp shadows, and it was with a genuine feeling of relief that I regained the sea-shore.

The vegetation of this subterranean region was not confined to mushrooms. Farther on a great many other trees with colourless foliage stood in groups. They were easy to recognize as the lowly shrubs of the earth, grown to phenomenal dimensions, lycopodiums a hundred feet high, giant sigillarias, tree-ferns as tall as the fir-trees in northern latitudes, and lepidodendrons with cylindrical forked stems, ending in long leaves and bristling with coarse hairs like monstrous cacti.

'Astonishing, magnificent, splendid!' cried my uncle. 'Here we have the entire flora of the Secondary Period of the world, the transitional period. Here are our humble garden plants which were trees in the early ages of the globe! Look, Axel, and admire it all! Never has a botanist had such a feast for the eyes.'

'You are right, Uncle. Providence seems to have wanted to preserve in this huge hot-house the antediluvian plants which scientists have so skilfully reconstructed.'

'As you say, my boy, it is a hot-house, but you might add that it may be a menagerie too.'

'A menagerie?'

'Yes, a menagerie. Look at this dust we are walking on, these bones scattered on the ground.'

'Bones?' I exclaimed. 'Why, yes, these are the bones of antediluvian animals!'

I fell on these primeval remains, composed of indestructible calcium phosphate, and unhesitatingly identified these gigantic bones, which looked like dried-up tree-trunks.

'Here is the lower jaw of a mastodon,' I said; 'and there is a femur which can only have belonged to the biggest of all those monsters, the megatherium. Yes, it certainly is a menagerie, for these bones can't have been brought here by a cataclysm. The animals they belonged to have lived on the shores of this subterranean sea, in the shade of these arborescent plants. Why, I can even see some whole skeletons. And yet . . .'

'Yet what?' asked my uncle.

'I can't understand the presence of such huge quadrupeds in this granite cavern.'

'Why?'

'Because animal life existed on earth only in the Secondary Period, when a sediment of soil had been deposited by the flood-waters and had taken the place of the incandescent rocks of the Primitive Period.'

'Well, Axel, there is a very simple answer to your objection, and that is that this soil is alluvial.'

'What! At this depth below the surface of the earth?'

'Why, yes, and there is a geological explanation of the fact. At a certain period the earth consisted only of an elastic crust, which moved alternatively upwards or downwards according to the laws of attraction and gravitation. Probably subsidences of the crust occurred and some of the alluvial soil was carried to the bottom of the abysses which suddenly opened up.'

'That must be it. But if antediluvian animals have lived in these subterranean regions, how do we know that some of those monsters are not still roaming about in these gloomy forests or behind these steep rocks?'

As this idea occurred to me, I examined, not without a certain alarm, the various points of the horizon, but no living creature could be seen on those deserted shores.

I was rather tired, so I went and sat down at the end of a promontory, at the foot of which the waves were breaking noisily. From there I could see the whole of the bay formed by an indentation of the coast. In its crook a little harbour had been formed by the pyramidal rocks, where still waters slept sheltered from the wind. A brig and two or three schooners could have anchored there with room to spare. I almost expected to see some ship emerge from it under full sail and take to the open sea with the southern breeze behind her.

But this illusion rapidly faded. We were indeed the only living creatures in this subterranean world. When the wind dropped, a silence deeper than that of the desert fell over the arid rocks and weighed on the surface of the ocean. Then I tried to penetrate the mists in the distance, and to tear away the curtain which hung across the mysterious horizon. A whole succession of questions rose to my lips. Where did the sea end? Where did it lead? Could we ever hope to reach its opposite shores?

My uncle, for his part, had no doubt that we could. As for myself, I was torn between hope and fear.

After spending an hour in the contemplation of this wonderful sight, we returned by way of the beach to the grotto, and it was under the influence of the strangest thoughts that I fell into a deep sleep.

31
The Raft

The next day I awoke completely cured. I thought that a bathe would do me good, so I went and immersed myself for a few minutes in the waters of this Mediterranean Sea – a name which it certainly deserved more than any other sea.

I came back with a good appetite for breakfast. Hans did the cooking; he had water and fire at his disposal, so that he was able to vary our usual diet somewhat. For dessert, he served us a few cups of coffee, and never did that beverage strike me as so delicious.

'Now,' said my uncle, 'the tide is rising, and we must not miss the opportunity of studying this phenomenon.'

'The tide?' I exclaimed.

'Yes, of course.'

'You mean that the influence of the moon and sun can be felt down here?'

'Why not? Aren't all bodies subject throughout their mass to the power of universal attraction? And why should this mass of water escape the general law? So in spite of the great atmospheric pressure on its surface, you will see it rise like the Atlantic itself.'

At that moment we were walking on the sandy beach, and the waves were gradually moving up the shore.

'You are right,' I cried. 'The tide is beginning to rise.'

'Yes, Axel, and judging by the ridges of foam I estimate that the sea will rise about ten feet.'

'That's wonderful!'

'No, it's perfectly natural.'

'You may say what you like, Uncle, but it all seems extraordinary to me, and I can scarcely believe my eyes. Who would ever have imagined that inside the earth's crust there was a real ocean, with ebbing and flowing tides, winds and storms?'

'Why not? Is there any scientific reason against it?'

'None that I can see, provided we abandon the idea of central heat.'

'Then so far Davy's theory is confirmed?'

'Clearly, and in that case there is no reason why there shouldn't be other seas and continents in the interior of the globe.'

'Quite – but uninhabited, of course.'

'Oh? But why shouldn't these waters contain fish of some unknown species?'

'At any rate we haven't seen any yet.'

'Well, let's make some lines and hooks, and see if they will have as much success down here as up above.'

'We will try, Axel, for we must penetrate all the secrets of these newly discovered regions.'

'But where are we, Uncle? That's a question I haven't asked you yet, and one to which your instruments must have given the answer.'

'Horizontally, we are 875 miles from Iceland.'

'As far as that?'

'I am sure I am not more than a mile out.'

'And the compass still shows our direction as south-east?'

'Yes, with a deviation to the west of 19 degrees 45 minutes, just as on earth. As for its dip, a curious phenomenon is taking place which I have observed with the greatest attention.'

'And what is that?'

'The needle, instead of dipping towards the Pole, as it does in the northern hemisphere, is pointing upwards instead.'

'Does that mean that the magnetic pole is somewhere between the surface of the earth and the point we have reached?'

'Exactly, and no doubt if we were under the polar regions, near that seventieth parallel where James Ross discovered the magnetic pole, we should see the needle point straight up. Therefore that mysterious centre of attraction obviously isn't situated at a very great depth.'

'Evidently, and that is a fact which science has never suspected.'

'Science, my boy, is made up of mistakes, but they are mistakes which it is useful to make, because they lead little by little to the truth.'

'And how deep down are we?'

'Eighty-eight miles.'

'So,' I said, examining the map, 'the mountainous part of Scotland is above us, and the Grampians are raising their snow-covered peaks at an incredible height over our heads.'

'Yes,' replied the Professor with a laugh. 'It's rather a heavy weight to carry, but the ceiling is solid; the great architect of the universe has built it with the best materials, and certainly man could never have given it such an enormous span. What are the arches of bridges and the naves of cathedrals compared with this vault, with its radius of at least eight miles and room for an ocean and its storms underneath?'

'Oh, I'm not afraid of the roof caving in. But now, Uncle, what are your plans? Aren't you thinking of returning to the surface of the earth?'

'Returning? Certainly not! On the contrary, we shall continue our journey, seeing that everything has gone so well so far.'

'But I don't see how we are going to get down below this liquid plain.'

'Oh, I've no intention of diving into it head first. But if all oceans are properly speaking just lakes, since they are surrounded by land, that is all the more reason why this internal sea should be circumscribed by a mass of granite.'

'Yes, I can see that.'

'Well, on the opposite shore I feel sure we shall find fresh openings.'

'How long do you suppose this sea to be?'

'Between seventy and a hundred miles.'

'Ah!' I said, thinking to myself that this estimate could be hopelessly wrong.

'So there's no time to lose, and we must set sail tomorrow.'

I automatically looked around for the ship which was to carry us.

'Oh,' I said, 'so we must set sail, must we? All right! But what about a boat?'

'It won't be a boat, my boy, but a good solid raft.'

'A raft?' I cried. 'But a raft is just as impossible to build as a boat, and I don't see . . .'

'You don't see, Axel, but if you listened, you might hear.'

'Hear?'

'Yes, hear some hammering which would tell you that Hans is already at work.'

'Building a raft?'

'Yes.'

'What! Has he already felled some trees?'

'Oh, the trees were already down. Come along and you will see for yourself.'

After walking for a quarter of an hour, I caught sight of Hans at work on the other side of the promontory which formed the little natural harbour. A few more steps and I was at his side. To my surprise a half-finished raft was lying on the sand; it was made of beams of a special kind of wood, and the ground was literally strewn with planks, knees, and frames of all sorts. There was enough material there to build a whole fleet of rafts.

'Uncle,' I said, 'what wood is this?'

'It's pine, fir, and birch, all the various northern conifers, mineralized by the action of the sea-water.'

'Really?'

'It's what is known as surturbrand or fossil wood.'

'But then, like lignite, it must be as hard as stone and too heavy to float?'

'That sometimes happens; some of these woods have become real anthracites; but others, like these we have here, are only partially fossilized so far. Look,' added my uncle, throwing one of these precious spars into the sea.

The piece of wood, after disappearing from sight, rose again to the surface and rocked up and down with the movement of the waves.

'Are you convinced?' asked my uncle.

'I'm convinced that it's incredible!'

The next evening, thanks to the guide's skill, the raft was finished. It was ten feet long and five feet wide; the beams of surturbrand, bound together by strong ropes, formed a solid surface, and, once launched, this improvised vessel floated peacefully on the waters of the Lidenbrock Sea.

32
We Set Sail

On 13 August we awoke early in the morning, eager to adopt a new mode of travelling which was both rapid and easy.

The raft's rigging consisted of a mast made of two staves lashed together, a yard made of a third, and a sail borrowed from our stock of rugs. There was no lack of ropes and the whole vessel was well made.

The provisions, baggage, instruments, arms, and a large amount of fresh water were put on board, and at six o'clock the Professor gave the order to embark.

Hans had fitted up a rudder which enabled him to steer his vessel, and he took the tiller. I cast off the rope mooring us to the shore, the sail was set, and we put off quickly.

Just as we were leaving the little harbour, my uncle, who liked naming places, suggested giving it a name, and proposed mine among others.

'I've a better name to propose to you,' I said.

'And what's that?'

'Gräuben. Port Gräuben would look very well on the map.'

'Port Gräuben it shall be.'

And that is how the memory of my dear Virlandaise was associated with our adventurous expedition.

The wind was blowing from the north-west. We sailed before it at a great speed. The dense atmosphere had tremendous force and acted on the sail like a powerful fan. After an hour my uncle had been able to calculate our speed.

'If we go on at this rate,' he said, 'we shall cover at least seventy-five miles in twenty-four hours, and it won't be long before we reach the opposite shore.'

I did not reply, but went and sat forward. Already the north shore was sinking on the horizon, and the shores to the east and west were opening outwards as if to facilitate our departure. Before my eyes there stretched a vast sea; the greyish shadows of great clouds swept across its surface, and seemed to weigh down on the gloomy waters. The silvery beams of the electric light, reflected here and there by drops of spray, produced luminous points in the eddies created by the raft. Soon all land was lost to view, no fixed object could be seen, and if it had not been for our foaming wake I might have thought that our raft was perfectly still.

About midday, some huge shoals of seaweed came in sight, floating on the surface of the waves. I was aware of the prolific nature of these plants, which grow at a depth of twelve thousand feet at the bottom of the sea, reproduce themselves under a pressure of four hundred atmospheres, and often form shoals big enough to impede the course of a ship; but never, I think, was there any seaweed as gigantic as that which we saw on the Lidenbrock Sea.

Our raft skirted fuci three or four thousand feet long, huge serpents stretching away out of sight; I amused myself by following with my eyes these endless ribbons, constantly thinking that I had reached the end of them, but for hours on end my patience was exercised as much as my surprise.

What natural force could produce such plants, and what must the earth have looked like in the first periods of its formation, when, under the action of heat and moisture, the vegetable kingdom above was developing on its surface?

Evening came, but, as I had noticed the previous day, the luminosity of the air was in no way diminished. This was a constant phenomenon, the permanency of which could be relied on. After supper I stretched out at the foot of the mast, and it was not long before I fell into a sleep full of pleasant dreams.

Hans, motionless at the tiller, let the raft run on; with the wind blowing aft, there was no need for steering.

As soon as we had left Port Gräuben, my uncle had

instructed me to keep the log, noting down every observation and recording interesting phenomena; the direction of the wind, the speed of our raft, the distance covered, in fact every particular of our strange voyage.

I shall therefore confine myself to reproducing here these daily notes, written down, so to speak, at the dictation of events, in order to furnish an exact record of our passage.

Friday, 14 August. Steady NW wind. Raft sailing fast and straight. Coast seventy-five miles to leeward. Nothing on the horizon. Intensity of light constant. Weather fine, in other words the clouds are high up, fleecy, and bathed in a white atmosphere like melting silver. Thermometer at 32° Centigrade.

At midday Hans fastened a hook at the end of a line, baited it with a small piece of meat, and threw it into the sea. For two hours he caught nothing, and we began to think that these waters were uninhabited. But then there was a pull at the line. Hans drew it in and brought a struggling fish out of the water.

'A fish!' cried my uncle.

'It's a sturgeon!' I cried in my turn. 'A small sturgeon!'

The Professor examined the creature carefully and came to a different conclusion. This fish had a flat, rounded head, and the front part of its body was covered with bony scales; it had fairly well-developed pectoral fins but no teeth or tail. It certainly belonged to the family in which naturalists have classed the sturgeon, but differed from that fish in some essential details.

My uncle noted this, for after a brief examination he said:

'This fish belongs to a family which has long been extinct and which is to be found only in a fossil state in the Devonian strata.'

'What!' I cried. 'You mean we've taken alive one of the inhabitants of those primitive seas?'

'Yes,' replied the Professor, continuing his observations, 'and you can see that these fossil fishes are quite unlike the present-day species. Finding one of these creatures alive is sheer bliss for a naturalist.'

'But to what family does it belong?'

'To the order of the ganoids, the family of the cephalisphides, the genus . . .'

'Well?'

'The genus of the *pterychtis*, I'd swear to that! But this displays a peculiarity common, so they say, to the fishes that inhabit subterranean waters.'

'What's that?'

'It's blind!'

'Blind?'

'It's not only blind, but it has no eyes at all.'

I looked at the fish. What my uncle had said was perfectly true. But this might be an exceptional case, so the hook was baited again and thrown back into the sea.

This ocean is certainly well stocked, for in two hours we caught a considerable quantity of *pterychtis*, as well as some fish belonging to another extinct family, the *dipterides*, but of a genus which my uncle could not identify. None of them had eyes. This unexpected haul was extremely beneficial to our food stocks.

Thus it seems clear that this sea contains nothing but fossil species, in which fishes like reptiles are all the more completely developed the farther back they were created. Perhaps we may yet come across some of those saurians which scientists have reconstructed on the basis of a bit of bone or cartilage.

I took the telescope and examined the sea. It was deserted. No doubt we are still too near the shore.

I looked up in the air. Why should not some of those birds reconstructed by the immortal Cuvier be beating their wings in this dense atmosphere? The fish would provide them with sufficient food. I searched the space above me, but the air was as uninhabited as the shore.

Now, however, my imagination carried me away among the wonderful hypotheses of palaeontology, and I had a prehistoric daydream. I fancied I could see floating on the water some huge *chersites*, antediluvian tortoises like floating islands. Along the dark shore there passed the great mammals of early times, the *leptotherium*, found in the caves of Brazil, and the *merycotherium*, found in the icy regions of Siberia. Farther on, the *pachydermatous lophiodon*, a gigantic tapir, was hiding behind the rocks, ready to dispute its prey with the *anoplotherium*, a strange animal which looked like an amalgam of rhinoceros, horse, hippopotamus, and camel, as if the Creator, in too much of a hurry during the first hours of the world, had combined several animals in one. The giant mastodon waved its trunk and pounded the rocks on the shore with its tusks, while the megatherium, buttressed on its enormous legs, burrowed in the earth, rousing the echoes of the granite rocks with its roars. Higher up, the *protopitheca*, the first monkey to appear on earth, was climbing on the steep peaks. Higher still, the pterodactyl, with its winged claws, glided like a huge bat through the dense air. And finally, in the upper strata of the atmosphere, some enormous birds, more powerful than the cassowary and bigger than the ostrich, spread their vast wings and soared upwards to touch with their heads the ceiling of the granite vault.

The whole of this fossil world came to life again in my imagination. I went back to the scriptural periods of creation, long before the birth of man, when the unfinished world was not yet ready for him. Then my dream took me even farther back into the ages before the appearance of living creatures. The mammals disappeared, then the birds, then the reptiles of the Secondary Period, and finally the fishes, crustaceans, molluscs, and articulated creatures. The zoophytes of the transitional period returned to nothingness in their turn. The whole of life was concentrated in me, and my heart was the only one beating in that depopulated world. There were no more seasons or climates; the heat of the globe steadily increased and neutralized that of the sun. The vegetation grew to gigantic proportions, and I passed like a ghost among arborescent ferns, treading uncertainly on iridescent marl and mottled stone; I leaned against the trunks of huge conifers; I lay down in the shade of *sphenophyllas, asterophyllas,* and *lycopods* a hundred feet high.

Centuries passed by like days. I went back through the long series of terrestrial changes. The plants disappeared; the granite rocks softened; solid matter turned to liquid under the action of intense heat; water covered the surface of the globe, boiling and volatilizing; steam enveloped the earth, which gradually turned into a gaseous mass, white-hot, as big and bright as the sun.

In the centre of this nebula, which was fourteen hundred thousand times as large as the globe it would one day form, I was carried through interplanetary space. My body was volatilized in its turn and mingled like an imponderable atom with these vast vapours tracing their flaming orbits through infinity.

What a dream this was! Where was it taking me? My feverish hand noted down on paper the strange details of my journey. I had forgotten everything else – the

Professor, the guide, and the raft. A hallucination had taken hold of me.

'What's the matter?' asked my uncle.

My staring eyes looked at him without seeing him.

'Take care, Axel, or you'll fall overboard!'

At the same time I felt Hans seizing me. But for him, I would have thrown myself into the sea, under the influence of my dream.

'Has he gone mad?' cried the Professor.

'What is it?' I said at last, coming to.

'Are you ill?'

'No. I've had a brief hallucination, but it is over now. Is everything all right?'

'Yes, there's a fair wind and a fine sea, we are making good headway, and unless my calculations are wrong, we shall soon make land.'

At these words I stood up and gazed at the horizon; but there was still nothing to be seen between water and clouds.

33
A Battle of Monsters

Saturday, 15 August. The sea retained its monotonous uniformity. There was no land in sight. The horizon seemed far away.

My head was still dazed by the vivid impression made by my dream.

My uncle had not been dreaming, but he was in a bad temper. He kept sweeping the horizon with his telescope and then folding his arms with a look of annoyance.

I find that Professor Lidenbrock is tending to revert to his old mood of impatience, and I note this observation in my log. It required my danger and sufferings to strike a spark of humanity out of him; but since I recovered, Nature had resumed its sway. And yet, what reason had he to feel annoyed? Our voyage was proceeding in the most favourable conditions that could be imagined, and the raft was moving wonderfully fast.

'You seem anxious, Uncle,' I said, seeing him repeatedly putting the telescope to his eye.

'Anxious? No, not a bit of it.'

'Impatient, then.'

'I've good reason to be.'

'But we are going very fast . . .'

'What's the good of that? It isn't our speed that's too small, but the sea that is too big!'

I then remembered that before we set sail the Professor had estimated the length of this subterranean sea at about seventy-five miles. Now we had covered three times that distance, yet there was still no sign of the south shore.

'And we aren't going down!' the Professor went on. 'All this is a waste of time, because, after all, I didn't come all this way just to go for an outing on a pond!'

He called this voyage an outing, and this sea a pond!

'But,' I said, 'seeing that we've followed the course indicated by Saknussemm . . .'

'That's just the question. Have we followed that route? Did Saknussemm meet this stretch of water? Did he cross it? Has that stream we took as a guide led us astray?'

'In any case we can't regret having come so far. The view here is magnificent, and . . .'

'I don't give a damn for views. I set myself an object, and I mean to attain it. So don't talk to me about magnificent views . . .'

I took him at his word, and left the Professor to bite his lips with impatience. At six in the evening, Hans claimed his wages, and three rix-dollars were counted out to him.

*   *   *

Sunday, 16 August. Nothing new. The same weather. The wind freshened slightly. When I awoke, my first thought was to observe the intensity of the light. I lived in dread that the electric light might grow dim and then go out altogether, but there seemed to be no reason for fear. The shadow of the raft was clearly outlined on the surface of the waves.

This sea really seems infinite. It must be as wide as the Mediterranean or even the Atlantic – and why not?

My uncle took soundings several times, tying one of the heaviest pickaxes to the end of a cord which he let down two hundred fathoms. No bottom. We had some difficulty in hauling up our weight.

When the pickaxe was back on board, Hans showed me some deep imprints on its surface. It was as if that piece of iron had been squeezed between two hard bodies.

I looked at the guide.

'*Tänder*,' he said.

I did not understand and turned to my uncle, who was deep in his calculations. I decided not to disturb him and returned to the Icelander, who by opening and shutting his mouth several times conveyed his meaning to me.

'Teeth!' I said in amazement, looking more closely at the iron bar.

Yes, those were definitely the marks of teeth imprinted on the metal. The jaws which contained them must have been incredibly powerful. Were they the teeth of some monster of a prehistoric species which lived deep down under the surface, a monster more voracious than the shark, more formidable than the whale? I could not take my eyes off this bar which had been half gnawed away. Was my dream of the previous night going to come true?

These thoughts plagued me all day, and my imagination scarcely calmed down after a few hours' sleep.

Monday, 17 August. Today I tried to remember the peculiar instincts of the antediluvian monsters of the Secondary Period, which, coming after the molluscs, the crustaceans, and the fishes, preceded the mammals on earth. The world belonged at that time to the reptiles. Those monsters held absolute sway over the Jurassic seas. Nature had endowed them with a perfect constitution, gigantic proportions, and prodigious strength. The saurians of our days, the biggest and most terrible alligators and crocodiles, are only feeble, reduced copies of their ancestors of primitive times.

I shuddered at the evocation of those monsters. No human eye has ever seen them alive. They appeared on earth a thousand centuries before man, but their fossilized bones, found in the clayey limestone which the English call lias, have made it possible to reconstruct their anatomy and ascertain their colossal structure.

I had seen in the Hamburg museum the skeleton of one of these saurians which was thirty feet long. Was I destined – I, an inhabitant of this earth – to find myself face to face with these representatives of an antediluvian family? No, that was impossible. Yet the iron bar bore the mark of strong teeth, and I could see from the impression they had left that they were conical like those of the crocodile.

I gazed in terror at the sea, dreading to see one of those inhabitants of the underwater caves leap into sight. I imagine that the same idea, if not the same fear, had occurred to Professor Lidenbrock, for after examining the pickaxe he kept watching the ocean closely.

'Why the devil,' I said to myself, 'did he have to go and take soundings? He has obviously disturbed some creature in its lair, and we may well be attacked on our way . . .'

I had a look at our guns to make sure they were in good condition. My uncle noticed what I was doing and gave an approving nod.

Already the surface of the water has begun moving over a wide area, indicating some disturbance down below. Danger is near. We must keep a sharp lookout.

Tuesday, 18 August. Evening came, or rather the moment when sleep weights down our eyelids, for there is no night on this ocean, and the implacable light tires our eyes with its persistency, as if we were sailing under the Arctic sun. Hans was at the tiller. During his watch I fell asleep.

Two hours later a violent shock awoke me. The raft had been lifted up above the water with indescribable force and hurled a hundred feet or more.

'What's the matter?' cried my uncle. 'Have we run aground?'

Hans pointed to a dark mass rising and falling about a quarter of a mile away. I looked and cried:

'It's a colossal porpoise!'

'Yes,' replied my uncle, 'and there there's an enormous sea-lizard.'

'And farther on a monstrous crocodile! Look at its huge jaws and its rows of teeth! Oh, it's disappearing!'

'A whale! A whale!' cried the Professor. 'I can see its enormous fins. Look at the air and the water it's throwing out through its blowers!'

Sure enough, two liquid columns were rising to a considerable height above the sea. We stood there surprised, stupefied, horrified by this herd of marine monsters. They were of supernatural dimensions, and the smallest of them could have broken the raft with one snap of its jaws. Hans wanted to put the helm up to get away from this dangerous region; but in the other direction he saw some more enemies which were just as terrifying – a turtle forty feet long, and a serpent thirty feet long, darting its enormous head to and fro above the waves.

Flight was out of the question. The reptiles came nearer and moved around the raft at a speed greater than that of any express train, in gradually narrowing circles. I picked up my rifle. But what effect could a bullet have on the scales with which these animals were covered?

We were speechless with fright. They drew closer – the crocodile on one side, the serpent on the other. The rest of the herd had disappeared. I got ready to fire, but Hans motioned me to stop. The two monsters passed within a hundred yards of the raft and hurled themselves on one another with a fury which prevented them from seeing us.

The battle began two hundred yards away. We could distinctly see the two monsters at grips with each other. But then it seemed to me that the other animals were coming and joining in the struggle – the porpoise, the whale, the lizard, and the turtle. Every moment I caught a glimpse of one or other of them. I pointed them out to the Icelander, but he shook his head.

'*Iva*,' he said.

'What, two? He says there are only two animals . . .'

'He's right,' cried my uncle, whose telescope had not left his eye.

'He can't be!'

'Yes, he is. The first of those monsters has the snout of a porpoise, the head of a lizard and the teeth of a crocodile: that is what put us out. It's the most formidable of the antediluvian reptiles, the ichthyosaurus!'

'And the other?'

'The other is a serpent with a turtle's shell, the mortal enemy of the first – the plesiosaurus!'

Hans had been right. Only two monsters were disturbing the surface of the sea, and before my eyes I had two reptiles of primitive oceans. I made out the bloodshot eye of the ichthyosaurus, as big as a man's head. Nature has endowed it with an extremely powerful optical apparatus capable of withstanding the pressure of the water in the depth at which it lives. It has appropriately been called the saurian whale, for it has the whale's speed and size. This one measured not less than a hundred feet, and I could gauge its size when it raised its vertical tail-fins above the waves. Its jaws were enormous, and according to the naturalists they contain not less than 182 teeth.

The plesiosaurus, a serpent with a cylindrical body and a short tail, had four flappers spread out like oars. Its body was entirely covered with a carapace, and its neck, which was flexible as a swan's, rose thirty feet above the water.

Those two animals attacked each other with indescribable fury. They raised mountainous waves which rolled as far as the raft, so that a score of times we were on the point of capsizing. Hissing noises of tremendous intensity reached our ears. The two monsters were locked together, and could no longer be distinguished from one another. We realized that we had everything to fear from the victor's rage.

One hour, two hours went by, and the fight went on with unabated fury, the combatants alternately nearing the raft and moving away. We remained motionless, ready to open fire.

Suddenly the ichthyosaurus and the plesiosaurus disappeared, creating a positive whirlpool in the water. Several minutes passed. Was the fight going to end in the depths of the sea?

All of a sudden an enormous head shot out of the water, the head of the plesiosaurus. The monster was mortally wounded. I could no longer see its huge shell, but just its long neck rising, falling, coiling, and uncoiling, lashing the waves like a gigantic whip and writhing like a worm cut in two. The water spurted all around and almost blinded us. But soon the reptile's death-agony drew to an end, its movements grew less violent, its contortions became feebler, and the long serpentine form stretched out in an inert mass on the calm waves.

As for the ichthyosaurus, has it returned to its submarine cave, or will it reappear on the surface of the sea?

34

The Great Geyser

*W*ednesday, *19 August.* Fortunately the wind, which is blowing hard, has enabled us to get away quickly from the scene of the battle. Hans is still at the tiller, and my uncle, whom the fight had distracted from his all-absorbing thoughts, has returned to his impatient examination of the sea.

The voyage has resumed its uniform tenor, which I have no desire to see disturbed by dangers such as we underwent yesterday.

Thursday, 20 August. Wind N.N.E., variable. Temperature high. Speed about nine knots.

Towards midday we heard a very distant noise, a continuous roar which I could not identify.

'There must be some rock or islet in the distance,' said the Professor, 'against which the sea is breaking.'

Hans climbed to the top of the mast but could not make out any reef. The ocean stretched away unbroken to the skyline.

Three hours went by. The roar seemed to be coming from a distant waterfall. I said as much to my uncle, who shook his head. All the same I felt sure that I was right, and wondered whether we might not be sailing towards some cataract which would hurl us into the abyss. I had no doubt that this method of descent would please the Professor, because it would be nearly vertical, but for my part . . .

At any rate there was definitely a very noisy phenomenon a good few miles to leeward, for now the roaring noise was clearly audible. Did it come from the sky or the sea?

I looked up at the vapours hanging in the atmosphere and tried to penetrate their depths. The sky was calm; the clouds, as high up in the vault as they could go, seemed motionless and almost invisible in the bright glare of the light. It was therefore necessary to look elsewhere for the explanation of the phenomenon.

I then examined the horizon, which was unbroken and free from mist. Its appearance had not changed in any way. But if the noise came from a waterfall, a cataract, if the whole sea was flowing into a lower basin, if that roar was produced by a mass of falling water, then there was bound to be a current, and its increasing speed would give me the measure of the danger threatening us. I consulted the current: it was nil. I threw an empty bottle into the sea: it lay still.

About four o'clock Hans stood up, clutched hold of the mast, and climbed up to the top again. From that position his eyes swept the horizon in front of the raft and stopped at a certain point. His face showed no surprise, but his eyes remained motionless.

'He has seen something,' said my uncle.

'Yes, I do believe he has.'

Hans came down and stretched his arm out to the south, saying:

'*Der nere!*'

'Over there?' repeated my uncle.

Seizing his telescope, he gazed hard for a minute which seemed an age to me.

'Yes, yes!' he cried.

'What can you see?'

'A huge jet of water rising above the waves.'

'Another sea monster?'

'Perhaps.'

'Then let us steer more to the west, because we know now how dangerous those antediluvian monsters are!'

'No, let us go straight ahead,' replied my uncle.

I turned to Hans, but he held his tiller with inflexible determination.

Yet if at the distance which separated us from the animal – a distance I estimated at thirty miles at least – we could see the column of water expelled by its blowers, then it must be of supernatural dimensions. The most ordinary prudence would dictate immediate flight, but we had not come so far to be prudent.

We therefore pressed on. The nearer we got to the jet, the bigger it seemed. What monster, we wondered, could take in such a quantity of water and shoot it out without a moment's interruption?

At eight o'clock in the evening we were less than five miles from it. Its huge, dark, hillocky body lay in the sea like an island. Illusion or fear gave me the impression that it was over a mile long. What could this cetacean be, which neither Cuvier nor Blumenbach knew anything about? It was motionless and apparently asleep; the sea seemed to be incapable of moving it, and it was the waves that lapped against its sides. The column of water, thrown up to a height of five hundred feet, was falling in the form of rain with a deafening roar. And there we were, speeding like lunatics towards that powerful monster which a hundred whales a day would be insufficient to satisfy.

Terror seized me. I refused to go any farther and swore that I would cut the halyards if necessary. I expressed my mutinous feelings to the Professor, but he made no reply.

All of a sudden Hans stood up, pointed at the menacing object, and said:

'*Holme.*'

'An island!' cried my uncle.

'An island?' I said with a sceptical shrug of the shoulders.

'Why, yes!' replied the Professor, roaring with laughter.

'But that column of water?'

'*Geyser*,' said Hans.

'Yes, of course, it must be a geyser,' said my uncle, 'a geyser like those in Iceland.'

At first I refused to believe that I had been so grossly mistaken as to take an islet for a sea monster. But the proof was there before me, and finally I had to admit my error. What we could see was just a natural phenomenon.

As we drew nearer the dimensions of the liquid column were revealed as truly magnificent. The islet looked exactly like a huge cetacean whose head was sixty feet above the waves. The geyser – a word which means 'fury' – rose majestically at one end. Now and then we could hear muffled explosions, and the enormous jet, seized with a more violent rage, shook its vaporous plume and shot up as far as the lowest stratum of clouds. It was all alone. There were no wreaths of steam, no hot springs around it, and all the volcanic power of the island was concentrated in its jet. The rays of electric light mingled with that dazzling sheaf of liquid, every drop of which took on all the colours of the spectrum.

'Let us land,' said the Professor.

We had to be careful to avoid the waterspout, which could have sunk the raft in a moment. Steering skilfully, Hans brought us to the end of the islet.

I jumped on to the rock, and my uncle followed nimbly,

while the guide remained at his post, like a man above curiosity.

We found ourselves walking on granite mingled with siliceous tufa. The ground was trembling under our feet like the sides of an overheated boiler full of steam; it was burning hot. We came in sight of a little central basin from which the geyser rose. I plunged a thermometer into the boiling water; it registered 163°C.

This water was coming from a blazing furnace, and this was in complete contradiction with Professor Lidenbrock's theories. I could not refrain from pointing this out to him.

'Well,' he said, 'what does that prove against my theory?'

'Nothing,' I said curtly, seeing that I was faced with absolute stubbornness.

All the same I was forced to admit that we had been singularly favoured so far, and that for some reason which escaped me we had travelled in perfectly tolerable conditions of temperature. But it struck me as obvious and certain that some day or other we would reach regions where the central heat attained the highest limits and went beyond the temperature registered by any thermometer.

'We shall see.'

That was all the Professor would say; and after naming the volcanic islet after his nephew, he gave the signal to re-embark.

I went on looking at the geyser for a few minutes. I

noticed that its jet varied in height, sometimes diminishing in force, then shooting up again, a fact I attributed to variations in the pressure of the vapours accumulated in its reservoir.

At last we set sail again, skirting the sheer rocks at the southern end of the island. Hans had taken advantage of our absence to put the raft in order.

Before putting off, I made a few observations to calculate the distance we had come, and I now note these down in my journal. We have sailed 675 miles from Port Gräuben, and we are 1,550 miles from Iceland, under England.

35
The Storm

Friday, 21 August. Today the magnificent geyser had disappeared. The wind had freshened and had rapidly carried us away from Axel Island, while the roar of the geyser had gradually grown fainter.

The weather, if I may use that term, was to change before long. The atmosphere grew heavy with vapours charged with the electricity generated by the evaporation of the salt water; the clouds sank perceptibly and took on a uniformly olive hue; the electric light could scarcely pierce this opaque curtain lowered over the stage on which the drama of the elements was about to be performed.

I felt overawed, as most people do on earth at the approach of a cataclysm. The cumulus clouds piled up in the south had a sinister look – that pitiless appearance I had often noticed at the beginning of a storm. The air was heavy, the sea calm.

In the distance, the clouds looked like huge wool-packs heaped up in picturesque disorder; little by little they swelled up, gaining in size what they lost in number. They were so heavy that they seemed unable to rise above the horizon; but gradually, under the influence of the breezes, they merged together, growing darker all the time, until they soon formed a single menacing mass. Now and then a fleecy ball of mist, still illumined by the electric light, dropped on to this greyish carpet and soon lost itself in the opaque mass.

Naturally the atmosphere was full of electricity; my own body was saturated with it, and my hair was standing on end as if it were close to an electrical machine. It seemed to me that if my companions touched me they would receive a violent shock.

At ten in the morning the signs became more decisive; it was as if the wind were dropping only in order to draw breath, and the bank of cloud looked like a huge leather bottle in which hurricanes were accumulating.

I was reluctant to believe in the sky's threats, but I could not help saying:

'There's bad weather on the way.'

The Professor made no answer. He was in a dreadful temper at seeing the ocean stretching away into infinity before his eyes. He simply shrugged his shoulders.

'We're going to have a storm,' I said, pointing at the horizon. 'Those clouds are weighing down on the sea as if they wanted to crush it.'

There was a general silence. The wind dropped completely. Nature seemed to have stopped breathing and to be utterly dead. On the mast, where a hint of St Elmo's fire was already shining, the sail hung in heavy folds. The raft lay motionless on the sluggish, waveless sea. Why, I thought, if we had come to a standstill, did we keep up that sail, which could capsize us at the first impact of the storm?

'Let us reef the sail and take down the mast,' I said. 'That would be the sensible thing to do.'

'No, damnit, no!' cried my uncle. 'A hundred times no! Let the wind seize us! Let the storm carry us away! Provided I set eyes on a rocky shore, I don't care if it smashes our raft to smithereens!'

These words were scarcely out of his mouth before a sudden change took place on the southern horizon. The accumulated vapours condensed into water, and the air, rushing from the farthest extremities of the cavern to fill the voids left by this condensation, blew with hurricane force. The darkness deepened until I could do no more than jot down a few hurried notes.

The raft rose into the air and bounded forward, flinging my uncle headlong. I crawled over to him, and found him clinging to a cable and apparently enjoying the sight of the elements unleashed.

Hans did not budge. His long hair, blown forward by the hurricane over his motionless features, gave him an odd appearance, for the end of every hair was tipped with little luminous plumes. This frightening mask reminded me of the face of antediluvian man, the contemporary of the ichthyosaurus and the megatherium.

Meanwhile the mast held firm, although the sail swelled out like a bubble on the point of bursting. The raft flew along at a speed I could not calculate, but not as fast as the water it displaced, which was thrown up in clean straight lines.

'The sail! The sail!' I cried, making as if to lower it.

'No!' replied my uncle.

'*Nej!*' repeated Hans, gently shaking his head.

By now the rain had formed a roaring cataract in front of that horizon towards which we were speeding madly. But before it could reach us the curtain of cloud was torn apart, the sea boiled, and a vast chemical action taking place in the upper regions brought electrical forces into play. Brilliant flashes of lightning mingled with the rolls of thunder, criss-crossing in the midst of the loud crashes; the vaporous mass became incandescent, and the hail-stones striking the metal of our tools or guns flashed with light; while the heaving waves looked like miniature volcanoes, each hillock containing an inner fire, each crest plumed with a flame.

My eyes were dazzled by the intensity of the light, my ears deafened by the din of the thunder. I had to cling to the mast, which bent like a reed before the violence of the storm.

*   *   *

(Here my notes became very vague. I have only been able to find a few brief observations, which I had jotted down almost unconsciously. But their brevity and even their incoherence reveal the emotion which gripped me and give a better idea of the atmosphere than my memory could.)

Sunday, 23 August. Where are we? We have been carried along with indescribable rapidity.

Last night was dreadful, and the storm has not abated. We are living in a continuous din and uproar, our ears are bleeding, and it is impossible to exchange a single word.

The lightning is flashing all the time. I see zigzags which, after hurtling downwards, rebound and shoot up towards the granite ceiling. What if it should fall in? Other flashes of lightning fork or take the form of globes of fire which burst like bombs. But the general din does not appear to get any louder; it has passed the limit of intensity within which the human ear can hear, and if all the powder magazines in the world were to blow up together, we would not be able to make out more than we can now.

There is a constant emission of light from the under-surface of the clouds; electric matter is constantly being given off by their molecules. The gaseous elements of the air have obviously changed, for countless columns of water are soaring into the air and falling back in a foaming mass.

Where are we going? . . . My uncle is stretched out at full length at the end of the raft.

It is getting hotter. I look at the thermometer; it registers . . . (the figure is illegible).

Monday, 24 August. Will this never end? Is this dense atmosphere, now that it has changed, going to remain in this condition?

We are utterly worn out. Hans is the same as ever. The raft is still heading south-east, and we have travelled over 500 miles from Axel Island.

At midday the storm increased in violence. We had to make fast all our cargo, and we all lashed ourselves to the raft as well. The waves passed over our heads.

For three days we had not been able to exchange a single word. We opened our mouths and moved our lips, but no sound could be heard. We could not even make ourselves heard by shouting into one another's ears.

My uncle came over to me and pronounced a few words. I think he said, 'We are done for,' but I am not sure.

I wrote down these words for him to read: 'Let us lower the sail.'

He nodded in agreement.

He had scarcely lifted his head again before a ball of fire appeared on board the raft. The mast and the sail vanished together, and I saw them rising to a prodigious height, looking like the pterodactyl, that fantastic bird of prehistoric times.

We were paralysed with fear. The fireball, half white, half blue, and the size of a ten-inch shell, moved slowly over the raft, slowly, but revolving at an astonishing speed under the lash of the hurricane. It floated here and there, perched on one of the supports, leapt on to the provision bag, jumped lightly down, rebounded, and touched the powder canister. For a horrible moment I thought we were going to be blown up; but no, the dazzling ball moved away and approached Hans, who simply stared at it, my uncle, who fell on his knees to avoid it, and myself, pale and trembling under its hot glare. It pirouetted near my foot, which I tried to pull away, but in vain.

A smell of nitrous gas filled the air, entering our throats and filling our lungs to suffocation.

Why was I unable to move my foot? Was it riveted to the raft? Then I realized that the electric fireball had magnetized all the iron on board; the instruments, tools, and guns were moving about and clinking as they collided; the nails of my boots were clinging to an iron plate let into the wood.

At last, with a violent effort, I managed to pull my foot away just as the ball was going to seize it in its gyrations and carry me away too.

Suddenly there was a blaze of light. The ball had burst and we were covered with tongues of fire.

Then everything went dark. I just had time to make out my uncle stretched out on the raft, and Hans still at his tiller but 'spitting fire' under the influence of the electricity with which he was saturated.

Where are we going? Where are we going?

Tuesday, 25 August. I have just emerged from a long swoon. The storm is still raging; the forks of lightning are flashing about like a brood of serpents let loose in the sky.

Are we still at sea? Yes, and moving at an incalculable speed. We have passed under England, under the Channel, under France, perhaps under the whole of Europe.

I can hear a new noise! Surely it is the sound of the sea breaking on rocks! But then . . .

36
An Unpleasant Shock

Here ends what I have called the log, happily saved from the wreck, and I resume my narrative as before.

What happened when the raft was dashed against the reefs on the coast I cannot say. I felt myself being flung into the sea, and if I escaped death, if my body was not torn to pieces on the sharp rocks, that was because Hans's strong arm snatched me from the abyss.

The brave Icelander carried me out of reach of the waves to a hot sandy beach where I found myself lying side by side with my uncle.

Then he returned to the rocks on which the furious waves were beating, to save what he could from the wreck. I was unable to speak, overcome as I was by fatigue and excitement; it took me a whole hour to recover.

Meanwhile the rain went on falling in a positive deluge, though with that violence which usually indicates that a storm is nearly over. A few overhanging rocks offered us a shelter from the torrential downpour. Hans prepared some food, which I could not even touch, and each of us, exhausted by three wakeful nights, fell into a painful sleep.

The next day the weather was magnificent. The sky and sea had calmed down with one accord. Every trace of the storm had disappeared when I awoke, to be greeted by the Professor's cheerful voice. He was ominously gay.

'Well, my boy,' he cried, 'have you slept well?'

I could almost have imagined that we were in the house in the Königstrasse, that I was coming down to breakfast, and that I was going to marry poor Gräuben that very day.

Alas, if the tempest had sent the raft eastwards, we had passed under Germany, under my beloved city of Hamburg, under the street where there lived all that I loved most in the world. In that case we were separated by barely a hundred miles! But they were a hundred vertical miles of solid granite, and in reality we were more than two thousand miles apart.

All these painful thoughts crossed rapidly through my mind before I could answer my uncle's question.

'Well,' he said, 'don't you want to tell me how you've slept?'

'Very well,' I replied. 'I still feel rather done in, but that will pass.'

'Of course it will. You're just a little tired, that's all.'

'But you seem in very good spirits this morning, Uncle.'

'Delighted, my boy, delighted! We've arrived!'

'At the end of our expedition?'

'No, but at the end of that apparently endless sea. Now we can start travelling by land again and really plunge into the bowels of the earth.'

'Uncle, may I ask you a question?'

'You may, Axel, you may.'

'What about our return journey?'

'Our return journey? You mean to say you are thinking about the return journey before we have even arrived?'

'No, I only want to know how we are going to manage it.'

'In the simplest way possible. Once we have reached the centre of the globe, we shall either find some new route to the surface, or we shall return in very humdrum fashion by the way we have come. I don't imagine that it will close up behind us.'

'Then we shall have to repair the raft.'

'Of course.'

'But have we got enough provisions to go on with the journey?'

'Oh, yes. Hans is an able fellow, and I'm sure he will have saved most of the cargo. But let us go and make sure.'

We left the open grotto. I cherished the hope which was a fear at the same time: it seemed to me impossible that the terrible wreck of the raft should not have destroyed everything on board.

I was mistaken. On my arrival on the shore, I found

Hans in the midst of a host of neatly arranged articles. My uncle shook hands with him with fervent gratitude, for with superhuman devotion, of which it would be difficult to find the equal, he had worked while we were asleep and had saved the most precious articles at the risk of his life.

Not that we had not suffered some serious losses, for instance our guns; but in the last analysis we could do without them. Our stock of powder, after nearly exploding during the storm, was intact.

'Well,' exclaimed the Professor, 'if we haven't any guns, we can't go hunting, that's all.'

'Yes, but what about the instruments?'

'Here is the manometer, the most useful of all, and the one for which I would willingly have given all the others. With it I can calculate how deep we are and know when we have reached the centre. Without it we might go too far and come out at the Antipodes!'

His gaiety was really ferocious.

'But where's the compass?' I asked.

'Here it is on this rock, in perfect condition, as well as the chronometer and the thermometers. Oh, that guide is a splendid fellow!'

There was no denying it: none of the instruments was missing, while, as for the tools and equipment, I could see the ladders, ropes, pickaxes, and so on laid out on the sand.

However, the question of provisions still had to be cleared up.

'What about the provisions?' I asked.

'Let us see,' replied the Professor.

The crates which contained them were arranged in a row on the shore in a perfect state of preservation; for the most part the sea had spared them, and what with biscuits, salt meat, gin, and dried fish, we had enough food for another four months.

'Four months!' cried the Professor. 'Why, we have time to get there and back; and with what is left I will give a great dinner to my colleagues at the Johannaeum!'

I ought to have been used to my uncle's character by now, yet the man still astonished me.

'Now,' he said, 'we must replenish our stock of water with the rain the storm has left in all these granite basins so that we have no reason to be afraid of going thirsty. As for the raft, I will ask Hans to repair it as best he can, although I don't imagine we shall need it again.'

'Why not?' I cried.

'Just an idea of mine, my boy. I don't think we shall get out by the way we came in.'

I looked at the Professor rather suspiciously, wondering whether he had not gone out of his mind. Yet he little knew how right he was.

'Let's go and have breakfast,' he said.

I followed him on to a promontory, after he had given instructions to the guide. There, preserved meat, biscuits, and tea provided us with an excellent meal, indeed one of the best I have ever had. Hunger, the fresh air, peace and quiet after all the excitement of the past few days, all contributed to give me a good appetite.

During breakfast I asked the Professor where he thought we were.

'That,' I said, 'strikes me as rather difficult to work out.'

'Yes,' he replied, 'it is certainly difficult to calculate exactly, indeed impossible, seeing that during these three days of storm I have been unable to keep a record of the raft's speed and direction. All the same, we can make a rough estimate.'

'Well, the last observation was made on the island with the geyser . . . !'

'Axel Island, my boy. Don't spurn the honour of having given your name to the first island discovered in the interior of the earth.'

'All right, at Axel Island we had covered about 675 miles of this sea, and we were over 1,500 miles from Iceland.'

'Good. Let us start from that point and count four days of storm, during which our rate cannot have been less than 200 miles every twenty-four hours.'

'I agree. That would make 800 miles to be added.'

'Yes, and the Lidenbrock Sea would be about 1,500 miles from shore to shore. Do you realize, Axel, that it can compete with the Mediterranean in size?'

'Yes, especially if we have only crossed the width of it!'

'Which is perfectly possible.'

'Another curious thing,' I added, 'is that if our calculations are correct, we have now got the Mediterranean over our heads.'

'Really?'

'Yes, because we are 2,250 miles from Reykjavik.'

'That's a tidy distance, my boy; but we can't say for sure that we are under the Mediterranean and not under Turkey or the Atlantic unless we are certain that our direction has not changed.'

'I feel sure it hasn't. The wind seemed to be constant, so I think this shore must be south-east of Port Gräuben.'

'Well, we can easily find out by consulting the compass. Let us go and see what it says.'

The Professor made for the rock on which Hans had placed the instruments. He was gay and cheerful, rubbing his hands and striking attitudes like a young man. I followed him, curious to know whether I had been right in my estimate.

Arriving at the rock, my uncle took the compass, and examined the needle, which after a few oscillations took up a fixed position.

My uncle looked, rubbed his eyes, and looked again. Then he turned to me in amazement.

'What's the matter?' I asked.

He motioned to me to examine the instrument. I gave an exclamation of surprise. The north tip of the needle was pointing to what we supposed to be the south! It was pointing inland instead of out to sea!

I shook the compass and examined it carefully; it was in perfect condition. In whatever position I placed the compass, the needle stubbornly returned to this unexpected direction.

There seemed to be no doubt that during the storm a sudden change of wind had occurred which we had not noticed, and had brought the raft back to the shore which my uncle thought he had left behind him.

37

A Human Skull

It would be impossible to describe the succession of emotions which seized hold of Professor Lidenbrock – stupefaction, incredulity, and finally anger. I have never seen a man so startled at first, and so furious afterwards. The fatigues of the crossing, the dangers we had undergone, had all to be repeated.

But my uncle rapidly regained control of himself.

'So. Fate is having fun with me, is it?' he cried. 'The elements are in league against me! Air, fire, and water combine to block my way! Well, they are going to find out just how strong-willed I am! I won't give in, I won't move back an inch, and we shall see whether man or Nature will get the upper hand!'

Standing on the rock, angry and menacing, Otto Lidenbrock, like Ajax, seemed to be hurling defiance at the gods. But I thought it best to intervene and put a check on his wild fury.

'Listen to me,' I said firmly. 'There is a limit to every sort of ambition in this world, and we can't do the impossible. We are ill-equipped for a sea voyage, because nobody can sail a thousand miles on a collection of rotten beams, with a blanket for a sail, a stick for a mast, and a contrary wind blowing. Unable to steer, and at the mercy of every storm, we should be mad to try that impossible crossing a second time!'

I was able to expound these irrefutable arguments for ten minutes without interruption, but simply because the Professor was not taking any notice of me and did not hear a single word I said.

'To the raft!' he cried.

That was his only reply. It was no use my arguing, begging, losing my temper: I came up against a will harder than granite.

Hans had just finished repairing the raft, as if the strange creature had guessed my uncle's intentions. He strengthened the craft with a few pieces of surturbrand. A sail had already been run up and the wind was playing in its folds.

The Professor said a few words to the guide, who promptly placed all our effects on board and got ready to cast off. The sky was fairly clear and the wind blowing steadily from the north-west.

What could I do? Stand up to the two of them? That was impossible. If only Hans had taken my side! But the Icelander seemed to have renounced all will of his own and taken a vow of abnegation. I could not get anything out of a servant so feudally devoted to his master. There was nothing to be done but press on.

I was therefore going to take my usual place on the raft when my uncle placed his hand on my shoulder.

'We shan't leave till tomorrow,' he said.

I made a gesture of complete resignation.

'I must neglect nothing,' he went on, 'and since Fate has driven me on to this part of the coast, I won't leave it until I have explored it.'

This remark will be understood when I explain that, if we had returned to the north shore, it was not at the place from which we had started. Port Gräuben, we decided, must be farther west. Nothing could be more sensible, therefore, than to make a thorough inspection of this new region.

'Let's start exploring!' I said.

And leaving Hans to his work, we set off. The space between the water and the foot of the cliffs was extremely wide at this point. It would take half an hour to reach the wall of rock. We were crushing underfoot countless shells of all shapes and sizes, in which prehistoric creatures had lived. I also noticed some huge carapaces, often over fifteen feet in diameter, which had belonged to those gigantic glyptodons of the Pleiocene Period of which the modern tortoise is just a greatly reduced copy. The ground was also strewn with stones, arranged in rows and looking like pebbles rounded by the waves. This led me to think that the sea must have covered this region at one time. On the scattered rocks, which were now out of their reach, the waves had left clear traces of their passage.

This could explain up to a certain point the existence of this ocean a hundred miles below the surface of the earth. This liquid mass, which, in my opinion, was bound to flow away gradually into the bowels of the earth, had obviously penetrated from the sea above through some fissure. Yet it had to be supposed that that fissure was now closed, for otherwise the whole of this cavern, or rather this huge reservoir, would have filled up in a fairly short time. Perhaps too this water, subjected to the action of the subterranean fires, had evaporated to some extent. This would account for the clouds over our heads and the development of that electricity which created storms in the interior of the earth.

This theory about the phenomena we had witnessed struck me as satisfactory, for however great the wonders of Nature may be, they can always be explained by physical laws.

We were therefore walking on a sort of sedimentary soil, deposited by the waters like all the terranes of that period on the surface of the globe. The Professor carefully examined every fissure in the rocks. Whenever he saw a hole it became a matter of importance for him to discover its depth.

We had followed the shores of the Lidenbrock Sea for

a mile when the ground suddenly changed in appearance. It looked as if it had been shaken and convulsed by a violent upheaval of the lower strata. In a good many places hollows or hillocks bore witness to a massive dislocation of the rock. We were advancing with difficulty over these granite fragments, mingled with flint, quartz, and alluvial deposits, when we were suddenly confronted with a field, or rather a plain, covered with bones. It looked like a huge cemetery, containing the remains of twenty centuries of mankind. Great mounds of bones were piled up in row after row, stretching away to the horizon, where they disappeared into the mist. There, within perhaps three square miles, was accumulated the entire history of animal life, a history scarcely sketched out in the too-recent strata of the inhabited world.

A burning curiosity impelled us forward. Our feet noisily cracked and crushed fossils and bones of pre-historic animals whose rare and interesting remains are a subject of contention between the museums of our great cities. A thousand Cuviers working all their lives could not have constructed all the skeletons which lay in that magnificent ossuary.

I was stupefied. My uncle had raised his long arms towards the thick vault which served us as a sky. His gaping mouth, his eyes flashing behind his spectacles, his head nodding up and down, and indeed his whole attitude denoted utter astonishment. He was faced with a priceless collection of *lepthotheria, mericotheria, lophiodia, anoplotheria, megatheria,* mastodons, *protopithecae,* pterodactyls, *and* other antediluvian monsters, all heaped up there for his personal satisfaction. Imagine a fanatical bibliomaniac suddenly transported into the middle of the famous library of Alexandria which Omar burnt and which had suddenly been miraculously resurrected from its ashes: that was what my uncle was like.

But he displayed amazement of a very different sort a little later, when, running through all this organic dust, he seized a bare skull and cried out in a voice trembling with excitement:

'Axel! Axel! A human head!'

'A human head, Uncle?' I replied, no less astonished.

'Yes, my boy. Oh, Mr Milne-Edwards! Oh, Monsieur de Quatrefages! If only you could be standing where I, Otto Lidenbrock, am standing now!'

38

The Professor Gives a Lecture

To understand this evocation of two illustrious scientists by my uncle, it is necessary to know that an event of the highest importance from the palaeontological point of view had occurred a short time before our departure.

On 28 March 1863, some labourers working under the direction of Monsieur Boucher de Perthes, in the quarries of Moulin-Quignon, near Abbeville, in the Department of the Somme in France, found a human jaw-bone fourteen feet below the surface. It was the first fossil of this sort that had ever been brought to light. Near it were found some stone axes and carved flints, all coloured and clothed by the passage of time with a uniform patina.

This discovery caused a great stir, not only in France, but also in Britain and Germany. Several scientists of the Institut Français including Messrs Milne-Edwards and de Quatrefages, took the affair very much to heart, demonstrated the incontestable authenticity of the bone in question, and became the most ardent defence witnesses in what the English called the 'trial of the jawbone'.

Those geologists in the United Kingdom who believed the jaw-bone to be genuine – Messrs Falconer, Busk, Carpenter, and others – were joined by German scientists, and among these the most eminent, the most ardent, and the most enthusiastic was my uncle Lidenbrock.

The authenticity of a human fossil of the Quaternary Period therefore seemed to be incontestably proved and recognized.

Admittedly this theory had had a fanatical opponent in Monsieur Élie de Beaumont. This leading authority maintained that the soil of Moulin-Quignon was not diluvial at all, but was of much more recent formation, and, agreeing on this point with Cuvier, he refused to admit that the human race could have been contemporary with the animals of the Quaternary Period. My uncle, together with the vast majority of geologists, had stood his ground, argued, and discussed, and Monsieur Élie de Beaumont had remained practically alone in his opinion.

We knew all these details of the affair, but we were unaware that, since our departure, further progress had been made in the matter. Other jaw-bones of an identical nature, though belonging to individuals of various types and different countries, were found in the loose grey soil of certain grottos in France, Switzerland, and Belgium, as well as weapons, utensils, tools, and bones of children, adolescents, adults and old people. The existence of Quaternary man was therefore becoming more certain every day.

And that was not all. Fresh remains exhumed from tertiary Pliocene terrane had enabled even bolder geologists to attribute a still greater age to the human race. It is true that these remains were not human bones, but just products of man's handiwork, fossil tibias and femurs of animals scratched in regular patterns, carved, so to speak, and bearing traces of human activity.

Thus, at one bound, man leapt a long way up the ladder of time; he was shown to be a predecessor of the mastodon, a contemporary of the *elephas meridionalis*; he was seen to be 100,000 years old, since that was the age attributed by the most famous geologists to the Pliocene terrane.

Such was the state of palaeontological science at that time, and what we knew of it was sufficient to explain our behaviour in the presence of that ossuary of the Lidenbrock Sea. The reader will therefore understand my uncle's joy and stupefaction, especially when, a few yards farther on, he found himself literally face to face with a specimen of Quaternary man.

It was an absolutely recognizable human body, perfectly preserved down the ages, though whether by some special soil, like that of the cemetery of Saint-Michel at Bordeaux, or by some other agency, I cannot say. At any rate this corpse, with its taut, parchment-like skin, its limbs still covered with flesh – at least as far as we could see – its perfect teeth, abundant hair, and fearfully long nails on fingers and toes, presented itself to our eyes as in life.

I stood speechless before this apparition from another age. My uncle, usually so talkative, so impetuously garrulous, was also silent. We lifted the body and stood it up against a rock. It looked at us out of its hollow eye-sockets. We tapped on its echoing chest.

After a brief silence my uncle became the Professor once more. Otto Lidenbrock, carried away by his temperament, forgot the circumstances of our journey, the place where we were, the cavern which contained us. No doubt he thought he was at the Johannaeum, lecturing to his pupils, for he assumed a magisterial air, and, addressing an imaginary audience, he said:

'Gentlemen, I have the honour to introduce to you a man of the Quaternary Period. Eminent geologists have denied his existence, and others no less eminent have affirmed it. The St Thomases of palaeontology, if they were here, would touch him with their fingers, and would have no option but to recognize their error. I am well aware that science has to be on its guard with discoveries of this kind. I know what capital Barnum and other charlatans of his ilk have made out of fossil men. I have heard all about Ajax's knee-cap, about the body of Orestes supposed to have been found by the Spartans, and about the body of Asterius, ten cubits long, which is mentioned by Pausanias. I have read the reports on the skeleton found at Trapani in the fourteenth century, and identified at first as that of Polyphemus; and the story of the giant unearthed in the sixteenth century in the neighbourhood of Palermo. You know as well as I do, gentlemen, the analysis made near Lucerne in 1577, of those huge bones which the famous doctor Felix Plater declared to be those of a giant nineteen feet tall. I have read the treatises of Cassanion, and all the memoirs, pamphlets, papers, and rejoinders published on the subject of the skeleton of the King of the Cimbrians, Teutobochus, the invader of Gaul, which was dug out of a sandpit in the Dauphiné in 1613. In the eighteenth century I would have joined with Petrus Camper in contesting the existence of Scheuchzer's primitive men. I have studied the work entitled *Gigan* . . .'

Here there reappeared my uncle's natural infirmity, his inability to pronounce difficult words in public.

'The work entitled *Gigan* . . .' he repeated.

He could not get any farther.

'*Giganto* . . .'

It was impossible. The wretched word would not come out. At the Johannaeum the audience would have roared with laughter.

'*Gigantosteology,*' Professor Lidenbrock finally managed to bring out, in between a couple of oaths.

Then, carrying on with renewed vigour, and getting steadily more animated:

'Yes, gentlemen, I know all these things. I know too that Cuvier and Blumenbach have identified these bones as nothing more than the bones of the mammoth and other animals of the Quaternary Period. But here doubt itself would be an insult to science! The body stands before you! You can see it, touch it! It is not just a skeleton, but an entire body, preserved for a purely anthropological purpose.'

I thought fit not to contradict this assertion.

'If I could wash it in a solution of sulphuric acid,' my uncle went on, 'I should be able to get rid of all the particles of earth and sparkling shells which are encrusted in it. But I have none of that precious solvent with me. Even so, such as it is, this body shall tell us its own story.'

Here the Professor seized the fossil skeleton and handled it with the dexterity of a fairground showman.

'As you can see,' he continued, 'it is less than six feet tall, and we are a long way from the alleged race of giants. As for the race to which it belongs, it is incontestably Caucasian, the white race, our own. The skull of this fossil is a regular ovoid, without either prominent cheek bones or projecting jaws. It offers no sign of that prognathism which modifies the facial angle.* Measure that angle: it is nearly 90 degrees. But I will go even farther in my

---

* The facial angle is formed by two lines: one more or less vertical, touching the forehead and the front teeth; the other horizontal, from the orifice of the ear to the lower line of the nostrils. The greater this angle, the higher the intelligence indicated by the formation of the skull. Prognathism is that projection of the jaw-bone which modifies the facial angle.

deductions and venture to say that this specimen of humanity belongs to the Japhetic race, which is to be found from the Indies to the Atlantic. Don't smile, gentlemen.'

Nobody was smiling, but the Professor was so used to seeing faces light up with amusement during his learned dissertations that he said this out of force of habit.

'Yes,' he went on with fresh animation, 'this is a fossil man, a contemporary of the mastodons whose bones fill this amphitheatre. But if you ask me how he got here, how those strata in which he was buried slipped down as far as this huge cavity in the globe, I will not presume to answer your question. No doubt in the Quaternary Period considerable disturbances were still occurring in the crust of the earth, and the prolonged cooling of the earth produced chasms, fissures, and faults, into which portions of the upper terrane probably fell. I refuse to commit myself, but after all, there is the man, surrounded by his own handiwork, those axes and carved flints which are characteristic of the Stone Age. And unless he came here like myself as a mere tourist, a pioneer of science, I have no reason to cast doubt on the authenticity of his remote origin.'

The Professor fell silent, and I broke into loud and unanimous applause. For my uncle was quite right, and more learned men than his nephew would have been hard put to it to refute his statements.

Further evidence in support of what he had said came with the discovery that this fossilized body was not the only one in that huge ossuary. We came across more bodies with every step we took through the dust, and my uncle was at liberty to choose the finest of these specimens in order to convince the sceptics.

It was indeed an astonishing sight, that spectacle of generations of men and animals mingled together in a common cemetery. But then a serious question occurred to us, to which we did not dare to give an answer. Had these creatures slipped through a fissure in the earth to the shores of the Lidenbrock Sea when they were already dead? Or had they lived here, in this subterranean world, under this false sky, being born and dying like the inhabitants of the upper earth? So far only sea monsters and fishes had appeared to us alive. Might not some human being, some native of the abyss, still be roaming these desolate shores?

39
Man Alive

For another half-hour we walked over these layers of bones, impelled by our burning curiosity. What other marvels did this cavern contain? What new treasures might we discover to offer up to science? My eyes were prepared to be surprised, my imagination to be astonished.

The sea shore had long since disappeared behind the hills of the ossuary. The rash Professor, heedless of the risk of losing our way, led me farther and farther. We pressed on in silence, bathed in the waves of electric light. By some phenomenon which I cannot explain, and thanks to its complete diffusion, this light shone uniformly on all the sides of every object. As it did not come from any one spot in space, it produced no shadows. You might have thought yourself in the tropics, at midday in the height of summer, under the vertical rays of the sun. There was no vapour to be seen. The rocks, the distant mountains, a few patches of forest a long way off, presented a peculiar appearance under the even distribution of the light. We resembled that fantastic character in Hoffmann's tale who had lost his shadow.

After walking a mile we reached the edge of a huge forest, but this time not one of those forests of mushrooms which we had seen near Port Gräuben.

Here we had the vegetation of the Tertiary Period in all its splendour. Tall palms, of species which have now disappeared, splendid palmacites, pines, yews, cypress trees, and thuyas represented the conifer family and were linked together by a network of inextricable creepers. A carpet of moss and hepaticas covered the ground. A few streams murmured in what would have been the shade of the trees if they had cast any shadows, and on the banks grew tree-ferns similar to those which are cultivated in our hothouses. The only difference was that there was no colour in all these trees, shrubs, and plants, deprived as they were of the vivifying heat of the sun. Everything merged together in one uniform hue, brownish and faded-looking. The leaves had no green, and the very flowers, though abundant enough in that Tertiary Period which saw their birth, had neither colour nor perfume, and looked as if they were made of a paper bleached by the atmosphere.

My uncle plunged boldly into this gigantic thicket, and I followed him, though not without a certain apprehension. Since Nature had provided ample stocks of vegetable food, might we not meet some fearful mammals? In the broad clearings left by the trees which time had felled and eaten away, I could see leguminous plants, *acerineae, rubiaceae*, and countless edible shrubs, dear to the ruminant animals of every period. Then, mixed up and tangled together, I saw trees from very different countries on the surface of the globe, the oak growing near to the palm, the Australian eucalyptus leaning against the Norwegian fir, the northern birch tree mingling its branches with those of the Dutch kauris. It was enough to drive to distraction the most ingenious classifiers of terrestrial botany.

Suddenly I stopped short, holding my uncle back.

The diffused light made it possible to make out the smallest objects in the depths of the thickets. I thought I had seen – no, I did see, with my own eyes – some huge shapes moving about beneath the trees. Sure enough, it was a whole herd of gigantic animals, of mastodons, not fossils this time but living creatures, and resembling those whose bones were found in the marshes of Ohio in 1801. I saw those huge elephants whose trunks were twisting about under the trees like a legion of serpents. I heard the noise of their long tusks whose ivory was tearing at the old trunks. The branches were cracking and the leaves, torn away in huge masses, were disappearing into the cavernous maws of the monsters.

So that dream in which I had had a vision of the prehistoric world, of the Tertiary and Quaternary Periods, was finally coming true. And there we were, alone in the bowels of the earth, at the mercy of its fierce inhabitants!

My uncle looked and looked again.

'Come along!' he said all of a sudden, seizing me by the arm. 'Forward! Forward!'

'No!' I cried. 'No! We are unarmed. What could we do in the midst of that herd of giant quadrupeds? Come along, Uncle, come along! No human being could brave the anger of those monsters with impunity.'

'No human being?' replied my uncle, lowering his voice. 'You are wrong, Axel! Look, look, over there! It seems to me that I can see a living creature, a creature similar to ourselves – a man!'

I looked, shrugging my shoulders, and determined to carry incredulity to its uttermost limits. But however sceptical I tried to be, I had to accept the evidence of my eyes.

For there, less than a quarter of a mile away, leaning against the trunk of an enormous kauris, stood a human being, a Proteus of those subterranean regions, a new son of Neptune, watching over that great herd of mastodons.

Immanis pecoris custos, immanior ipse . . . Yes, indeed, the shepherd was bigger than his flock. This was not something like the fossil creature whose corpse we had found in the ossuary; it was a giant capable of mastering those monsters. He was over twelve feet tall. His head, which was as big as a buffalo's, was half hidden in the tangled growth of his unkempt hair – a positive mane, like that of the primitive elephant. In his hand he was brandishing an enormous bough, a crook worthy of this antediluvian shepherd.

We had remained motionless and stupefied. But he might see us; we must take to our heels.

'Come on, come on!' I cried, pulling my uncle, who for the first time in his life allowed himself to be persuaded.

A quarter of an hour later we were out of sight of that redoubtable enemy.

Now that I can think about it unemotionally, now that I am quite calm again, now that months have gone by since that strange, extraordinary encounter, what am I to think, what am I to believe? Was it a man we saw? No, that is impossible! Our senses were deceived, our eyes did not see what we thought they saw. No human being could exist in that subterranean world; no generation of men could live in those deep caverns of the globe, caring nothing about the inhabitants of its surface and having no communication with them. The very idea is insane!

I would rather believe that it was some animal whose build resembles that of a human being, some monkey of the early geological ages, some *protopitheca* or *mesopitheca* like the one Monsieur Lartet discovered in the ossiferous cave at Sansan. But the creature we saw surpassed in stature all the measurements known to modern palaeontology. Never mind! It must have been a monkey, however improbable that may seem. The idea that a man, a living man, and with him a whole generation, should be buried down there in the bowels of the earth is unacceptable.

We left the bright, luminous forest, dumb with astonishment, overwhelmed by an amazement which bordered on stupefaction. We ran in spite of ourselves. It was a positive rout, similar to those horrible flights which occur in nightmares. Instinctively we made our way towards the Lidenbrock Sea, and I cannot say what vagaries my mind would have indulged in if a particular preoccupation had not repeatedly brought me back to practical matters.

Although I was certain that we were treading ground on which we had not set foot before, I kept noticing groups of rocks whose shape reminded me of those at Port Gräuben. This, of course, seemed to confirm the indication given by the compass that we had involuntarily returned to the north coast of the Lidenbrock Sea. Occasionally there seemed to be no doubt about it. Hundreds of brooks and waterfalls were tumbling from the projections of the rocks. I thought I recognized the layer of surturbrand, our faithful Hansbach, and the grotto in which I had returned to life and consciousness. Then, a few paces farther on, the arrangement of the cliffs, the appearance of a stream, or the surprising outline of a rock plunged me back into doubt.

I told my uncle about my bewilderment. Like myself

he was undecided: he could not find his bearings in this uniform panorama.

'Clearly,' I said to him, 'we haven't landed at our point of departure, but the storm has carried us a little farther down, and if we follow the coast we shall probably come to Port Gräuben.'

'In that case,' said my uncle, 'it is no use our continuing with our exploration, and the best thing to do would be to return to the raft. But are you sure you are right, Axel?'

'It's hard to be sure, Uncle, because all these rocks are so much alike. But I think I can recognize the promontory at the foot of which Hans built the raft. We must be near the little port, if indeed this isn't it,' I added, examining a creek which I thought looked familiar.

'No, Axel, we should at least find our own traces, and I can see nothing . . .'

'But *I* can!' I cried, rushing towards an object which was shining on the sand.

'What?'

'This!' I replied.

And I showed my uncle a rusty dagger which I had just picked up.

'Well, well!' he said. 'So you had this weapon with you?'

'I hadn't. But you . . .'

'Not to my knowledge,' said the Professor. 'I have never had this object in my possession.'

'Well, that's very strange.'

'No, Axel, it's perfectly simple. The Icelanders often carry weapons of this kind. This belongs to Hans, and he must have dropped it.'

I shook my head. Hans had never had that dagger with him.

'Did it belong to some antediluvian warrior then?' I cried. 'To a living man, a contemporary of that gigantic shepherd? But no. This isn't a weapon of the Stone Age, or even of the Iron Age. This blade is steel . . .'

My uncle cut short this new train of thought and said in his coldest voice:

'Calm down, Axel, and think. This dagger is a sixteenth-century weapon, a real poniard such as gentlemen carried in their belts to give the *coup de grâce*. It belongs neither to you, nor to me, nor to our guide, nor even to the human beings who may inhabit the bowels of the earth.'

'You mean to say . . . ?'

'Look, it didn't get twisted like that by plunging into people's throats; its blade is coated with a layer of rust that is more than a day, a year, or even a hundred years old!'

The Professor was getting excited as usual, as he allowed his imagination to run away with him.

'Axel,' he went on, 'we are on the way to a great discovery! This blade has remained on the sand here for one, two, three hundred years, and has been blunted on the rocks bordering this subterranean sea!'

'But it didn't get here by itself!' I cried. 'It didn't twist itself out of shape! Somebody has been here before us!'

'Yes, a man.'

'And that man?'

'That man has carved his name somewhere with this dagger. He wanted to indicate the way to the centre of the earth once more. Let us look around.'

Tremendously excited, we skirted the high cliff, peering into every fissure which might lead into a gallery.

Presently we reached a place where the beach narrowed; the sea almost came up to the foot of the cliffs, leaving a passage no wider than a couple of yards. Between two projecting rocks we caught sight of the entrance to a dark tunnel.

There, on a slab of granite, appeared two mysterious letters, half eaten away by time – the two initials of the bold, adventurous traveller:

$$\cdot \; \text{ᚴ} \; \cdot \; \text{ᚻ} \; \cdot$$

'A.S.,' cried my uncle. 'Arne Saknussemm! Arne Saknussemm again!'

40

We Meet an Obstacle

Since the beginning of our journey I had had so many surprises that I might be forgiven for thinking myself immune to astonishment and incapable of amazement. Yet at the sight of those two letters, carved there three hundred years before, I stood in utter stupefaction. Not only was the signature of the learned alchemist legible on the rock, but I held in my hand the dagger which had traced it. Without showing the most appalling bad faith, I could no longer doubt the existence of the traveller and the reality of his journey.

While these thoughts were whirling about in my head, Professor Lidenbrock was indulging in a somewhat rhapsodical panegyric on Arne Saknussemm.

'Marvellous genius,' he cried, 'you have neglected nothing which might open up to other mortals the road through the crust of the earth, and even now, after three centuries, your fellow humans can follow your footsteps through these subterranean passages. You have made it possible for other eyes besides your own to contemplate these wonders. Your name, engraved here and there, leads the traveller bold enough to follow you straight to his objective, and at the very centre of our planet it will be found again, inscribed by your own hand. Well, I too will sign my name on that last page of granite. As for this cape seen by you in this sea discovered by you, let it be known henceforth for ever as Cape Saknussemm!'

This, or something like it, is what I heard, and I felt myself being infected by the enthusiasm which filled my uncle's words. An inner fire was kindled again in my heart. I forgot everything, both the dangers of the journey and the perils of the return. What another had done I would do too, and nothing that was not superhuman appeared impossible to me.

'Forward! Forward!' I cried.

I was already rushing towards the dark gallery when the Professor stopped me; he, the impulsive one, counselled patience and calm.

'Let us go back to Hans first,' he said, 'and bring the raft to this spot.'

I obeyed, not without a certain reluctance, and hurried off among the rocks on the shore.

'Do you know, Uncle,' I said as we walked along, 'we have been singularly favoured by circumstances so far.'

'You think so, Axel?'

'Why yes. Even the storm has put us on the right path. Thank heaven for that storm! It brought us back to this coast, from which fine weather would have taken us far away. If we had landed on the south shore of the Lidenbrock Sea, what would have become of us? We should never have seen the name of Saknussemm, and at this moment we should be lost on a rockbound beach.'

'Yes, Axel, there is something providential in the fact that, sailing south, we should have been carried north and reached Cape Saknussemm. I must say that it's more than astonishing, and that I can't find any explanation for it.'

'Well, what does that matter? Our business is not to explain facts but to take advantage of them.'

'You may be right, my boy, but . . .'

'But now we are going to go north again, and pass under the northern countries of Europe, under Sweden, Russia, Siberia, and heaven knows where else, instead of burrowing under the deserts of Africa or the waves of the Atlantic; and that is all I want to know.'

'Yes, Axel, you are right, and everything has worked out for the best, seeing that we are leaving this horizontal sea which could not lead us anywhere. Now we shall go down, and down, and down! Do you realize that we're less than four thousand miles from the centre now?'

'Is that all?' I cried. 'Why, that's nothing. Let's be on our way!'

This crazy conversation was still going on when we rejoined the guide. Everything was ready for an immediate start; there was not a single package that had not been put on board. We took our places on the raft, the sail was hoisted, and Hans set his course along the coast for Cape Saknussemm.

The wind was unfavourable for a craft that could not hug the shore, so in many places we were obliged to push ourselves along with our iron-shod sticks. Often the rocks, which were just below the surface of the water, forced us to make fairly long detours. Finally, after three hours at sea, that is about six in the evening, we reached the place where we could disembark.

I jumped ashore, followed by my uncle and the Icelander. This short journey had not calmed my ardour. On the contrary, I actually suggested 'burning our boats' so as to cut off all possibility of retreat, but my uncle demurred. I thought him singularly lukewarm.

'At least,' I said, 'let's start without delay.'

'Yes, my boy; but first of all let us examine this new gallery, to see if we shall need our ladders.'

My uncle started up his Ruhmkorff apparatus. The raft, moored to the shore, was left by itself; in any case, the opening of the gallery was less than twenty yards away, and our little party, with myself at the head, made for it without a moment's delay.

The opening, which was roughly circular, was about five feet across; the dark tunnel plunged straight into the rock, smoothly bored by the eruptive matter which had once passed through it; the lower part was level with the ground outside, so that we were able to enter it without any difficulty.

We were following an almost horizontal course when, after about half a dozen paces, our progress was interrupted by a huge block.

'Damn this rock!' I cried angrily, finding myself suddenly halted by an insurmountable obstacle.

We searched in vain to right and left, up and down, for a way through; there was no chink. I was bitterly disappointed and refused to admit the reality of the obstacle. I bent down and looked underneath the block. There was no gap. Up above, there was the same barrier of granite. Hans passed the light of the lamp over every portion of the wall, but without revealing any gap. We had to abandon any hope of getting through.

I sat down on the ground. My uncle strode up and down the passage.

'But what about Saknussemm?' I cried.

'Yes,' said my uncle, 'does this mean he was stopped by this stone barrier?'

'No, no!' I exclaimed. 'This piece of rock must have been loosened by some shock or by one of those magnetic storms which affect these regions, and suddenly blocked this passage. A good many years elapsed between Saknussemm's return to the surface and the fall of this rock. Isn't it obvious that this gallery was once a route taken by lava, and that at that time eruptive matter passed freely through it? Look, there are recent fissures furrowing this granite ceiling. The roof itself is made up of fragments of rock, of huge stones, as if some giant had built it; but one day the pressure on it was too great, and this block, like a falling keystone, slipped to the ground and blocked the way. It's an accidental obstacle which Saknussemm didn't meet; and if we don't destroy it, we are unworthy to reach the centre of the earth!'

That was how I spoke! The Professor's soul had passed straight into me, and the spirit of discovery inspired me. I forgot the past and scorned the future. Nothing existed any longer for me on the surface of this globe into which I had penetrated, neither town nor country, nor Hamburg, nor the Königstrasse, nor even poor Gräuben, who must have given me up for lost in the bowels of the earth.

'Well,' said my uncle, 'let us make our way through with our pickaxes.'

'It's too hard for pickaxes.'

'Then our mattocks.'

'That would take too long.'

'Then what?'

'Why, gun-cotton of course! Let's mine the obstacle and blow it up!'

'Gun-cotton?'

'Yes, it's only a bit of rock to blast!'

'Hans, to work!' cried my uncle.

The Icelander returned to the raft and soon came back

with a pickaxe which he used to hollow out a hole for the charge. This was no easy task; he had to make a hole big enough to hold fifty pounds of gun-cotton, the explosive force of which is four times that of gunpowder.

I was tremendously excited. While Hans was at work, I helped my uncle to prepare a slow match made of damp gunpowder in a linen tube.

'We shall get through!' I said.

'We shall get through!' repeated my uncle.

By midnight our mining preparations were finished; the charge of gun-cotton was packed inside the hollow, and the slow match wound its way along the gallery to a point just outside.

One spark would now be enough to set off the whole contraption.

'Tomorrow,' said the Professor.

I had no option but to resign myself to waiting another six long hours.

41

Down the Tunnel

The next day, Thursday, 27 August, was a great date in our subterranean journey. I cannot recall it even now without feeling my heart beating with fear. From that time on, our reason, judgement, and ingenuity counted for nothing, and we became the playthings of the elements.

At six o'clock we were up and about. The time had come to blast a way through the granite obstruction.

I begged for the honour of lighting the fuse. Once I had done this, I was to join my companions on the raft, which had not yet been unloaded; then we were to put out to sea, to avoid the dangers of the explosion, whose effects might not be confined to the interior of the rock.

According to our calculations the match would burn for ten minutes before setting fire to the gun-cotton, so I had enough time to reach the raft.

I got ready to carry out my task, not without some emotion.

After a hasty meal, my uncle and the guide embarked, while I remained on shore.

'Off you go, my boy,' said my uncle, 'and come back and join us straight away.'

'Don't worry,' I replied. 'I won't stop to play.'

I promptly went to the mouth of the tunnel, opened my lantern, and picked up the end of the match.

The Professor was holding his chronometer in his hand.

'Ready?' he called out.

'Yes, I'm ready.'

'Well, then, fire, my boy!'

I plunged the end of the match into the flame, saw it light up, and ran back to the water's edge.

'Come on board,' said my uncle, 'and let's push off.'

With a vigorous shove, Hans sent the raft about sixty feet out to sea.

It was an exciting moment. The Professor was watching the hand of the chronometer.

'Another five minutes,' he said. 'Another four . . . Another three.'

My pulse was beating half-seconds.

'Another two . . . one . . . Now, you granite mountains, down you go!'

What happened then? I don't think I heard the noise of the explosion. But the shape of the rocks suddenly changed before my eyes; they opened like a curtain. I caught sight of a bottomless pit which appeared in the very shore. The sea, seized with a fit of giddiness, turned into a single enormous wave, on the ridge of which the raft stood up perpendicularly.

All three of us were thrown flat on our faces. In less than a second the light was replaced by total darkness. Then I felt that not only I, but the raft too, had no support underneath. I thought it was sinking, but this was not the case. I wanted to speak to my uncle, but the roar of the water would have prevented him from hearing me.

In spite of the darkness, noise, surprise, and terror, I realized what had happened.

On the other side of the rock which had just blown up, there was an abyss. The explosion had caused a sort of earthquake in this much-fissured rock, the abyss had opened up, and the sea, turning into a torrent, was pouring into it and carrying us with it.

I gave myself up for lost.

An hour went by – two hours, perhaps – I cannot tell. We closed up and held each other's hands, to save ourselves from being thrown off the raft. Violent shocks occurred whenever it struck the wall, but this did not happen often, from which I concluded that the gallery was widening considerably. This was undoubtedly the way Saknussemm had come; but instead of following by ourselves, we had, by our imprudence, brought a whole sea along with us.

These ideas, of course, occurred to me in a vague and obscure form. I had difficulty in putting them together during that dizzy rush which seemed like a vertical descent. Judging by the air which was whipping my face, we were moving faster than the fastest of express trains. It was impossible to light a torch under these conditions, and our last electric apparatus had been broken by the explosion.

I was therefore extremely surprised to see a bright light suddenly appear near me. It lit up Hans's calm face. The skilful guide had succeeded in lighting the lantern, and although its flame flickered so much that it nearly went out, it none the less shed a little light in the terrifying blackness.

I had been right in thinking that the gallery was a wide one. The dim light did not enable us to see both sides at once. The water was falling at an angle steeper than that of the swiftest rapids in America. Its surface looked as if it were composed of a sheaf of liquid arrows shot with incredible force; I cannot think of a better comparison to convey the impression it made on me. The raft was occasionally caught by an eddy and spun round as it sped along. When it went near the walls of the gallery, I threw the light of the lantern on them, and I obtained some idea of our speed by seeing the way in which the projections of rock appeared as continuous ribbons, so that we seemed to be confined within a network of moving lines. I estimated that we must be travelling at something like eighty miles an hour.

My uncle and I gazed about us with haggard eyes, clinging to the stump of the mast, which had snapped in two at the moment of the catastrophe. We kept our backs to the rush of air, to avoid being suffocated by the speed of a movement which no human power could check. Meanwhile the hours went by. There was no change in our situation, but I made a discovery which complicated matters.

In trying to put a little order into our cargo, I found that most of the objects which we had taken on board had disappeared at the moment of the explosion, when the sea had struck us so violently. I wanted to know exactly what we had left, and with the lantern in my hand I began my examination. Of our instruments, only the compass and the chronometer remained. Our stock of ladders and ropes was reduced to a bit of cord tied round the stump of the mast. There was not a single pickaxe, not a single mattock, not a single hammer; and worst of all, we had only one day's provisions left.

I searched every crack and cranny in the raft, the tiniest corners formed by the beams and the joints of the planks. There was nothing. Our provisions consisted of nothing more than a piece of salt meat and a few biscuits.

I stared stupidly at this minute stock, unwilling to understand. Yet what danger was I worrying about? Even if we had enough provisions for months or years, how could we get out of the abysses into which this irresistible torrent was sweeping us? Why should we be afraid of hunger when death was already threatening us in so many other forms? Would we have enough time to die of starvation?

Yet by an inexplicable freak of the imagination I forgot the immediate peril to contemplate the dangers of the future, which appeared to me in all their horror. Besides, perhaps we might be able to escape from the fury of the torrent and return to the surface of the earth? How? I didn't know. By what route? What did it matter? One chance in a thousand was still a chance, whereas death from starvation would leave us no hope at all.

The thought occurred to me to tell my uncle everything, to show him the terrible straits to which we were reduced, to calculate exactly how much longer we had to live. But I had the courage to remain silent. I wanted to leave him cool and self-possessed.

At that moment the light of the lantern grew fainter and then went out. The wick had burnt away, and we were plunged back into total darkness, which we had no hope of being able to dissipate. We still had a torch left, but we could not have kept it alight. So, like a child, I closed my eyes so as not to see all that darkness.

After a fairly long interval our speed increased, as I noticed from the wind in my face. The descent became steeper, and I really believe that we were no longer gliding but falling. I had the impression of an almost vertical drop. My uncle and Hans held me firmly by the arms.

Suddenly, after a lapse of time I could not measure, I felt a shock. The raft had not collided with a solid object, but its fall had suddenly been arrested. A waterspout, a huge liquid column, struck its surface and I felt as if I was suffocating, drowning.

However, this sudden inundation did not last. A few seconds later I found myself gulping in fresh air again. My uncle and Hans were gripping my arms hard enough to break them, and the raft was still carrying all three of us.

42

Going Up

I suppose it was then about ten o'clock at night. The first of my senses which came into play after this last experience was the sense of hearing. Almost immediately I heard – for it was a real act of hearing – I heard silence fall in the gallery, taking the place of the roar which had filled my ears for hours. Then these words of my uncle's came to me like a murmur:

'We are going up!'

'What do you mean,' I cried.

'Yes, we are going up, we are going up!'

I stretched out my arm and touched the wall, grazing my hand. We were rising, extremely fast.

'The torch! The torch!' cried the Professor.

Hans managed to light it, not without difficulty, and the flame, rising in spite of our upward movement, gave enough light to illuminate the whole scene.

'Just as I thought,' said my uncle. 'We are in a narrow shaft, about twenty feet across. The water has reached the bottom of the abyss and is now rising to find its own level, taking us with it.'

'Where to?'

'That I don't know, but we must be ready for anything. We are rising at a speed which I estimate at twelve feet a second, or about eight miles an hour. At this rate we shall get a long way.'

'Yes, provided that nothing stops us and this shaft has an outlet. But if it's stopped up, if the air is gradually compressed by the pressure of this column of water, then we shall be crushed.'

'Axel,' the Professor replied very calmly, 'our situation is almost desperate, but there are a few chances of our escaping, and I am considering these. If we may die at any moment, we may also be saved at any moment. So let us be prepared to seize the slightest opportunity.'

'But what shall we do now?'

'Recruit our strength by eating.'

At these words I gazed at my uncle with haggard eyes. What I had not wanted to confess had at last to be told.

'Eating?' I repeated.

'Yes, straight away.'

The Professor added a few words in Danish. Hans shook his head.

'What!' cried my uncle. 'Are all our provisions gone?'

'Yes, this is all the food we have left – one piece of salt meat for the three of us!'

My uncle looked at me as if he did not want to understand.

'Well,' I said, 'do you still think we can be saved?'

My question went unanswered.

An hour went by. I began to feel terribly hungry. My companions were suffering too, but none of us dared to touch the wretched remnant of our stock of food.

Meanwhile we were still rising fast. Occasionally the air cut our breath short, as it does with aeronauts when they go up too quickly. But while they get colder the higher they go, we were beginning to feel a contrary effect. The temperature was rising at an alarming rate, and at that moment it must have been about 40° Centigrade.

What could be the meaning of such a change? So far our experience had tended to confirm the theories of Davy and Lidenbrock; until now special conditions of non-conducting rocks, electricity, and magnetism had modified the laws of Nature, providing us with a moderate temperature, for the theory of a central fire remained in my opinion the only one that was sound and reasonable. Were we therefore coming to a terrain where the phenomena of central heat occurred in full force, and where the heat reduced the rocks to the state of molten liquid? I feared as much, and said to the Professor:

'If we are neither drowned nor crushed, and if we don't starve to death, we may still manage to be burnt alive.'

He simply shrugged his shoulders and returned to his thoughts.

Another hour went by, and apart from a slight rise in temperature nothing happened to change the situation. At last my uncle broke the silence.

'Look here,' he said, 'we must take action.'

'Take action?' I said.

'Yes. We must recruit our strength. If we try to prolong our existence by a few hours by husbanding this bit of food, we shall feel weak up to the very end.'

'Oh, the end won't be a long time coming!'

'Perhaps not. But if a chance of saving our lives presents itself, and if it becomes necessary to take sudden action, where shall we find the required strength if we have allowed ourselves to be weakened by hunger?'

'But once we have eaten this bit of meat, Uncle, what shall we have left?'

'Nothing, Axel, nothing. But will it do you any more good to devour it with your eyes? You are reasoning like a man with no will-power or energy.'

'Then haven't you given up hope?' I cried irritably.

'No, certainly not,' the Professor replied in a firm voice.

'What! You still think there's a chance of escape?'

'Yes, I do. As long as this heart goes on beating, I can't admit that any creature endowed with will-power should ever despair.'

What splendid words! The man who could utter them

in such circumstances was certainly of no common stamp.

'Then what do you suggest we do?'

'Eat the food that is left down to the last crumb and restore our failing strength. This may be our last meal, but at any rate we shall have become men again, instead of exhausted weaklings.'

'Very well then, let us eat,' I said.

My uncle took the piece of meat and the few biscuits which had escaped destruction, divided them into three equal portions, and handed them out. This made about a pound of food for each of us. The Professor ate his ration greedily, with a sort of feverish excitement; I ate without pleasure, in spite of my hunger, and almost with distaste; while Hans ate quietly and slowly, silently chewing small mouthfuls and relishing them with the calm of a man whom anxiety about the future could never worry. By searching diligently he had found a flask half-full of gin; he offered it to us, and it succeeded in reviving my spirits slightly.

'*Förträfflig*,' said Hans, taking his turn with the flask.

'Excellent,' repeated my uncle.

A little hope had returned to me. But our last meal was just over. It was five in the morning.

Man is so constituted that his health is a purely negative state; once his hunger is satisfied, it is difficult for him to imagine the horrors of starvation; without feeling them, he cannot understand them. Consequently, after a long fast, a few mouthfuls of meat and biscuits banished the memory of our past privations.

However, when the meal was over, each of us abandoned himself to his reflections. What were those of Hans, I wondered, that man of the far West endowed with the fatalistic resignation of the East?

For my part, my thoughts were all memories, and these took me up to the surface of the globe which I ought never to have left. The house in the Königstrasse, poor Gräuben, and dear old Martha passed like visions before my eyes, and in the dismal rumblings which sounded through the rock I imagined I could hear the noise of the cities of the earth.

As for my uncle, who never forgot his work, he was carefully examining the nature of the terrain, torch in hand, trying to discover where he was from observation of the strata. This calculation, or rather this estimate, could only be a rough approximation; but a scientist is always a scientist as long as he retains his composure, and Professor Lidenbrock certainly possessed this quality to an extraordinary degree.

I heard him murmuring geological terms which I understood, and in spite of myself I began to take an interest in this final piece of research.

'Eruptive granite,' he said. 'We are still in the Primitive Period. But we are going up, we are going up! Who knows?'

He had still not abandoned hope. With his hand he

was feeling the perpendicular wall, and a few moments later he went on:

'This is gneiss! And this is mica schist! Good! Soon we shall come to the terrane of the Transition Period, and then . . .'

What did the Professor mean? Could he measure the thickness of the earth's crust above us? Had he some means of making this calculation? No: he no longer had the manometer, and no calculation could take its place.

Meanwhile the temperature was rising fast, and I felt bathed in a burning atmosphere like the heat given off by the furnace in the foundry when the molten metal is being poured into the moulds. Gradually Hans, my uncle, and I were obliged to take off our jackets and waistcoats, as the lightest covering became a source of discomfort, not to say pain.

'Are we going up towards a furnace?' I cried, at a moment when the temperature rose steeply.

'No,' replied my uncle. 'That's impossible, impossible!'

'All the same,' I said, feeling the side of the shaft, 'this wall is burning hot.'

Just as I said this, my hand touched the water and I hurriedly withdrew it.

'The water is boiling!' I cried.

This time the Professor's only answer was an angry gesture.

Then an invincible terror took hold of me, and would

not be shaken off. I felt that a catastrophe was approaching such as even the liveliest imagination could never have conceived. An idea, vague and uncertain at first, became a conviction in my mind. I thrust it away, but it stubbornly returned. I did not dare to put it into words, but a few involuntary observations confirmed me in my opinion. In the flickering light of the torch I noticed some convulsive movements in the layers of granite. A phenomenon was obviously going to take place in which electricity would play some part. And then there was this unbearable heat, this boiling water . . . I decided to consult the compass.

It had gone mad!

43

Shot Out of a Volcano

Yes, the compass had gone mad! The needle was swinging jerkily from one pole to the other, indicating every point of the compass in turn, and spinning around as if it were giddy.

I was well aware that, according to generally accepted theories, the mineral crust of the globe is never in a state of complete rest; the changes produced by the decomposition of its constituent matter, the agitation caused by great liquid currents, and the action of magnetic forces all tend to disturb it, even though the creatures living on the surface may imagine that all is quiet down below. This phenomenon by itself would therefore not have alarmed me, or at least it would not have suggested to my mind the dreadful suspicion which occurred to it.

But there were other facts, other circumstances of a special kind which I could no longer ignore. Loud explosions could be heard with increasing frequency; I could only compare them with the noise which would be made by a great number of waggons driven at full speed along a cobbled street. Before long this noise had become a continuous roll of thunder.

Then the maddened compass, shaken by the electric phenomena, confirmed me in my opinion. The mineral crust was threatening to burst, the granite masses to join up, the fissure to close and the void to be filled while we poor atoms would be crushed in this formidable embrace.

'Uncle, Uncle,' I cried, 'we are done for!'

'What are you so frightened about now?' he replied with astonishing calm. 'What's the matter?'

'What's the matter? Look at these shaking walls, this quivering rock, this torrid heat, this boiling water, these clouds of steam, this crazy needle – all the usual signs of an earthquake!'

My uncle gently shook his head.

'An earthquake?' he said.

'Yes!'

'My boy, I think you are mistaken.'

'What! Don't you recognize the symptoms?'

'Of an earthquake? No. I am expecting something better than that.'

'What do you mean?'

'An eruption, Axel.'

'An eruption? You mean you think we are in the shaft of an active volcano?'

'I do,' said the Professor with a smile. 'And I think it's the best thing that could happen to us.'

The best thing! Had my uncle gone out of his mind? What did he mean? And how could he be so calm and smiling?

'What!' I exclaimed. 'We are caught in the midst of an eruption! Fate has flung us in the path of burning lava, molten rock, boiling water, and all sorts of eruptive matter! We are going to be thrown out, expelled, rejected, vomited, spat into the air, along with fragments of rock and a rain of ashes and cinders, in a whirlwind of flame! And you say that that is the best thing that could happen to us!'

'Yes,' replied the Professor, looking at me over the top of his spectacles. 'Because it's the only chance we have of returning to the surface of the earth.'

I will say nothing of the countless ideas which then crossed each other in my mind. My uncle was right, absolutely right; and never had he struck me as bolder or more self-assured than at that moment when he was calmly working out the chances of being involved in an eruption.

In the meantime we went on rising: the night went by in this continued ascent, with the din around us growing louder all the time. I was almost suffocated and thought my last hour was approaching; yet imagination is such a strange thing that I devoted myself to a really childish speculation. But I was the victim, not the master of my thoughts.

It was obvious that we were being carried upwards by an eruptive thrust; under the raft there was boiling water, and under that a whole mass of lava, an agglomeration of rocks, which, when expelled from the crater, would be scattered in all directions. We were therefore in the chimney of a volcano; there was no room for doubt on that score.

But this time, instead of an extinct volcano like Sneffels, we were inside a fully active one. I therefore began wondering where this mountain could be, and in what part of the world we were going to be shot out.

I had no doubt that it would be in some northern region. Before it had gone mad the compass needle had consistently indicated that we were heading in that direction. From Cape Saknussemm we had been carried due north for hundreds of miles. Had we returned under Iceland? Were we going to be shot out of the crater of Hecla or one of the seven other volcanoes on the island? Within a radius of 1,500 miles I could think of nothing to the west, in that latitude, but the little-known volcanoes on the north-east coast of America. To the east, there was only one, Esk, in Jan Mayen's Land, not far from Spitzbergen. Certainly there was no lack of craters, and some of them were big enough to spew out a whole army. But what I wanted to know was which of them was going to serve us as an exit.

Towards morning our upward movement was accelerated. If the temperature was increasing, instead of diminishing, as we drew nearer to the surface of the earth, this was purely a local phenomenon due to volcanic activity. Our means of ascent left me with no doubts about that. An enormous force, a force of several hundred atmospheres, generated by the vapours accumulated in the bowels of the earth, was pushing us irresistibly upwards. But to what countless dangers it exposed us!

Soon lurid lights began to appear in the vertical gallery, which was growing wider; on both right and left I noticed deep corridors like huge tunnels from which thick clouds of vapour were pouring, while crackling tongues of flame were licking their walls.

'Look, look, Uncle!' I cried.

'Those are just sulphurous flames. Nothing could be more natural in an eruption.'

'But what if they envelop us?'

'They won't envelop us.'

'But what if we are suffocated?'

'We shan't be suffocated, the shaft is getting wider, and if necessary we'll leave the raft and take shelter in some crevice.'

'And what about the rising water?'

'There's no water left, Axel, but a sort of lava paste which is carrying us up with it to the mouth of the crater.'

The liquid column had indeed disappeared, giving

place to fairly solid, though boiling, eruptive matter. The temperature was becoming unbearable, and if we had had a thermometer it would have registered over 70°C. I was bathed in sweat. If we had not been rising so fast, we should undoubtedly have been suffocated.

However, the Professor did not put into practice his idea of abandoning the raft, and it was just as well. However roughly joined together they were, those few beams provided us with a solid surface and a firm support which we could not have found anywhere else.

About eight in the morning a fresh incident occurred for the first time. The ascent suddenly stopped and the raft lay absolutely motionless.

'What is it?' I asked, shaken by this sudden stoppage.

'A halt,' replied my uncle.

'Is the eruption calming down?'

'I sincerely hope not.'

I stood up and tried to look around me. Perhaps the raft had caught on a projection and was momentarily checking the eruptive mass. If so it was essential to release it as quickly as possible.

But this was not the case. The column of ashes, cinders, and rocks had itself ceased to rise.

'Has the eruption stopped?' I cried.

'Ah,' said my uncle, gritting his teeth, 'you are afraid it has, aren't you, my boy? But don't worry, this lull is only temporary. It has already lasted five minutes, and before long we shall be resuming our journey towards the mouth of the crater.'

While he was speaking the Professor kept his eye on his chronometer, and once again he was to be proved right. Soon the raft started moving again, and rose swiftly but jerkily for about two minutes. Then it stopped once more.

'Good,' said my uncle, noting the time. 'Ten minutes from now it will start again.'

'Ten minutes?'

'Yes. This is a volcano with an intermittent eruption. It lets us draw breath every now and then at the same time as itself.'

This was perfectly true. At the given moment we were shot upwards again at tremendous speed, and we had to cling to the beams to avoid being flung off the raft. Then the thrust stopped.

I have since thought about this strange phenomenon without being able to find a satisfactory explanation of it. All the same, it seems clear to me that we were not in the main shaft of the volcano, but in a lateral gallery where a sort of recoil effect was produced.

How many times this happened I cannot say. All I know is that at each fresh impulse we were sent upwards with increased force as if we were on an actual projectile. During the short halts we were nearly suffocated; and while we were moving the burning air took my breath away. I thought for a moment of the bliss of suddenly finding myself in the polar regions at a temperature of 30° below zero. My excited imagination pictured the snowy plains of the arctic countries, and I longed for the moment when I should be able to roll on the icy carpet of the Pole. Little by little, in fact, my brain, weakened by so many repeated shocks, was giving way. But for Hans's arms, my skull would have been broken more than once against the granite wall.

I have therefore no clear recollection of what happened during the following hours, but just a vague impression of continuous explosions, shifting rocks, and a spinning movement in which our raft was whirled around. It rocked about on waves of lava, in the midst of a rain of ashes. Roaring flames enveloped it. A hurricane which seemed as if it came from a huge pair of bellows was keeping up the subterranean fires. For the last time I caught a glimpse of Hans's face in the light of the flames, and after that the only feeling I had was the terror of a condemned man tied to the mouth of a cannon, just as the shot is fired and his limbs are scattered to the winds.

44
Back to the Surface

When I opened my eyes again I felt the guide's strong hand holding my belt. With his other hand he was supporting my uncle. I was not seriously injured, but simply bruised all over. I found myself lying on a mountain slope, only a few feet from an abyss into which I would have fallen at the slightest movement. Hans had saved my life while I was rolling down the side of the crater.

'Where are we?' asked my uncle, who seemed to be extremely annoyed at being back on the surface of the earth.

The guide shrugged his shoulders to express complete ignorance.

'In Iceland,' I said.

'*Nej!*' retorted Hans.

'What, not in Iceland?' cried the Professor.

'Hans must be wrong,' I said, sitting up.

After the countless surprises of our journey, one more had been reserved for us. I expected to see a cone covered with perpetual snow, in the midst of the barren deserts of the north, under the pale rays of the polar sky, and beyond the highest latitudes; but contrary to all these expectations, my uncle, the Icelander, and I were lying half-way down a mountain baked by the rays of a scorching sun.

I could not believe my eyes, but the absolute roasting to which my body was being subjected left no room for doubt. We had come out of the crater half-naked, and the radiant orb, from which we had demanded nothing for two months, was lavishing a fierce light on us.

When my eyes had grown accustomed to this brilliance with which they had become unfamiliar, I used them to rectify the errors of my imagination. I wanted to be at Spitzbergen at the very least, and I was in no mood to accept anything else.

The Professor was the first to speak up, saying:

'It certainly doesn't look like Iceland.'

'What about Jan Mayen's Land?' I asked.

'It doesn't look like that either, my boy. This isn't a northern volcano with granite slopes and a skull-cap of snow.'

'All the same . . .'

'Look, Axel, look!'

Above our heads, not more than five hundred feet up, there was a volcano, through which, every quarter of an hour, with a loud explosion, there emerged a tall column of flame, mingled with pumice-stones, ashes, and lava. I could feel the convulsions of the mountain, which seemed to be breathing like a whale, and puffing out fire and air through its huge blowers. Below us, on a fairly steep slope, streams of eruptive matter stretched for a distance of seven or eight hundred feet, giving the mountain a height of about 1,800 feet. Its base was hidden in a regular bower of green trees, among which I made out olives, figs, and vines laden with purple grapes.

I had to admit that this was not at all an arctic scene.

When one's gaze passed beyond this green girdle, it plunged away into the waters of an exquisite sea or lake, in which this enchanted land appeared as an island barely a few miles wide. To the east there was a little harbour, with a few houses scattered around it, and some ships of a peculiar kind rocking on its blue waves. Beyond it, some groups of islets rose from the liquid plain in such numbers that they looked like a vast ant-heap. To the west, distant coasts lined the horizon; on some of them gently curving mountains were silhouetted; on others, farther away, there appeared a lofty cone with a waving plume of smoke. In the north, an immense sheet of water sparkled in the rays of the sun, its expanse broken here and there by the top of a mast or the curve of a sail swelling in the wind.

The unexpectedness of such a sight increased its wonderful beauty a hundredfold.

'Where are we? Where are we?' I kept asking in a murmur.

Hans closed his eyes with indifference, while my uncle gazed uncomprehendingly.

'Whatever this mountain may be,' he said at last, 'it's rather hot here. The explosions are still going on, and it would be a pity to come safely out of a volcano just to be hit on the head with a piece of rock. Let us go down, and then we shall know where we stand. Besides, I am dying of hunger and thirst.'

The Professor was definitely not a contemplative character. For my part, forgetting all my needs and fatigue, I could have stayed in that spot for hours, but I had to follow my companions.

The sides of the volcano were extremely steep; we kept slipping into regular quagmires of ash, trying to avoid the streams of lava which wound down the mountain like fiery serpents. As we went down, I chattered away volubly, for my imagination was too full not to spill over in words.

'We are in Asia,' I cried, 'on the Indian coast, in the Malay Archipelago, in Oceania! We have gone across the globe and come out at the antipodes of Europe.'

'But what about the compass?' said my uncle.

'Yes, of course, the compass,' I said with a puzzled air. 'According to the compass, we have been travelling north all the time.'

'Then was it lying?'

'Lying? No, how could it?'

'Then is this North Pole?'

'The Pole? No, but . . .'

There was a mystery here, and I did not know what to think.

Meanwhile we were getting nearer to that greenery which was such a treat for the eyes. I was tormented by hunger and thirst. Fortunately, after walking for two hours, we reached a lovely stretch of country, entirely covered with olive trees, pomegranate trees, and vines which seemed to be common property. At any rate, in our state of destitution we were in no mood to be over-scrupulous. What a joy it was to press that delicious fruit to our lips, and to bite off whole clusters of those purple grapes! Not far off, in the delightful grassy shade of the trees, I found a spring of fresh water, into which we joyfully plunged our faces and hands.

While we were enjoying the delights of repose in this way, a child appeared between two clumps of olive-trees.

'Ah!' I cried. 'A native of this happy land!'

He was a poor boy, wretchedly clothed, rather sickly-looking, and apparently greatly alarmed by our appearance; indeed, half-naked, with unkempt hair and beards, we looked anything but prepossessing, and unless this was a country of robbers we were likely to terrify the inhabitants.

Just as the boy was about to take to his heels, Hans ran after him and brought him back to us, kicking and screaming.

My uncle began by doing his best to reassure him, and asked him in German:

'What is the name of this mountain, my boy?'

The child made no reply.

'Good,' said my uncle, 'we are not in Germany.'

He then put the same question in English.

The child still did not answer. I was extremely puzzled.

'Is the boy dumb?' cried the Professor, who, very proud of his command of languages, repeated his question in French.

The same silence.

'Then let's try Italian,' said my uncle, and he asked:

'Dove noi siamo?'

'Yes, where are we?' I repeated impatiently.

The boy still made no reply.

'Will you answer when you're spoken to?' cried my uncle, beginning to lose his temper and shaking the child by the ears.

'Come si noma questa isola?'

'Stromboli,' replied the little shepherd-boy, slipping out of Hans's grasp and running off to the plain through the olive trees.

We gave no thought to him. Stromboli! What an effect this unexpected name produced on my imagination! We were in the middle of the Mediterranean, in the heart of the Aeolian archipelago of mythological memory, in that ancient Strongyle where Aeolus kept the winds and storms on a chain. And those blue mountains in the east were the mountains of Calabria! And that volcano on the southern horizon was none other than the fierce and frightening Etna!

'Stromboli! Stromboli!' I repeated.

My uncle accompanied me with his words and gestures, so that we seemed to be singing a chorus.

Oh, what a journey! What a wonderful journey! We had gone in by one volcano and come out by another, and this other was more than three thousand miles from Sneffels, from that barren country of Iceland at the far limits of the inhabited world! The chances of our expedition had carried us into the heart of the most beautiful part of the world! We had exchanged the region of perpetual snow for that of infinite verdure, and the grey fog of the icy north for the blue skies of Sicily!

After our delicious meal of fruit and cold water, we set off again in the direction of the port of Stromboli. It seemed to us that it would be unwise to say how we had arrived on the island: the superstitious Italians would undoubtedly take us to be demons vomited out of hell, so we resigned ourselves to passing ourselves off as victims of a shipwreck. This was not so glorious but far safer.

On the way I heard my uncle murmuring:

'But the compass! The compass! It pointed north! How can we explain that fact?'

'Good Lord,' I said disdainfully, 'the best thing to do is not to explain it. That's the simplest solution.'

'What! A professor at the Johannaeum unable to explain a cosmic phenomenon! The idea is positively disgraceful!'

And as he spoke, my uncle, half-naked, with his leather money-belt round his waist, and settling his spectacles on his nose, became once more the awe-inspiring professor of mineralogy.

An hour after leaving the olive grove, we reached the port of San Vicenzo, where Hans claimed his thirteenth week's wages, which were counted out to him with hearty handshakes all round.

At that moment, if he did not altogether share our very natural emotion, at least he gave vent to an extraordinary display of feeling: he gently pressed our hands with the tips of his fingers, and began to smile.

45
Home Again

Such is the conclusion of a story which even those people who pride themselves on being astonished at nothing will refuse to believe. But I am hardened in advance against human incredulity.

We were received by the Stromboli fishermen with the kindness due to the victims of shipwreck. They gave us food and clothing, and after waiting forty-eight hours, a small craft took us on 31 August to Messina, where a few days' rest removed every trace of fatigue.

On Friday, 4 September, we embarked on the *Volturno*, one of the French Imperial packet-boats, and three days later landed at Marseilles, with nothing on our minds but the problem of our wretched compass. The mystery of its inexplicable behaviour plagued me all the time. In the evening of 9 September we arrived at Hamburg.

I cannot hope to describe Martha's astonishment and Gräuben's joy at our return.

'Now that you are a hero, Axel,' my dear fiancée said to me, 'you will never need to leave me again.'

I looked at her, and she smiled through her tears.

I leave the reader to imagine whether Professor Lidenbrock's return caused a sensation in Hamburg. As a result of Martha's gossiping, the news of his departure for the centre of the earth had spread all over the world. People had refused to believe it, and when they saw him again they did not believe it any the more.

However, the presence of Hans and various pieces of information from Iceland gradually modified public opinion.

My uncle then became a great man, and I the nephew of a great man, which is not something to be despised. Hamburg gave a banquet in our honour. A public meeting was held at the Johannaeum, at which the Professor told the story of his expedition, leaving nothing out but the mystery of the compass. On the same day he deposited Saknussemm's document in the city archives, and expressed his deep regret that circumstances, stronger than his will, had prevented him from following in the Dane's footsteps to the very centre of the earth. He was modest in his glory, and his reputation grew as a result.

So much honour inevitably aroused envy. There were some who could not forgive him his fame; and as his theories, based on established facts, contradicted scientific doctrine on the question of the central fire, he was obliged to engage in oral and written controversy with scientists all over the world.

For my part I cannot agree with his theory of gradual cooling: in spite of what I have seen, I still believe, and always shall believe, in the central fire. But I admit that certain circumstances, as yet imperfectly understood, may modify this law under the influence of natural phenomena.

While these questions were being fiercely debated, my uncle suffered a real sorrow. Hans, in spite of his entreaties, left Hamburg; the man to whom we owed everything would not allow us to pay our debt in hospitality. He was afflicted with home-sickness.

'*Färval*,' he said one day, and with that simple word he left for Reykjavik, where he arrived safely.

We were deeply attached to our worthy eider-hunter; though far away, he will never be forgotten by those whose lives he saved, and I certainly intend to see him again before I die.

In conclusion, I should add that this *Journey to the Centre of the Earth* created a tremendous sensation all over the world. It was translated into every other language; and the leading newspapers competed with one another in order to publish the most interesting passages, which were commented on, discussed, attacked, and defended with equal conviction on the part of believers and sceptics. My uncle had the rare privilege of enjoying in his lifetime the fame he had deservedly won, and even received an offer from Mr Barnum to 'exhibit' him in the United States.

But a nagging worry, I might almost say a torment, was mingled with all this glory. One aspect of the journey – the behaviour of the compass – remained a mystery, and for a scientist an unexplained phenomenon is a torture for the mind. Fortunately Providence was to make my uncle completely happy.

One day, while arranging a collection of minerals in his study, I noticed the famous compass and had a look at it.

It had been there for six months in its corner, never suspecting how much worry it was causing.

Suddenly I gave a cry of surprise. The Professor came running into the room.

'What's the matter?' he asked.

'The compass!'

'Well?'

'Well, the needle points south instead of north!'

'What's that you say?'

'Look, the poles are reversed.'

'Reversed!'

My uncle looked, compared the compass with another, and then gave a leap of joy which shook the whole house.

Light dawned at the same time in his mind and mine.

'So,' he exclaimed, as soon as he was able to speak again, 'after our arrival at Cape Saknussemm the needle of this confounded compass pointed south instead of north?'

'Obviously.'

'Then that explains our mistake. But what phenomenon could have caused this reversal of the poles?'

'It's all very simple.'

'Explain yourself, my boy.'

'During the storm on the Lidenbrock Sea, that fireball which magnetized all the iron on the raft simply reversed the poles of our compass!'

'Ah!' cried the Professor, bursting out laughing. 'So it was a practical joke that electricity played on us!'

From that day onward, my uncle was the happiest of scientists, and I the happiest of men; for my pretty Virlandaise, abdicating her position as ward, took her place in the Königstrasse house in the dual capacity of niece and wife. I need scarcely add that her uncle was the illustrious Professor Otto Lidenbrock, corresponding member of all the scientific, geographical, and mineralogical societies in the world.

JOURNEY to the CENTRE of the EARTH

With Puffin Classics, the adventure isn't
over when you reach the final page.
Want to discover more about your favourite
characters, their creators and their worlds?
Read on . . .

CONTENTS

Name: Jules Gabriel Verne
Born: 8 February 1828 in Nantes, France
Died: 24 March 1905 at his home, 44 Boulevard Longueville
(now Boulevard Jules-Verne) in Amiens, France
Nationality: French (*Journey to the Centre of the Earth* was
originally written in French)
Lived: in France
Married: to Honorine de Viane, a widow, in 1857
Children: one son, Michel, and two step-daughters, Suzanne
and Valentine

What was he like?

Jules was a man with an extraordinary imagination who never
gave up his dream of being a writer. His father was a lawyer
who sent Jules to law school in Paris. Once Jules had
graduated, though, he told his father he didn't want to carry
on the family business. He was going to be a writer.

Ten long, hard years followed. He wrote plays, poems and
short stories. Although some were published or performed,
none were successful, and Jules had to work as a stockbroker
to support his family. It wasn't until he was thirty-four that
the publisher Pierre-Jules Hetzel accepted Jules' novel *Five
Weeks in a Balloon*. It became an instant success.

Where did he grow up?

In Nantes, France, a port on the river Loire. Jules grew up
surrounded by great ships coming home from or embarking

for faraway places. Seeing these ships might be what made him interested in stories of travel and adventure.

What did he do apart from writing books?
Jules loved to sail his boats (the *Saint-Michel I, II* and *III*) around Europe. Unfortunately, there were also family problems to contend with. His son Michel was a rebellious teenager, while his mentally unstable nephew Gaston tried to murder Jules in 1886. Fortunately, one of his bullets missed and the other only hit Jules in the leg.

What did people think of Journey to the Centre of the Earth when it was first published in 1864?
Journey to the Centre of the Earth was part of Jules' *Les Voyages Extraordinaires* (*Extraordinary Voyages*) series of books. They combined up-to-date science with thrilling plots. In those days no one had seen anything quite like them before, and they sold like hotcakes.

Where did he get the idea for Journey to the Centre of the Earth?
Jules was not a scientist or an explorer, and he got his ideas through reading lots of newspapers, magazines and books. *Journey to the Centre of the Earth* would have been modern science to Jules' first readers. Today, of course, we know that much of the science in it is wrong.

What other books did he write?
He wrote over fifty novels, including the famous books

Around the World in Eighty Days and *Twenty Thousand Leagues Under the Sea*. Jules also adapted his novels for the stage and published a bestseller (the lost manuscript *Paris in the Twentieth Century*) nearly ninety years after his death.

Axel Lidenbrock – the teenage narrator of *Journey to the Centre of the Earth*. Dragged along on the expedition by his uncle, Axel is at first a reluctant explorer.

Professor Otto Lidenbrock – Axel's uncle and guardian, Professor Lidenbrock is a brilliant but eccentric scientist, often laughed at by his students. The fifty-year-old Professor is also impatient, quick to anger and can be a tyrant to his family. Only when Axel's life is in danger do the Professor's true feelings for him show.

Hans Bjelke – an Icelander whom the Professor engages as a guide. A man of few words, Hans is brave, strong and calm in the face of danger. He saves the day more than once, and in some ways is the true hero of the story.

Gräuben – the Professor's seventeen-year-old goddaughter and Axel's fiancée, Gräuben is left behind in Hamburg. Because she comes from a part of Estonia called Virland, Axel often calls her 'my Virlandaise'.

Martha – the Professor's elderly housekeeper.

Arne Saknussemm – long-dead Icelandic alchemist, and writer of the encrypted message that sends the Professor and Axel on their quest.

Professor Thomson – museum curator in Copenhagen, who helps the Professor and Axel find a ship to Reykjavik.

Captain Bjarne – Danish captain of the ship that takes the Professor and Axel to Reykjavik.

Baron Trampe, Mr Finsen, Mr Picturssen, Mr Fridriksson, Dr Hyaltalin – Icelanders whom the Professor and Axel meet on their journey.

Humphry Davy – an English scientist the Professor supposedly knows. Humphry Davy was a real person, still famous today for scientific discoveries such as the elements potassium and sodium. The Professor's description of Davy's theory about what lies in the centre of the Earth is accurate (although in later life Davy changed his mind). However, Jules seems to have made a mistake in his dates. As the book is set in 1863, but the Professor claims to have met Davy in 1825, the Professor must have been only twelve or thirteen when they met!

How believable is the story? What makes it believable/unbelievable?

Do you think Axel is brave or cowardly?

What kind of skills do you think you'd need to be a successful explorer?

What do you think of the relationship between the Professor and Axel? Is the Professor a good guardian to Axel?

'Rhombohedral'. 'Retinasphaltic'. 'Gehlenite'. Many of the scientific words in *Journey to the Centre of the Earth* wouldn't be understood by most grown-ups! Why do you think Jules uses so many difficult words? Does it make the book hard to understand?

What did you think of the ending of the book? Do you think that Axel and the Professor's expedition was a success or a failure?

There are many novels in which the characters go on journeys, and on the way they learn not only about life but about themselves. What do you think the Professor and Axel learn about their inner-selves? Do they change by the end of their journey?

You have been invited to take part on an intrepid journey to the centre of the Earth. What dangers do you face along the way? What type of plants and animals would you come across? Does the landscape change as you get nearer to the Earth's core?

Why do you think that Jules Verne is considered to be the 'father of science fiction'?

Make a cross-section map of the Professor and Axel's journey.

You are the set designer for a multimillion-dollar Hollywood movie of *Journey to the Centre of the Earth*. Choose a section of the story and draw detailed plans for the sets for it.

You own an adventure travel agency, offering trips down the underground route that Axel and the Professor took! Make a poster advertising your trips.

On their expedition, the Professor and Axel encounter many plants and animals thought to be extinct. Imagine you have become famous for (re)discovering a supposedly extinct animal. What animal could it be? How did you discover it? Write a newspaper article about your career and your discovery.

Imagine that you are leading an expedition as adventurous as Axel and the Professor's – to the North Pole, the Sahara Desert, into the Amazon jungle or even into outer space . . .

★ Make a list of all the things you'll need to take with you.

★ Create a logbook of your expedition, including dates, measurements and important events.

★ You've taken with you a miniature satellite-linked laptop that can send emails! Write an email to your best friend telling them how the expedition is going.

There were many real explorers in the nineteenth century – for example, Henry Morton Stanley and David Livingstone. Do some exploration of your own into some of the explorers of the time to find out more about the discoveries they made.

Read Jules Verne's other adventures such as *Around the World in Eighty Days* and *Twenty Thousand Leagues Under the Sea*. How do they compare to *Journey to the Centre of the Earth*?

Jules Verne researched his books carefully. Unfortunately, though, many of the theories scientists had in the 1800s about what was inside the Earth were wrong! Read on to find out what's *really* at the centre of the Earth.

★ If Axel and the Professor had really found a way to the centre of the Earth, there's no way they could have survived. Our Earth, which seems such a comfortable place to inhabit on the surface, is in truth a fire planet. Wherever you stand on the globe, less than fifty miles below your feet lies an inferno of red-hot rock!

★ This rock (known as the Earth's mantle) can reach temperatures of over 3500°C (6330°F). It's so hot that if the rock were at the surface, it would melt, or even boil and become a gas. The tremendous pressure of billions of tons of rock pressing down from above, though, keeps most of this red-hot rock in a solid state.

★ Beneath the Earth's mantle lies its core: the true centre of the Earth. Unlike the mantle, the core is made of metal (mostly iron). It's even hotter than the mantle – scientists estimate it may be as hot as 5000–7000°C (9030–12,630°F)! The inner core is solid metal and the outer core is liquid metal.

* The metal at the Earth's core is also a huge magnet. It's this enormous hidden magnet at the centre of the Earth that makes compass needles swing to magnetic north.

* The only thing protecting us from the Earth's red-hot interior is its crust: a thin but tough layer of solid basalt and granite rock. This layer can be as little as three miles thick under the oceans.

* If the crust of the Earth is breached, hot rock from the mantle escapes as molten lava, forming deadly volcanoes. Volcano eruptions are so powerful because they release part of the tremendous pressure in the mantle.

* The Professor tells Axel that the volcano Sneffels is extinct (and therefore safe) because it hasn't erupted since 1219. If Axel had known that today scientists consider the lifecycle of volcanoes to be so long that any volcano which has erupted within human history is still active, it probably would have made him even more nervous!

* Thin though the crust of the Earth is, no one has ever succeeded in drilling through it. The deep-sea mission Chikyu Hakken (Japanese for 'Earth Discovery') is scheduled to have another go in 2007.

* Thanks to the science of seismology, we know a great deal about the inside of the Earth without ever having gone there. Seismologists have been able to work out what's

inside the Earth by studying the waves of energy sent downwards through our planet by earthquakes. By looking at how and when these waves reach sensitive measuring stations all around the globe, seismologists can work out what sorts of material they travelled through and build up a 3D picture of the inside of the Earth.

Where and what is Iceland exactly?

Iceland is a large island in the far north of the Atlantic Ocean. Today an independent country, in Jules Verne's day Iceland was ruled by Denmark (this is probably why Axel and the Professor sail from Denmark).

Is Iceland as it is described in Journey to the Centre of the Earth?

Jules Verne drew on other travellers' tales rather than his personal experience or Icelanders' own accounts. The descriptions are, nevertheless, fairly accurate. Today, Iceland is a modern country and one of the richest in the world.

Is the volcano the Professor and Axel climb down a real place?

Yes, although there's no evidence that Sneffels has a passage to the centre of the Earth in it! Sneffels is only one of Iceland's many volcanoes, and much of Iceland is made from cooled, solidified lava.

Why does Iceland have so many volcanoes?

Because under Iceland lies a particularly hot and active part of the Earth's red-hot mantle. One advantage of living in one of the most volcanically active spots on Earth is that it's very cheap to heat your house in Iceland – Icelanders get over half their domestic power not from coal, oil or gas, but through tapping into free volcanic heat.

CRACK THE CODE!

Jules Verne loved secret codes, and Arne Saknussemm's
message is just one of many encoded messages in his books.
Here's how to create some secret codes of your own:

★ Make a simple code by writing out the alphabet and the
numbers 0 to 9 on a piece of paper, then writing them out
again in a different order underneath. This order can
either follow a pattern (making the code easier to break,
but also easier to remember), or be completely random.
One famous code in history of this type was Julius
Caesar's, in the days of the Roman Empire. Caesar
encoded important messages by substituting each letter
with a letter three places further along in the alphabet.

★ Use a boring-looking note or email to carry a secret message.
Somewhere on your note, perhaps disguised as part of a date
or address, write (for example) 5. This means that the person
you're sending the note to needs to read every fifth word to
discover the hidden message. For example,
*James, I hope to meet you this coming Tuesday, at the big
party for the opening of the museum garden. I'll wait at the
gate. It will start at nine and finish about twelve o'clock.
Love, Sarah.*
would mean, 'meet at the garden gate nine o'clock.'!

★ If you and a friend both own the same edition of a
dictionary (it must be exactly the same), it's easy to use

this as a secret codebook. Your code is the page and entry number of the word you want to encode. So, 145-8 would mean 'Go to page 145 and count down to entry number 8.'